Forgotten Boy

A Chicago Detective Thriller

Todd Luchik

Sleepless Night Press

For Rachel

ONE

I didn't like the looks of the kid standing by the jukebox. It wasn't his clothes or his hair or his face. The neighborhood was crawling with hipsters, and this variety was nothing I hadn't seen before. He was just another shaggy-haired kid in skinny pants.

No, it was the five-dollar bill in his hand. It represented commitment, a shotgun wedding over shots and cheap beer. I watched him feed the five into the jukebox and braced myself for an hour or more of his music, feeling violated.

Cleo's jukebox was just a little too eclectic for its own good, and I could only imagine what atrocities this kid was about to play. I briefly considered calling it a night when the opening notes of "Life on Mars?" by David Bowie came over the speakers. I guess I had sold the kid short, or at least his taste in music.

The bar had tuned the TVs to the national news with the sound down. Secretary of State Colin Powell's moon-shaped face filled the screen, all dour and gray. The closed captioning said he was speaking at the United Nations. Iraq again.

Powell peered down from the TV above me, his expression severe and disapproving. It was a judgmental face, a teetotaler's face, and it was making me feel self-conscious about my alcohol intake.

I caught the bartender's attention. "Anything else on?"

He glanced up at the screens. "Sure, just a second."

He retrieved the remote from under the counter and changed the channel to a pro bowling tournament on ESPN. "How's this?"

"Perfect."

I ordered another shot of the house bourbon. It was some cheap, off-brand poison they kept under the bar for only the most hardcore drinkers. This was my third of the evening. It tasted caustic and stale, like something siphoned out of the gas tank of a long-abandoned automobile. I chased it with the final lukewarm remnants of a Miller High Life and placed the empty on the bar.

The door behind me opened, letting in a cold winter draft that chilled the back of my neck. I turned around to see a man entering the bar. He was slender and small of stature, bigger than a lawn jockey but not by much. He had a slender hooknose, and his dark eyes were set too close together, giving his face a pinched, bird-like quality. His drab brown suit didn't fit him right, the jacket a little too large and the pants just a tad too short. Everything about him looked shabby. Then again, he was bound to look bad to me. The guy owed me money.

His name was Gary Grolczyk, and he was a former client. Gary owned a shop on Milwaukee Avenue that dealt in garish, overpriced eyesores: a mix of Rococo furniture, hotel art, and space-age bachelor pad kitsch. He suspected his wife of infidelity and had hired me to tail her. One look at her and I could see why he was insecure. She was way out of his league, 15 years his junior and half a foot taller with a slim but curvy figure. A week and a half on the case and I caught her rolling around half-naked with one of Gary's vendors in the back seat of her car. I snapped more than a dozen pictures of their little show and was gracious enough to give Gary most of them. When he confronted her, she came clean, telling him she wanted a divorce. Next thing he knew, she was asking for half of everything he owned, claiming neglect and emotional cruelty, or something like that. In the meantime, I waited and waited for my money.

Gary grabbed a stool at the other end of the bar and ordered a drink. I caught his eye and waved. You could almost see his heart rising into his throat. Call me cruel, but his discomfort brought a smile to my face. He turned away, pretending not to see me. I collected my things and moved into the seat next to him.

"When did you get here?" he asked.

"I've been here. I was here when you came in. Didn't you see me wave?"

"No, but I've got a lot on my mind, what with the divorce and all. Nothing personal."

"Oh, of course. Nothing personal, Gary. I just want my money." He was about to speak, but I cut him off. "You're a businessman. You understand the concept of supply and demand."

Gary nodded.

"You see, I'm a lazy man, and I don't part with my time easily. I charge what I charge, so I don't have to work too many hours, and by not working many hours and being selective about my choice of clientele, my time is just that much more valuable. Now, when a client neglects to pay me, it devalues my time. It forces me to work more and to be less selective about my clientele. That's not good, Gary. That's bad business."

The bartender stopped by to check on us. "You guys all right?"

"I think we could use a couple more drinks," I said. "What're you having, Gary?"

"I'm having the McClellands."

"Make it two McClellands and put it on his tab."

Gary looked like he was about to protest but thought better of it.

The bartender poured our drinks and moved to the other end of the bar. Gary sipped his Scotch. I downed mine in a single gulp. Gary watched me drink, a wide-eyed expression of disbelief on his pinched little face. He looked horrified when I flagged down the bartender and ordered another on his tab.

"Take it out of what you owe me," I said.

"Sure, it's just that those are ten dollars apiece, and I'm not sure I have enough cash on me."

"Put it on your credit card."

Gary looked like he was about to object but remained silent.

"All right, then we're good. Now, about the money you owe me."

"I'll put a check in the mail first thing tomorrow morning."

I shook my head. "That's no good. I'm having trouble with my mail carrier. He doesn't deliver if the weather's too nice or too shitty, and it's usually one or the other in this town. No, I'd rather pick it up."

"Okay, then stop by the store on Thursday and I'll cut you a check."

"Or how 'bout this? We'll have a few more drinks, and when we're done, we'll stop by an ATM."

Gary hemmed and hawed about different accounts and the divorce and how it would have to be Thursday, to which I responded by downing my Scotch and ordering another one. By then, I figured I had recouped about one percent of what he owed me, along with the more valuable satisfaction of watching the cheap little bastard squirm.

"We live in a marvelous age of technology, Gary. You can make all the necessary arrangements, all the transfers and whatnot, at the ATM."

Gary slumped in his seat. Seeing that we had settled our plans for the evening, I changed the subject. I spent the rest of the evening regaling him with stories of my days on the police force, most of them made up, each ending with me playing the tough guy. That segued into an informative lecture on police brutality in the Chicago PD. I told Gary stories I had heard during my career. I told him about how the cops could beat a guy senseless without leaving a single mark, using little more than your run-of-the-mill phonebook. I told him how a plastic typewriter cover placed over the face of an uncooperative suspect can be an effective way of eliciting a confession and explained how one sick, devious officer fashioned an electroshock device from an old WWII field phone. All the while, Gary nervously wrung a cocktail napkin between his hands, twisting it into a tight little knot. Every so often, he'd peer longingly at the exit.

Before long, I had drunk so much that my tales turned to nonsense, and my nonsense had made the short jump to gibberish. I was deranged with drink and the sadistic joy of ruining Gary's evening. By last call, I had forgotten entirely about collecting my money and was encouraging my unwilling companion to take the party to a four o'clock bar. "Just one more drink and we'll ca-hawl it a night."

"Sure, Glenn, just let me make a quick trip to the washroom and we'll go."

I didn't notice him take his coat, but the state I was in, I wouldn't have noticed if he had taken my pants. I waited a few minutes for Gary to return, and then a few minutes more. I laid my head on the bar, just to rest my eyes.

The bartender came by and tapped me on the shoulder. "Hey, buddy, you better get going," he said.

I squinted up at him, his image hazy and haloed by the bar lights he had just turned on. "Oh, hey, have you seen Gary?"

"Gary?"

"The guy I was with."

"He left about ten minutes ago."

I slammed an open palm on the bar. "Damn it! I'm going to go over to his house and beat the living crap out of him. But first, one more drink."

"Sorry, we're closed. You don't have to go home, but you can't stay here."

I uttered something I must've found hilarious because it had me doubled over with laughter. The bartender wasn't amused. Realizing that I was wasting my charm on the bar staff, I headed for the door.

Outside, honeycomb crystals of frost formed on storefront windows and twinkled in the stark light of the street lamps. There was no one around, just the occasional drinker heading home from the bars or a third-shift worker waiting for a bus.

The cold air helped revive me. I briefly considered going home before remembering that I had almost a full bottle of Irish whiskey at the office. I headed there for a nightcap.

My progress was slow and intermittent—a couple of steps forward followed by a sharp veer to the right, a step back, and then another couple of steps forward. It was a lovely dance that made the few non-psychotics out this time of night cross to the opposite side of the street.

My office was on the fourteenth floor of a tall art déco building at the corner of North and Milwaukee. I passed the usual collection of transients, deadbeats, and lunatics out front. Normally, these guys would hit me up for cigarettes or a few bucks, but not this time. I guess the shape I was in, they mistook me for one of their own. Thank goodness for small blessings. I don't think I could have handled even the most insignificant amount of human interaction at that point. My tongue felt dry and heavy in my mouth, and I couldn't see straight. Somewhere deep inside my psyche, my better judgment was drowning in a pool of booze, its garbled prophecies of tomorrow morning's pain sounding like,

'Just one more drink before I hit the sack,' to my drunken ears.

I don't remember entering the building or riding the elevator up to the floor of my office, but I'm sure I did. I recall making a detour to the washroom. I can picture myself now, standing in front of the urinal, one hand pressed against the wall to steady me. And I'm sure I made it to my office and had that last drink because I was head down at my desk drooling on the keyboard of my computer next to an open bottle of Powers Irish Whiskey when the phone rang at 8:30 in the morning. If I had known then what I know now, I wouldn't have answered it.

TWO

I answered on the fourth ring with a guttural noise that sounded like the word, 'what'—the final consonant coated in phlegm. The man on the other end paused for a moment before speaking. He had a deep, sonorous voice, which sounded like a foghorn in my head.

"I'm sorry. I'm trying to reach a Mr. Glenn Wozniak."

"Speaking."

"Mr. Wozniak, my name is Edgar Marsh." He paused before adding with a note of hesitancy, "Lisa Benton referred me to you."

There was a name I hadn't heard in a while. Lisa was a former client, an executive for a large insurance firm. I worked on some fraud cases for her once upon a time. I'd tail guys who claimed they couldn't walk or stand up straight and try to catch them doing things they shouldn't be able to do in their condition. It was pure tedium, a lot of driving around and snapping pictures, but the money was good. Besides, Lisa was a good-looking girl. She was tall and pretty with a nice pair of legs. I pondered them for a moment, a smile forming on my face.

"Mr. Wozniak, are you still there?"

"Huh? Yes, sorry."

"Are you taking any new clients at this time?"

I hesitated for a moment, a part of me wanting to say no until I remembered the sorry state of my finances. "Sure, how can I help you, Mr. Marsh?"

"I have a case I'd like you to work on. It's a delicate matter of great urgency, and I'd rather not discuss it over the phone. Are you available to meet sometime this morning?"

"Sure, no problem. Let me give you directions to my office. I'm at—"

"No, I think it'd be better if you came here. I have a conference call in a few minutes and a board meeting at noon."

For a delicate matter of great urgency, it sure didn't seem to be his top priority. I was grateful for the chance to run home and clean myself up a little. If I looked anything like I felt, I was sure to lose the job. We settled on a 10:30 meeting time. I took down his address. Marsh's office was on the 75th floor of the Sears Tower.

I hung up, and an all-too-familiar feeling of regret moved in on my hangover's territory. I lit a cigarette with trembling hands and took a swig of whiskey straight from the bottle. My head cleared, and I felt like I could handle just about anything. My legs disagreed, but fuck 'em. They weren't in charge. I was going to be pretty busy over the next few days, and my body was just going to have to get with the program.

I rushed home, washed up, and changed into a charcoal-gray suit with white pinstripes and a red power tie. The outfit was something I kept in the event I had to meet with a guy like Marsh, a guy who held conference calls and attended board meetings. I looked every bit the clean-cut, well-put-together small business owner, the kind of guy a man could entrust with a delicate matter of great urgency.

I took the El downtown. The trains were running about ten minutes behind schedule, so I had to rush to make the appointment on time. I arrived red-faced, my neck slick with sweat.

Marsh's offices were swanky and stuffy all at once, like a private men's club. The reception area was a melange of earth colors accented with hints of scarlet. It had soft leather chairs and wood paneling. Dour-looking portraits of various Marshes covered the walls.

The receptionist was a short, white-haired woman shaped like a stack of tires. She had a fleshy face, and her eyes appeared small behind glasses big enough to require windshield wipers. Two piles sat on her desk—one of letters, the other of envelopes—and she was feverishly signing the first and stuffing the second.

She looked like she had been in that seat all her life. I imagined she had once been an attractive woman. I imagined that old Mr. Marsh had kept her around a long time—long enough to have once found her desirable, long enough for her to have aged past the point of ever being seen in such a way again, long enough for him to have forgotten ever finding her attractive.

I approached her desk. "Hi, I have a 10:30 appointment with Mr. Marsh."

"Your name?" she asked without looking up.

"Glenn Wozniak."

She directed her eyes up at me, peering over the top of the dual magnifying glasses she was wearing, a skeptical expression on her face. "Please have a seat, and I'll ring Mr. Marsh."

A few minutes later, she walked me back to Marsh's office. Along the way, we passed a series of small offices on the right and a larger common area filled with cubicles to the left. It was a busy place with a good-sized staff.

"What do you do here?" I asked.

"We handle the Marsh family's investments and philanthropic activities."

"That's it?"

"That's it."

"All these people just to manage one family's money?"

The old lady smiled. "A very wealthy family's money."

We stopped at an oak door with a gold S-shaped handle. The receptionist opened the door, revealing a lush corner office with floor to ceiling windows. The room looked more like a den than an office, a place where a man could kick back and while away the time with a brandy snifter and a pipe. A bookcase took up one wall, and there was a globe that I suspected was one of those stealth Italian mini-bars. My mouth watered at the thought. I glanced out at the city below, everything in miniature, like an elaborate model train set. Edgar Marsh's elaborate model train set.

Marsh sat behind a large mahogany desk. He stood up as I entered.

Edgar was a tall man, lanky and long-limbed, with enormous hands. He looked younger than I had imagined, no older than in his mid to late fifties. He had a full head of thick, dark hair with only trace amounts of graying at the temples. His face was long, and his complexion pale.

"Mr. Wozniak," he said, extending his hand. I gave it a quick shake and took a seat in a burgundy leather chair across from him. Marsh sat and eyed me across the vast expanse of his desk as the receptionist departed, closing the door behind her.

"What can I do for you, Mr. Marsh?"

Edgar reached into his desk and retrieved a photograph. He handed it to me. It was of an unsmiling young woman with jet-black hair and dark eyes. She was a petite girl with a boyish figure and delicate features. I suppose she was attractive in a gloomy kind of way. I pictured a girl with multiple eating disorders and a procession of increasingly tortured boyfriends.

"That's my daughter, Alison," Edgar said. "She's gone missing, and I would like you to find her."

I studied the photo for what must've been a long time, because when I looked up, Marsh was glaring at me as though he suspected I had been picturing his little girl in the buff.

"How long has she been missing?" I asked, shifting in my seat.

"Her roommate last saw her a week ago yesterday. She hasn't reported to work, and she hasn't attended class. She's a student at the Art Institute."

"Have you contacted the police?"

Edgar clasped his hands in front of him on the desk and leaned forward in his seat. "Of course, but I'm not the kind to rely on the government to solve my problems."

"What have the cops told you?"

"Not much. They keep telling me they'll call me when they hear something. For all I know, they're not even working on the case. That's why I called you. I want my man on the job so I can be certain something is being done."

I didn't like him referring to me as his man. I didn't like the idea of someone breathing down my neck. I had a bad feeling about the guy, and I liked the prospect of working for him less and less with every passing second.

"I don't usually work this kind of case," I said.

"You used to be in homicide. Is that correct?"

"You think your daughter's been murdered?"

"No, I mean... I don't know what to think." Marsh paused and peered at me with moist eyes. "What I meant was that I would think this kind of investigation would not be beyond your abilities."

"You'd think right, but like I said, I don't normally work these kinds of cases."

"How much are you asking?"

I thought for a moment. "I'd want $50 an hour, plus a thousand upfront."

Marsh accepted quickly enough to make me wonder if I could've gotten more. As it was, I knew I was in for some actual work, and a lot of it. I felt my chest tighten at the thought.

Marsh leaned forward in his seat, his forearms resting on the desk. "Just one thing, Mr. Wozniak: I want to make it clear that as long as you're on my payroll, you will do as I say. I'm a private man, and I do not wish to have my affairs discussed with anyone other than myself."

"I have no intention of speaking to anyone about your affairs. I always adhere to a strict code of client confidentiality."

"Good. The Marsh family's business is the Marsh family's business."

"I fully understand. Since we're on the subject, what exactly is the family business?"

"Now? Nothing really. I have many investments and a staff that watches them. I sit on several boards and do some philanthropic work. I guess you could call me semi-retired. I used to run Marsh Enterprises. We manufactured electrical components for the auto industry. My grandfather founded the business. My father ran the company after him, and I after him. We had a large industrial campus on the south side and employed over 1,000 people. A few years ago, I sold the business to Federated Components." Marsh paused and gazed out the window, a wistful, faraway look on his face. "They've since done away with the Marsh name and moved all operations to Mexico. I've heard that they're about to shut down there and move everything to China."

"That's globalization for you. You go where labor's the cheapest."

Marsh nodded, that same forlorn expression on his face.

I pulled a small notebook out of my inside coat pocket. "Tell me about your daughter."

"What would you like to know?"

"Where does she live? What does she do? What's her normal routine like?"

"She lives with a roommate on the far north side of the city. She goes to school."

"At the Art Institute."

"Right, and she works part-time at a cafe near her house."

"Has she ever taken off like this in the past?"

Marsh poured himself a glass of water from a crystal carafe dappled with condensation and took a sip before answering. "It's not like Alison to take off like this without at least telling her mother. I mean, she ran away once as a teenager, but that was different. She was just a kid then."

"Why'd she run away?"

"Oh, it was nothing. Displeasure with the rules of the house. If I remember correctly, I forbade her going to a concert, and she just took off. She was only gone for a couple of days."

"Any boyfriends?"

Marsh's shoulders slumped. "Perhaps." He shook his head. "I don't know, no one she's mentioned to her mother or me. To be honest, my daughter and I don't talk much. We haven't for the last couple of years."

"Why's that?"

Marsh picked up his daughter's photograph and studied it for a moment as if trying to find the answers there. "I don't know. We're just different people. I don't approve of her choice of studies, and she doesn't approve of me."

"What do you mean?"

"She resents me for selling the business and losing people's jobs, for one thing. Or at least that's what she told me. Of course, she's benefited from the business decisions I've made. She's always had the best of everything, and she'll never want for anything. All she has to do is ask, and it's hers, though she's been less inclined to do so the last couple of years."

"I'm sure she's just going through a phase."

Marsh sighed. The sky grew overcast outside, casting half his face in shadow. "I hope so. The last time we spoke, we had a huge argument about Iraq, of all things. Believe me, I'm not unsympathetic to her beliefs. No one is pro-war. Heck, I even marched against the Vietnam War in '68. You catch Colin Powell's presentation to the UN Security Council?"

I shook my head.

"Masterful, simply masterful. He does a great job of laying out the case for war. I don't see how any right-thinking person could find otherwise. We can't leave a dangerous man like Saddam Hussein in power, not after 9/11. Don't you agree?"

"Sure," I muttered, too tired to feign an interest in politics.

Edgar shook his head. "I'm sorry, I'm rambling."

"That's okay. Let's get back to your daughter. Can you think of anyone who might want to harm her? Perhaps someone who had it out for your family, like a disgruntled former employee?"

Edgar rubbed his chin and considered my question. "I suppose that's possible," he said. "No one comes to mind."

"When was the last time you or your wife saw her?"

"Three weeks ago. Alison came over for dinner and to do some laundry. There's no washer and dryer in her building. She went shopping with her mother a few days after that."

"Did either of you notice anything out of the ordinary? Did she seem depressed?"

"No, I wouldn't say she seemed any different from any other time I saw her, though I suppose it would be hard to tell if she were depressed. She's always been a somber, introverted girl."

"You said she has a roommate. What can you tell me about her?"

"Not much. Her name is Maya Garcia. Alison met her when she answered an ad in the paper. They live in the Rogers Park neighborhood. I'll get you the address."

"Thanks, and if you have the address of this cafe where she works, that would be great."

"Certainly," Edgar said as he jotted down the information.

There was a photo of what I took to be Mrs. Marsh on a credenza behind his desk. She was on the deck of a boat, flashing a toothy smile, her hair blowing in the wind. She looked young, younger than him, not much older than the daughter.

"I would like to speak with your wife," I said.

"Of course, I will have her get in touch with you."

"Great; the sooner I can talk to her, the better. Time is of the essence in these kinds of cases."

"Yes, yes, of course."

"I think I have all that I need to get started, everything but the retainer."

Marsh rang his assistant and asked her to cut me a check. He looked up at me, and his long face seemed to droop just a little further, his eyes moist. It was a look that I could only take for so long. I gathered up my papers and rose to my feet.

"I'll call you to set up an interview with your wife." I fumbled about in my pockets and retrieved my card. "That's my cell phone. Call me if you have any questions."

Marsh took the card. "I will expect regular updates from you," he said.

Get out now, I thought. This is your last chance.

"Of course," I said before walking out, slump-shouldered with my head down, feeling like a condemned man.

THREE

Maya Garcia opened the door a crack, the security chain drawn taut across the narrow opening. She was a petite woman, the eye peering out at me barely reaching chest level.

"Sorry to bother you," I said. "My name is Glenn Wozniak. I'm a private investigator. Edgar Marsh hired me to find his daughter, and I was wondering if you might have a minute to talk."

I reached inside my coat pocket and retrieved a business card and passed it through the crack in the door. Maya studied it for a moment before unfastening the chain to let me in.

She was a nice-looking girl, about five feet tall with long, raven-colored hair. To my surprise, she wore nothing but a T-shirt and a pair of blue cotton panties. I wasn't complaining. She was just my type: round butt, thick thighs, and tiny ankles. Her skin was a warm olive color, and she smelled of vanilla. I noticed the scent as I brushed past her to enter the apartment.

"I just got out of the shower," she explained.

"Oh, I'm sorry. I probably should've called first."

"That's okay," she said, looking me up and down. "To be honest, I'm glad you're here. I'm a little nervous about being alone right now."

"That's understandable."

Maya took my coat and hung it in the front closet. Again, she gave me the once-over, almost as if she were interested in me. I dismissed the idea as wishful thinking. My mind had a way of inventing distractions when there was work to do.

I followed her into a sparsely furnished living room. The apartment was spacious and well-kept. The hallway led into a large living room. Beyond that was an eat-in kitchen and a couple of bedrooms. A cherry wood entertainment center sat against one wall, and opposite that was a burgundy sofa with a simple mission-style coffee table in between. The tabletop was clear except for a couple of Cosmopolitan magazines, a votive in a translucent green acrylic cup, and a half-empty glass of red wine.

Maya took a seat on the sofa. She nestled into a corner, curling one leg underneath her with the other dangling off the couch. I remained standing a safe distance away. I could see her inner thigh and the crotch of her cotton panties and did my best to look elsewhere. I had a bad habit of staring when I saw a nice pair of legs or cleavage or a bare midriff. In short, I have a staring problem. A little bare flesh and I stare like a starving street urchin pressed against a candy store window.

"Can I get you anything?" she asked. "A glass of wine?"

"No, I'm fine," I said, taking a seat on the sofa. I sat at the far end with my back flush against the armrest. "I'll try not to take up too much of your time."

"It's fine. Mr. Marsh said you might visit me, though I'd be a little annoyed if you were with the police. I already spoke to them twice."

"Twice?"

"Yes, two different detectives. They both asked me the same kinds of things, which is kind of weird. I mean, why didn't the second guy just talk to the first guy?"

"Did you get their names?"

"The first guy left his card. The second didn't. Hold on a second."

Maya padded off to the kitchen, returning a moment later with the card. "Detective Conrad was his name."

Conrad. There was a name I hadn't heard in a while. He wouldn't exactly be my first choice for a missing person case. Time was of the essence, and Conrad was never in a hurry. The man liked his overtime.

"And the second guy?"

Maya shook her head. "I don't know. I can't remember. The first guy came by here last night after work. The second guy came to my office this morning. Like I said, they both asked a lot of the same questions. When I asked him why I needed to go through all of this again, he said he was just following up. I'm not up on how the police do things. Is that standard?"

"No, not really."

"Weird."

"I appreciate you taking the time to talk to me. Let's start with when you last saw Alison."

Maya reached for her glass of wine. "Last Thursday, the 29th," she said.

"Did you notice anything different about her behavior? Anything out of the ordinary?"

Maya raised a finger, signaling she needed a moment, and took a sip before answering.

I leaned forward in my seat, resting my forearms on my knees, and watched her drink.

"No, it was like any other Tuesday or Thursday morning," she said. "Alison has class on those days. I was getting ready for work. She was getting ready for school. We were both rushing around, waiting for the washroom, getting in each other's way. The usual roommate stuff."

"Did she seem sad? Depressed? Anxious?"

Maya shook her head.

"Would you say the two of you were close?"

"No. She answered an ad I posted for a roommate when my ex moved out. I mean, we're cool with each other, but we don't hang out or anything."

"What do you know about her social life? Did she have any boyfriends?"

"No one that I had met, though I think she might've started seeing someone." She leaned in, her voice dropping to a whisper, and added, "A married man."

"Really?"

Maya nodded. "One day, I was walking past her bedroom, and I caught the tail end of a conversation she was having with this guy. I think I heard her call him Bill. Anyway, I distinctly heard her say, 'What about your wife?'"

"What about your wife?"

"Uh-huh."

"Anything else?"

"No, that's all I could make out. She must've known I was around because she shut the door to her room."

"Did she ever mention this guy at any other time or say anything about seeing someone?"

"No, I'm afraid that's all I know. I imagine he was older, being married and all. That's probably the one thing we do have in common."

"You're seeing a married man?"

Maya laughed. "No, that's a little too complicated for my tastes. I meant we both like older men."

I froze for a moment. Was she coming on to me?

"Are you okay?" Maya asked. "You're sweating bullets."

I was. Dark circles of moisture had formed in my shirt's armpits, and my face tingled as if all the blood had rushed from my head.

"I'm fine," I said. "Do you mind if I look around?"

"Suit yourself. Alison's bedroom is down the hall, first door to the left."

"Thanks," I said, making a quick getaway.

Alison's room was more amply decorated than the rest of the apartment. A motley collection of knickknacks covered the shelves of a bookcase against one wall and the top of her dresser. A CD rack and a couple of milk crates filled with albums occupied a corner of the room. I browsed her vinyl collection. She had eclectic tastes in music, everything from classical to punk.

One album caught my eye—a rare recording of the Dead Boys at CBGB's. It was the Johnny Blitz benefit concert. Blitz, the band's drummer, had been injured in a knife fight, and the show was to raise money for his medical bills. John Belushi sat in on drums for a part of the set. Divine performed a duet with Stiv Bators. It was the stuff of legends.

I continued thumbing through her collection before remembering why I was there. Some of her artwork sat stacked against the wall just to the right of the milk crates. I gave them a look. Most were paintings of commonplace urban environments: bus stops, grocery stores, subway cars. They were ultra-realistic, like photographs, except for the people. Each figure appeared in silhouette as if a human-shaped hole had been ripped in the space-time continuum, leaving a void.

Towards the end of the stack, I found something a little different, a mixed-media piece—part painting, part collage. It depicted what looked like an image of hell, a fiery swirl of reds and oranges with stalactites sprouting from the ground. A tall, thin man with dark, spiky hair loomed over a doe-eyed little girl in a frilly, baby blue dress. The man bore a vague resemblance to Edgar Marsh, only younger, his features more delicate, almost feminine. Scattered about the piece were phrases clipped out of various women's magazines. 'Ten ways to please your man,' read one. 'A penny for his thoughts,' read another. I turned it over. She had written the title in the upper right-hand corner. Alison had taken it from one of my favorite Stooges songs: "Your Pretty Face is Going to Hell."

I snapped some photos of the room and jotted down a few notes. Wherever Alison went, she didn't intend to be gone for long. An entire set of luggage sat unused in her bedroom closet, and she had left her birth control pills in one of her dresser drawers.

I rummaged through her nightstand, finding her passport, birth certificate, some outstanding bills, and various receipts. I also found a stack of flyers from a group called the International League of Spartacists. They were for a "teach-in" on the impending war in Iraq. The meeting was the following evening at the Green Briar Park field house. I took a flyer and stuck it in my pocket.

The sound of bare feet padding across a hardwood floor came from behind me. I turned around to find Maya, still half-naked, leaning in the doorway. She stretched, revealing a plump yet appealing midriff. "Find anything interesting?" she asked.

I did, which was the problem. I was supposed to be looking for Edgar Marsh's daughter, not ogling some girl half my age. I turned away, flustered, and pretended to examine the contents of Alison's nightstand.

"I don't know," I said. "I should probably get going. You have my card. Call me if you think of anything you'd like to add."

"Are you sure you have to leave so soon?"

"I'm afraid so. I've got a bunch more people to question."

She looked disappointed. "Oh, okay. Give me a call if you have any more questions."

She peered up at me, and I made the mistake of returning her gaze. Maya must've sensed what I was thinking, seen the blue movie playing in my head reflected in the darks of my eyes. She looked away, staring at her bare feet.

I grabbed my coat out of the closet and headed for the door. "Thanks for taking the time to speak with me."

"No problem," Maya said. "I hope I was helpful."

"Yes, very," I said in a rush.

We stopped at the door. Maya stood so close that I could almost feel the warmth coming off her body. For a moment, I thought about making a move, perhaps just asking her if she wanted to meet for coffee, but the words caught in my throat.

"Thanks," I said, fumbling for the knob. The door wouldn't open. I turned what I thought was the deadbolt and tried again. Still no luck. I worked the lock on the knob and tried once more only to discover I had secured the deadbolt.

"Here, allow me," Maya said. She opened the door, and I stepped out onto the landing.

"Bye," I said.

Maya smiled and gave me a little wave. "Bye."

I headed down the stairs, the awkwardness of my exit trailing me like a foul odor. Outside, an icy wind blew. I turned the collar up on my coat and headed back to the car, lingering outside it for a moment with my hand on the door handle. My mind kept replaying Maya in the doorway to Alison's bedroom, each time her words tinged a little more with sex. Before long, I was kicking myself for not making a move. She said she liked older men. How much more obvious could she be?

I turned and looked up at what I assumed was her window, hoping to glimpse her. When she didn't appear, I opened the car door and took a seat. I peered up at the rearview mirror, catching my reflection. A middle-aged man with a pudgy face and thinning hair looked back at me. That cinched it. I turned my key in the ignition and headed for home.

FOUR

I'd lived in the same small four-room apartment for more than a decade. Over the years, the detritus of a lazy bachelor lifestyle had collected on every flat surface of the place as if alive and reproducing. Piles of books, newspapers, magazines, compact discs (both in and out of their cases), junk mail, and bills formed a rough topography throughout the space. Most nights, I slept on the sofa—my bed lost beneath a layer of clothes that spilled onto the floor—my bedroom part closet, part hamper, the distinction no longer clear as clean mingled with dirty.

I usually dozed with the television on, lulled to sleep by late-night talk shows and get-rich-quick infomercials. I ended my first night on the Marsh job much the same way, only less comfortably. I tossed and turned as I mulled over the work that lay ahead before finally coming to rest on my stomach with my head buried in the crook of my right arm. When I awoke, the limb hung limp and numb at my side; the feeling returning in waves of prickling heat.

I had slept later than I intended. The clock on my VCR read ten AM. I rummaged through the clutter on my coffee table, found a Stooges CD, and popped it in the stereo before fixing myself a pot of coffee. A cold draft ran across the floor, chilling my feet. I returned to the sofa and smoked cigarette after cigarette, trying to wake up as "Search and Destroy" played. A dull light leaked through the sides of the window shades, the walls of my living room appearing gray in the winter morning gloom. Smoke coiled from the tip of my cigarette towards the ceiling and dispersed. I watched it, thinking about Maya, and then about the case, before settling on how much I hated working and how unnecessary this job would've been had Gary simply paid me the money he owed.

Fucking Gary. Why didn't I turn the screws on him? I should've lied and said I still had friends with the city who could've made his life difficult. How would you like daily visits from the building inspector, Gary? How would you like to be fined for even the slightest traffic violation? Heck, you won't be able to get away with jaywalking if you don't pay up. That's what I should've said. Then I could've told Edgar Marsh thanks, but no thanks. Oh well, what's done is done. Playtime was over. I needed the work, needed the money, so I pushed myself. I pushed myself to shave, shower, and get dressed to do the fucking job. I pushed and pushed, and before I knew it, it was noon. The nine-to-fivers were already halfway through their workdays, and I was just leaving the house.

My first stop was the Art Institute of Chicago. I began by checking the school directory for professors named Bill, finding two. Unfortunately, neither fit the profile of Alison's married man. One was in his late seventies, and the other was, as one secretary in the front office put it, "as gay as the day is long." I questioned one of Alison's professors—a tall, husky woman with hands larger than mine. Her name was Bradshaw, and she taught something called intaglio printing. She knew little, though she confirmed Alison attended class from noon until 1:30 on January 29. I gave her my card and asked her to call me if she thought of anything else.

I kept pushing, driving north to pay Alison's work a visit. The Metropolitan Cafe was on Sheridan Road, near the lake. It was a sleepy storefront operation with a smattering of tables. I met with the proprietor, a man named Jeff Ledewski. He was short and stocky with a rosy complexion, a thick, white beard, and thinning hair, the top of his head baring a semi-circle of light red skin. He regarded me with moist, rheumy-looking eyes as we spoke, appearing as if he was on the brink of tears.

Alison was a good employee, he said—reliable, hard-working, a pleasure to be around. She had called in sick to work on the day of her disappearance, and that was the last he had heard from her. It was not like her to take off without telling anyone. And so on.

"Be honest with me," he said. "Her chances aren't good."

"Why do you say that?"

"I read that missing persons rarely turn up alive after the first 48 hours."

"Yeah, well..." I began before trailing off. I had nothing to say. He was right.

Jeff shook his head. "Why her? She was so smart and kind. She was super talented. Some of her artwork hangs in the front. She painted one of them for me, a city scene of Sheridan at night. You can see the cafe in it."

Jeff's eyes welled up with tears. He grabbed a handkerchief from his desk and dabbed at his eyes. I didn't like where this was going. The work was one thing, but I had a hard time with the emotions. I didn't know how to react. I wouldn't say I was unfeeling. I wasn't dead inside. It's more like whatever's inside me—in my heart, my head—was sleeping off a nasty hangover, and I wasn't ready to wake it, to feel all the pain that comes with returning to consciousness. Watching this little man shedding tears for Alison, I could feel a part of me stirring, and I wanted nothing more than to hit the snooze button and send it back to sleep.

“Did Alison give any indication that anything was wrong in her life?” I asked, trying to redirect the conversation. “Did she seem troubled or worried?”

“Not particularly, though there was one instance that’s been bothering me since she disappeared. It was about three weeks ago. I overheard Alison arguing with someone on the phone. It sounded like a boyfriend.”

“A boyfriend? Did you ever meet this guy?”

“No, I never met him, but I overheard her telling him she never wanted to see him again or something like that. She seemed pretty shaken up.”

“How so?”

“She was scared, so scared she asked me to drive her home that night, and she only lives a few blocks away.”

“Did she say anything about the call?”

“No, I asked, but she said she didn’t want to talk about it.”

“Did she ever mention someone named Bill?”

“Bill? No, I met a friend of hers from the anti-war group she belongs to. I think his name was Scott.”

“Could you describe him?”

“Sure, he was a big guy—must’ve been around 6‘1″, husky build, short brown hair, brown eyes, kind of clean-cut looking. He seemed nice.”

“Do you know how I might get in touch with him?”

Jeff shook his head. "I only met him once or twice. I suppose you could attend a meeting. I think they have one tonight."

Ledewski opened the top drawer of his desk and retrieved a pink sheet of paper. It was the flyer I had found in Alison's bedroom.

At first, I thought the International League of Spartacists got its name from the 1960 Stanley Kubrick film, *Spartacus*, starring Kirk Douglas as the titular hero. I was close. A small collection of University of Chicago students formed the ILS, as it was more commonly called, in the mid-90s. They named the group after the Spartacus League, a German Marxist movement that existed during the latter years of the First World War, which had derived its name from the leader of the Roman Empire's largest slave rebellion, the very guy Kirk Douglas played in the movie.

The International League of Spartacists was also something of a misnomer in that it was far from a global movement. At its height, its members spanned a few Chicago-area campuses stretching from Hyde Park to the near north side of the city. The group's initials spelled the French word for "they," and its followers would often signal their solidarity to the movement by greeting each other *en francais* with a seeming non-sequitur, *ils sont entre amis*. Translation: "They are among friends." The cloak-and-dagger act was little more than an affectation as the ILS held their meetings in the most public of places—libraries, coffee shops, university cafeterias—without otherwise bothering to code their language or even keep their voices down.

On this date, the group met at the Green Briar Park field house. The building sat at the end of an open, rectangular field surrounded by brick bungalows and three-flat apartment buildings. Inside, a children's basketball game was going on in the gym, and the intermittent squeak of shoes echoed throughout the building. The meeting room was across from there. The group configured it like a classroom with a blackboard and a large desk up front facing four rows of wooden chairs.

I appeared to be early. The only people in the room were two scruffy-looking men in their early twenties and an older woman with long, brittle gray hair. One of the guys was short and bespectacled with a shaved head and the beginnings of a beard, the hair on his scalp and face of an almost uniform length. The other man was lanky. He also wore a beard, his thicker and unkempt. The shorter of the two men sat atop the big wooden desk at the front of the room. I assumed he was the guy in charge, or at least as in charge as anyone could be in a group like this. They all turned as I entered and flashed big, toothy smiles.

"Are you here for the meeting?" asked the guy at the front of the room.

"Yes, I am," I said.

"Great, my name is Tim," he said and then motioning to the others, "This is Phillip and Brenda."

"Pleased to meet you. Is this everyone?"

Brenda laughed. "Oh no, more will be along shortly. I'm afraid we rarely get started on time. We have a lot of people coming here straight from work or school."

That figured. The people who opposed wars were never quite as organized as those who waged them.

"That's good," I said. "It'll give us a chance to talk. I wanted to ask you about one of your members, Alison Marsh."

"Are you guys fucking with us?" Phillip said, his face turning red. They closed ranks—the guys on either end of Brenda, arms crossed.

"Fucking with you? No, what are you talking about?"

"We already spoke to the police," Brenda said. "Twice!"

"Okay. Okay. I get it, sorry. I'm not a cop. I'm a private investigator. Alison's father hired me to find her." I handed each of them a card. Tim studied it, his eyes narrowing into slits.

"Sorry about jumping down your throat," Phillip said. "We're a little on edge. We've had some trouble with the police recently, and then two different detectives visited us when Alison disappeared, which seemed a little weird.

Here, I got one of their cards. Hold on a second." He picked up a weathered backpack off the floor and rummaged about, producing a business card. "Detective Conrad. That was the first guy we spoke to. The second guy didn't leave a card. I saw a badge. His name was West or Wellesley or something like that."

Those names didn't ring a bell. "I'm sorry to ask you guys to go through this again, but if you could help me out, I'd greatly appreciate it. The family is worried sick, as I'm sure you can imagine."

A tall kid with dark spiky hair and a pallid complexion entered the room. "Is this the International League of Spartacists meeting?" he asked.

"Yes, thanks for coming," Tim said. "Sit wherever you'd like. We should start shortly."

The kid walked over to a seat in the front row and then gave Tim a look as if he sought his approval.

"Yeah, that's cool," Tim said. "Anywhere is fine." He turned to me. "Sorry about that. How can we help you?"

I asked a few questions, and they answered, divulging nothing too revelatory: Alison was a dedicated and well-liked member of the group. Tim met her through his girlfriend, another Art Institute student. No one noticed anything out of the ordinary about her behavior in the days leading up to her disappearance. And so on. There were no aha moments, no tearful confessions, nothing to mercifully send me back to my comfortable existence of booze-soaked leisure. This interview was little different than the last two, little different, I imagined, than every other would be from here on out. I was at best, collecting half-heard conversations and background noise. Ledewski had it right. The trail had gone cold long ago.

"Did Alison ever mention someone named Bill to you?" I asked.

They shook their heads.

"Not that I remember," Tim said.

"Any boyfriends?"

Phillip folded his arms, a sour expression on his face. I'd struck a nerve.

"What's wrong?" I asked.

He shook his head. "Nothing, nothing at all."

"Alison was seeing someone in the group," Brenda said.

"Scott," Phillip said. "Scott Richter."

"She never actually said that they were dating," Brenda interjected. "But they'd been spending a lot of time together."

"What can you tell me about him?"

"I don't know," Phillip said. "There's not much to him. He's one of those big, beefy athletic types." Then with a shrug. "I guess that's what she's into."

Tim rolled his eyes.

"What?" Phillip said. "Don't tell me you like that ape."

"As a matter of fact, I do," Tim said. "He's a nice guy."

"Nice? More like crazy. Remember Greuning Corp?"

"What's Greuning Corp?" I asked.

"Nothing," Tim said. Then, turning to Phillip, "I'm sure the man isn't interested in what we do."

"Well, actually—" I said.

"He should be interested!" Phillip shouted. "Alison's missing, and I'm sure that nutcase had something to do with it."

"You don't mean that," Brenda said. "Scott would never hurt her. He's not that kind of guy."

"Give me a break!" Phillip scoffed. Then turning to me. "Look, man, I'll tell you what happened. A few weeks ago, we were organizing a demonstration at Greuning Corp.'s offices. They build planes for the military and stand to make a hefty profit off the war. So, of course, they've been lobbying pretty hard to remove Saddam Hussein from power. Anyway, the plan was to stage a demonstration in the lobby of their corporate offices. We were trying to decide whether we should enter the lobby one by one or as a group when Scott suggested we do something more provocative."

"Like what?" I asked.

"Like planting a pipe bomb somewhere on the premises. A pipe bomb! Can you believe that shit? The fucking nutjob said that we'd be giving them a taste of their own medicine."

"I think Scott just got carried away," Brenda said.

"Oh, please," Phillip said. "That's like saying Bin Laden just got carried away. We're not terrorists, for fuck's sake."

"So what happened at the protest?" I asked.

Tim chuckled. "We didn't plant any explosives. That's for sure. We wouldn't have had a chance even if we had wanted to."

"What do you mean?"

"The cops were waiting for us when we got there. They intercepted us the second we set foot on the property."

"You think someone tipped them off?"

"It would seem so. We don't know who, but we have our suspicions. There were some members who missed the demonstration and stopped showing up right after."

"So, what happened?"

"We all spent a night in jail," Brenda said with a shrug. "It goes with the territory."

"We'd still be there if we'd listened to Scott," Phillip said. "Can you imagine what would've happened if they'd found explosives on us, at the headquarters of a top government contractor no less?"

"It wouldn't have been pretty," Brenda conceded.

"Do you know how I might reach this Scott guy?" I asked.

"I suppose you could sit in on the meeting, see if he shows up."

"And if not?"

"Tim keeps a list of members' numbers," Phillip said.

Tim hesitated for a moment. "Right," he said, a look of resignation on his face. "I got it right here."

“Ten to one says you don’t reach him,” Phillip said. “He’s probably long gone by now. Perhaps the cops might’ve found his ass if they weren’t wasting their time fucking with us.”

“Perhaps,” I said.

Tim gave me the number, and I grabbed a seat. The room gradually filled over the next few minutes. Tim, Brenda, and Phillip took turns leading the meeting. All the while, I mentally undressed a cute young blonde sitting in the front row. She had to have been in her early twenties, slender yet busty, her hair in a ponytail.

“The Bush Administration is using Saddam’s pursuit of nuclear weapons as a justification for this war, but Iraq is further away from acquiring nuclear weapons than at least a hundred other nations,” Brenda said as I thought about how long it had been since I had last slept with a woman.

“The administration hasn’t provided a reason the UN inspectors shouldn’t finish the job they were sent there to do,” Tim said as I considered my prospects with Maya.

“Don’t let them fool you with talk of liberating the Iraqi people,” Phillip said as I pictured my hands cupping the blonde’s breasts.

“Let’s not forget that for many years the US supported Hussein,” Phillip continued, his every word mere white noise. I was in my own little world, my mind concocting all sorts of dirty scenarios involving Maya and the blonde.

They brought a smile to my face. In fact, I was grinning ear-to-ear—a twisted, lascivious smile—when the blonde caught me staring. My face went red, and my stomach did a flip. I tried to look nonchalant, but it was no use. She gave me a disgusted look as if she'd caught me picking my nose.

I tried to focus on the case, tuning in just in time to catch Phillip on a roll. "The US has supported countless dictators in the name of furthering the economic interests of the nation's elite," he said. "We've looked the other way as these totalitarian states slaughtered innocents. We've actively undermined democratically elected regimes. This is not about liberating oppressed people. America's military adventures never are!"

The tall, pale kid in the front raised his hand. It was an unusually large hand with long, slender fingers. "Excuse me," he said, his voice small and tentative.

"Yes," said Phillip.

The kid stood up. He was long-limbed and slump-shouldered, awkward yet oddly imposing. "I want to thank you," he said.

"I'm sorry. Thank me? For what?"

"Not just you," the kid said, his eyes moist with tears. "All of you. I'm moved. I'm moved." The kid paused for a moment before repeating, "I'm moved," once more. He trembled as he spoke, as though he were about to break down.

Phillip regarded him uncomfortably, unsure of what to say. I exchanged a glance with the guy next to me, and we both shrugged as if to say, what can you do? There's one in every crowd.

"I'm sorry," the kid said. "I'm not good with words. I just wanted to say I appreciate what you are doing here. You're trying to prevent a war and make the world a better place. I'm moved. Thank you."

"Thank you for coming out and supporting us," Phillip said. "This is a joint effort. We succeed by working together."

The kid reached into his coat pocket and pulled out a thick stack of cash bound by a rubber band. "I want you to have this," he said.

Tim stood up, waving off the money. "That's okay," he said. "We're not asking for donations."

"It costs money to spread the word," the kid said. "You print flyers, right? Those cost money. I heard you say you were recently arrested for protesting. You could use this to make bail next time or to hire an attorney. Please take it. I insist."

He walked to the front of the room, placed the money in Phillip's hand, and departed before anyone could say anything.

"That was weird," Brenda said.

Tim nodded. "Yeah."

"Nice of him," an attendee added.

"Oh definitely," Tim said. "It's just that's... never happened before."

Phillip thumbed through the stack of bills, a look of bewilderment on his face. "Holy shit! There must be a good five grand here." He paused for a moment. "And to think my parents keep bugging me to get a real job. I guess drinks are on me!"

We all had a big laugh at that.

"I guess on that note, we'll call it a meeting," Tim said. "Thanks for coming. If you haven't already, please give us your email so we can keep you abreast of our next action and, I guess, what we're going to be doing with our newfound finances."

The crowd thinned out until there was only Tim, Phillip, Brenda, and me.

"Hey, I don't know what to tell you," Tim said. "Scott hasn't missed a meeting in weeks."

"That's okay," I said. "I'll try calling him."

We said our goodbyes, and I headed back to my car. As I approached, I could hear the halting whine of an automobile struggling to start, and then its engine revving to life. I checked my side-view mirror. I could see a car idling halfway out of a parking space about a block behind me as though in the middle of pulling out. One headlight was dimmer than the other, looking like a lazy eye. I sat for a while and let my car warm up, checking behind me a few minutes later. The car hadn't moved. It just sat there idling, its front extending out into the street.

I pulled out, and Lazy Eye followed suit. We drove around the park. I turned onto Peterson Avenue and headed east. I checked my rearview mirror. Lazy Eye was still behind me, and I had the sinking suspicion I was being followed.

I stopped at Western Avenue, pulling into a gas station. Lazy Eye slowed and hesitated for a moment before pulling away. This gave me a chance to get a better look at the car. It was a burgundy Buick LeSabre. I tried to make out the license, but it was too dark.

I pulled out of the gas station and resumed my journey home. I hadn't gone more than a couple of blocks when a feeling of dread came over me. I checked my rearview mirror. Nothing. A minute passed, and I checked again, this time catching the Buick drift into view for a moment before disappearing behind another vehicle a few car lengths back. Now I was sure he was tailing me.

I turned and started heading back west and then north towards where I had come. The Buick slowed on turns, that dim headlight drifting out of view before reappearing. I sped up and made a quick turn down a side street, the car skidding on the icy road before I could right it again. I ducked down an alley, pulling the car in behind a large dumpster, and shut off the engine. A few moments later, I watched my old friend drive past. I turned the key in the ignition and pulled out of the alley to find him stopped at an intersection about a half-block ahead of me. Now it was my turn to do the following.

There's an art to tailing a car. You want to stay close enough that you don't lose the person you're following but not so close that they notice the pursuit. I always try to keep another car between me and my target. My friend in the Buick had that part down. He might've tailed me all the way home if it weren't for that dim headlight blowing his cover. I fared better, slowing on turns so that I would drift out of his rearview mirror's field of vision, only to reappear at a distance where my car could not be recognized at night. I'd let one or two cars pass me, always keeping track of my target.

I followed him back to Western Avenue. This time we headed north. The Buick turned right again onto Pratt Avenue upon reaching Warren Park. I could see in the distance a hill where children went sledding on snowy days. It appeared in silhouette, looking desolate against the night sky. We turned off Pratt at Ridge Avenue and headed north again. I passed large wood-frame houses and, to the left, cookie-cutter townhomes built during the late sixties. We turned right at Touhy Avenue, heading east once again towards the lake, zigzagging in such a way that I wondered if Lazy Eye was onto my tail job.

The Buick slowed down, and I followed suit. It stopped just before an empty spot on the street. The driver skillfully maneuvered the enormous vehicle into the space and got out. I turned on my flashers and double-parked a few car lengths back. The driver exited the Buick. He was middle-aged and stocky with a marshmallow complexion and a no-nonsense buzz cut. He looked familiar, but I couldn't place where I'd seen him before.

I watched him enter a brick apartment complex with a front courtyard and multiple entrances, following a couple minutes later, in time to see him go through the second door to the right. I waited a minute before doing the same. I scanned the names on the mailboxes, finding one that I recognized. It read: George Wesley.

Just then, it hit me. No wonder the guy looked familiar. George Wesley was a cop.

FIVE

Don's was a greasy fast-food joint within spitting distance of several Wicker Park bars and nightclubs. It was better lit than it had any right to be, the glare of fluorescent lights reflecting off canary yellow tables to illuminate an extensive collection of stains on the floors, walls, and furniture.

It was a little after midnight, and the place was crawling with drunks stuffing their faces and talking loudly, usually at the same time. A big, awkward-looking black man wearing Coke-bottle glasses occupied a booth in the back of the restaurant. His name was Todd Burton, and he was the reason for my visit.

Todd was my former partner. He was a hefty guy with a hearty appetite. I'd say outsized, but Todd had grown into it, especially around his midsection. He particularly loved a good Italian beef sandwich. It was enough motivation for him to brave the stupid and the drunk. He tuned out the din of the crowd, at one with his meal. Nothing fazed him, not the guy passed out and drooling on the table next to him or the filthy homeless man making the rounds in search of spare change. Todd took a bite out of his sandwich, grease dripping off his fingers, and closed his eyes for a moment, an almost Zen-like look of pure contentment on his face. That look disappeared the second he glimpsed me. He sank into his seat, raising his sandwich in front of his face as if trying to hide behind it. I pretended not to notice and sat down across from him.

"What do you want?" he said.

"What makes you think I want something?"

Todd chuckled and shook his head. We sat for a moment, not saying anything, the booth going as cold as the February night air outside. Todd took another bite of his sandwich, a placid smile forming on his lips despite me.

"That smells good," I said.

"Get your own," Todd said with his mouth full.

"I wasn't asking you to share. I was just saying it smells good."

"Best darn Italian beef in the city of Chicago."

"No kidding?"

"No kidding."

"Let me try it."

"Get the fuck out of here," Todd said. He held the sandwich away from me, a wide-eyed look of panic on his pudgy face. "I told you I'm not sharing."

"I'm just kidding," I said.

"That shit ain't funny. I've been craving this sandwich all day."

"Best in the city, huh?"

"Damn straight. Some people are partial to Mr. Beef, but for my money, nobody beats Don's."

"I'm more of an Al's guy myself."

"Al's is good."

"Or what's that place in Elmwood Park everyone is always raving about?"

"I don't know. I'm never out that way."

Todd took another bite out of his sandwich and returned to his happy place.

"You know what?" I said. "I enjoy watching you eat."

He looked at me incredulously.

"I'm serious. I've never seen anyone look so content. It's nice."

"What do you want, Glenn?"

"I just wanted to say hi."

"Okay, you said it, so I guess we're done here."

"Hey, man, what's with the attitude? I do something to upset you?"

Todd looked like he was about to say something and then caught himself.

"What?"

"What? All right, I didn't want to get into it, but since you asked, let's do this. How about two weeks ago? You remember that?"

I did. Not one of my finer moments. "What about it?"

Todd took a bite out of his Italian beef sandwich before responding. A brown-green wad of masticated bread, roast beef, and giardiniera tumbled between his lips as he spoke. "What about it? How about you dragging me out drinking on a Tuesday and leaving me passed out in front of my building? Does that ring a bell?"

"What did you want me to do? Carry you? You're not exactly petite. Besides, I was half in the bag myself."

"You were sober enough to go through my pockets and take my keys. You had no problem raiding my refrigerator and crashing in my bed."

"You're right, I'm sorry. That was selfish of me."

"Damn right, it was selfish."

"Let me make it up to you."

Todd laughed. "How is your broke ass going to make it up to me?"

"I just got a job. As soon as I'm done with this case, we'll go to Morton's and get porterhouses as big your head. My treat. For the record, that's *your* head we're talking about, okay? That's a big steak."

Todd was not amused. "What do you want?" he asked.

"I just need a small favor."

"Don't tell me, a couple of bucks to tide you over until you get paid."

"Not necessary. I got a healthy advance."

Todd looked surprised.

"I need you to check something for me."

"What?"

I told him about the case and my encounter with George Wesley. "What can you tell me about this guy?" I asked.

"Not much. He's in narcotics, been there for a few years now."

"So what's he doing poking around in Conrad's missing person case?"

"What do you mean?"

"Several people I've questioned mentioned getting visits from two detectives. One was Conrad."

"Old man Conrad? He's still working?"

"I guess if you call it that."

"And you think the other is Wesley?"

"Well, yeah, seeing as he tried to tail me."

"All right; let me see what I can find out."

I left Todd to his meal and headed out. It was late, but there was no way I was getting to sleep anytime soon. I stopped by one of my usual haunts—a smoky dive about two blocks from my apartment. The place was called Club Foot, though most patrons simply referred to it as "the Foot." I practically lived there.

My usual spot at the end of the bar was open. I grabbed it, slapped a few bills on the bar, and settled in for the night. By last call, I had reached that semi-depraved state where serving me caused the bartender a crisis of conscience. I threw down one last shot and beer combo for good measure and did the drunken cha-cha home before passing out on my couch.

The next morning, I woke up to the phone ringing. It rang four times before mercifully going to voicemail. I lay in bed for a while, my head pounding as I buried my eyes in the crook of my arm, trying to block out the light. A few minutes passed before I worked up the nerve to check the time. It was almost noon. I checked my messages. The call was from Edgar Marsh, and he wasn't happy.

"Wozniak," the message began. Wozniak! That's how he was addressing me now. "Wozniak, I would appreciate you giving me a call. I'd like to know what progress, if any, you've made. I trust your lack of communication will not become a habit. I expect daily updates on how the case is progressing. Get back to me as soon as possible."

He ended the message by rattling off his phone number so fast that it was unintelligible. I tracked down some scrap paper where I had written it earlier and gave him a call. One of the servants answered the phone. "Marsh residence," she said in a cheery singsong.

"Yes, may I speak to Mr. Marsh?"

"Who may I tell him is calling?"

"It's Glenn Wozniak returning his call."

"I'll see if he is available."

I listened to her shoes clicking off into the distance, walking on what sounded like a marble floor. I had to see that house. I made a mental note to visit Mrs. Marsh.

Edgar picked up. "Before you say anything, I want you to know that I am not a happy client. When I pay someone, I expect service, and in your case, that means information."

"Sorry, I intended to call you this evening."

"Tell you what, we're going to set a new rule. Starting now, you will provide daily reports regardless of what you've found. Is that understood?"

"Yes sir," I said through gritted teeth.

"Good, now where do things stand?"

"Well, I've assembled a rough timeline leading up to your daughter's disappearance. Alison was home getting ready for school around seven in the morning on the 29th. She had two classes that day: one in the morning, another at noon. One of her professors confirmed that she was in school. Around two or three in the afternoon, she called in sick to work, and that was the last anyone heard from her."

"Is that it? I got that much from the police."

"No, you didn't let me finish. Alison's roommate mentioned overhearing a phone conversation with a man named

Bill. From the sound of things, they were seeing each other, and he was married."

"Married?"

"Yeah, Maya heard your daughter ask the guy about his wife."

"What exactly did she say?"

"She said: 'What about your wife?'"

I waited a few seconds for a reaction, but Marsh had gone silent. I continued, "I asked around about this Bill guy, but no one else seems to remember meeting or hearing her speak of him. Some people mentioned that she had been seeing another man named Scott. She met him at an anti-war meeting. I attended a meeting of the same group last night, but he didn't attend."

"She was seeing two men?"

"It would appear so."

"Anything else?"

"Her boss said he overheard her breaking up with someone over the phone about two or three weeks ago. It sounds like she was pretty shaken up by the conversation because she asked him to drive her home after work, and she only lives a few blocks away from the cafe."

"What are you saying? She was scared?"

"It would appear so."

Marsh went quiet again.

"Hello?" I said after a while.

"Yes, I'm here," he said. "Just thinking. Alison must've come to her senses and was breaking it off with this married guy."

"Perhaps."

"Perhaps? There's no perhaps about it. Alison's not the type to sleep around, and she wouldn't get involved with a married man."

I didn't like where this was headed. "Of course," I said.

Marsh cleared his throat. "Look, just let me know as soon as you find anything out. And I'll expect regular calls from you, regardless."

We hung up, and I called the number Tim gave me for Scott Richter. It rang a few times before going to voicemail. I left a message introducing myself and asked him to call me. I then contemplated my next move and, realizing I didn't have one, dozed off on the couch only to be awoken a half-hour later by a call from Todd.

"You got a pen and paper?" he asked. "I got some info on your boy George Wesley."

"Yeah, sure, but let me ask you something," I said.

"I don't have a lot of time, Glenn. I just spent the last couple hours—"

"It'll only take a second. Do you think it would be wrong for me to ask out someone I met on the case?"

The line went silent for a moment. "Who?" Todd asked.

"The Marsh girl's roommate. She's kind of cute, and I sensed some chemistry between us when we met."

I could just picture Todd rolling his eyes. "Like that waitress at the Salt and Pepper Diner that wanted nothing to do with you?"

"No, this was different. This girl was giving off some serious signals. She answered the door wearing nothing but a T-shirt and panties and didn't put a stitch of clothing on the entire time I was there."

"How old was this chick?"

"Early twenties."

Another pause. "She probably thought you were a fag."

I don't know what bothered me more, the put-down or that it took him a moment to come up with such a weak burn. "Ha-ha, real funny."

"Look, I don't have time for this shit. I've got work to do, and I've already pissed away enough of my day chasing down leads for you."

"Come on, man, just tell me what you think, honestly."

"Honestly? I think you're imagining things, and I think it's a total conflict of interest."

Typical Todd, the overgrown boy scout. "I don't care what you think. This chick is interested in me, and what's wrong with that?"

"I'm sure she is. I just wonder what's doing it for her: the thinning hair, the beer gut, or that you're a barely employed man in his forties. What twenty-year-old girl could resist a package like that? And you don't see a conflict of interest? What if she's playing you? What if she's involved in the Marsh girl's disappearance? That's probably why she's coming on to you. She's a desperate criminal."

I lit a cigarette and took a deep drag. "Very funny," I said, smoke getting in my eyes.

"I'm not even smiling. Seriously, Glenn, I'd watch that shit."

"You don't know what you're talking about."

"You know what? I don't care."

"Okay fine. What did you find out?"

"All right, but listen carefully, because I'm only going to go over this once. I asked around about your boy George Wesley, and he had a partner assigned to this thing called the Joint Terrorism Task Force. It's a special project CPD's doing with the feds. The guy's name is Bill Bertram, and they assigned him to investigate that anti-war group."

"Did you say *Bill* Bertram?"

"Yes, do you know him?"

"No, I never heard of him, but Alison's roommate said she overheard her talking on the phone with a guy named Bill shortly before her disappearance. Why are the cops interested in these guys?"

"It's like anything else in this city; just follow the money. You see, under the Patriot Act, the feds are giving money to municipalities that can prove there's a terrorist threat in their area, so a lot of cities have been passing off lefty groups like the one you were at as persons of interest to justify the funding. They'll send in a young cop disguised as a protester to spy on them and perhaps stir up a little trouble. It's not legit police work, but it pays the bills."

I should've known. Federal dollars or not, Chicago was never kind to protesters or anyone looking to shake things up. This was the city of the Haymarket Riot and the 1968 Democratic Convention, the police force that murdered Fred Hampton in his sleep.

"So, what can you tell me about Bertram?"

"He's in his mid-thirties but looks younger. He could easily pass for mid-to-late-twenties. He's married and has one child: a son. Until recently, he worked for the Fourth District narcotics unit, but his commanding officer recommended him for the Joint Terrorism Task Force. They assigned him to the anti-war group the Marsh girl belonged to, where he went by an alias of Scott Richter."

So Scott and Bill were the same guy. That explained a lot.

Todd continued, "Here's the kicker. Bertram's been missing since January 29th."

"That's when Alison disappeared."

"Exactly. You'll want to follow up with Captain Montanez at the Belmont station. He's the guy heading up the task force. I told him to expect a visit from you."

We hung up. I sat and thought for a moment. Until now, I had been going through the motions, never really expecting to get anywhere with the case. I'd banked on a week, two weeks tops, of futility before Marsh wised up and fired me in favor of a more competent investigator with a better work ethic. But now I was stuck. I was seeing some genuine progress. I had found Alison's married man.

SIX

The Belmont Avenue police station had a familiar funk. I recognized it the moment I entered—a combination of stale air, male perspiration, and the ancient musk of yellowed papers filed away long ago and forgotten. The station walls reverberated with the usual bustle and racket. A tearful young woman reported a stolen car at the front desk, and I could hear the echoes of a man somewhere in the bowels of the building protesting his impending incarceration.

"Man, I told you that bag didn't belong to me," he cried.

An old homeless man with the beginnings of a beard dozed on a bench next to the front desk; one arm handcuffed to the armrest. His skin was ruddy and weatherworn—his clothes, torn and dingy. He wore an olive-drab jacket with a hood. Tufts of stuffing, turned gray by the elements, protruded from a series of holes in the fabric. The man mumbled obscenities to himself in a placid monotone—a deranged lullaby.

A tall, pimple-faced young cop, who seemed better suited for working the fry grill at a Mickey D's, manned the front desk.

"Can I help you?" he asked.

"Yes, I'm here to see Captain Montanez."

"Is he expecting you?"

"Yes, I have a one o'clock appointment."

"Your name?"

"Glenn Wozniak."

"I'll check to see if the captain is available." The kid motioned to the psychopath with a bench growing out of his arm. "Have a seat."

"Thanks, but I think I'll stand."

The kid peered over the desk at the homeless man. He had ceased his ranting, and was now sleeping, a long strand of drool extending from his chin to his chest like a spiderweb. The kid rolled his eyes before heading down the corridor towards the lock-up and offices. I leaned against the counter and waited. A few minutes later, the kid returned and shuffled me off to an interrogation room to continue my wait.

A long, gray Formica table sat in the center, surrounded by four hard plastic chairs. The room was more like a cubicle or a cell, eight feet by nine feet, the furniture crammed in tight enough to make the place suffocating. Fluorescent lights hummed overhead and bathed everything in a pale, sickly light. I sat facing the reflective end of what I figured to be a two-way mirror. The view wasn't good. I looked like shit, all pasty-faced and sweaty, with dark circles under my eyes. I sat with my hands folded in front of me and waited. About twenty minutes later, a stocky, potbellied man entered the room. He had thick, dark hair that started an inch above his eyebrows. Or eyebrow to be more exact.

"Mr. Wozniak?" he said.

I rose from my seat and extended a hand. "Captain Montanez?"

"Yes, pleased to meet you," he said, giving my hand a quick, firm shake. "I hope I didn't keep you waiting too long."

Of course, he had kept me waiting just long enough to put me in a sour mood, but I didn't let on. "No, not at all, though these rooms could use some reading material."

"It's not a hair salon, Wozniak."

Montanez dropped a thick, manila envelope on the table and slowly descended into the seat across from me. "Sergeant Burton tells me you wanted some info on Bill Bertram."

"Yes, I'm working on a missing person case, and I believe his disappearance may be connected."

"And who exactly is this missing person?"

"Alison Marsh."

"Sounds familiar. Rich girl?"

I nodded.

"I think Bertram mentioned her in one of his reports."

"So, what can you tell me about Detective Bertram?"

"Not a lot. He was on loan from narcotics. The Joint Terrorism Task Force has been pulling primarily from vice and narcotics. We need guys with surveillance and undercover experience."

"Who does he normally report to?"

"A Captain Dan Morrow in narcotics."

"How long has he been working for you?"

"A little over two months, though I'd hardly say he's been working for me. He filed his reports sporadically at best. They were sloppy and light on useful information."

"Any mention of Alison Marsh in these reports?"

"Only in the first. Bill started strong. His first report helped thwart a disruption the group was planning at Greuning Corp.'s offices. After that, nothing. If I'm to believe his last report, this group was planning little more than a potluck dinner." Montanez opened the manila file and read from it. "Tim promised to bring his spinach and artichoke dip. Marsha reminded the group that several vegans attended the meetings and encouraged the rest of us to plan our contributions accordingly."

He looked up at me wide-eyed. "What do you think? Sound like Bill might be holding back? The shit gets fucking surreal after that. A few paragraphs down, 'Carob chips, unbleached flour, two cups of sugar...' It goes on like that."

"Sounds like a recipe for some kind of dessert."

"That's right, and you know what? The Federal Government didn't give us extra funding to get crappy recipes from a bunch of dirtbags!"

"No, they didn't," I said, trying not to laugh.

"I wouldn't be the least bit surprised if Bill was fucking this Marsh chick. She got him all turned around, and he sold us, and the whole goddamn project out."

"Did you ask him about the report?"

"Of course. He said that was the most radical thing to come up in their meetings." Montanez leaned forward in his seat. "Look, I know as well as the next guy that this project is horseshit, but there's such a thing as a chain of command when you're a cop. There's such a thing as obeying your commanding officer and not causing him trouble with the boys upstairs. That asshole had a job to do, and he didn't fuckin' do it."

"Did you choose Bertram for this assignment?"

Montanez shook his head. "No, I didn't know the guy from a hole in the ground. His commanding officer volunteered him for the job. To be honest, I had Bertram pegged as some space case that Morrow was trying to pawn off on me, but then I did some checking around, and he's got a pretty impressive record. He made a lot of arrests last year."

"Why do you think Morrow volunteered him for your unit?"

Montanez shrugged. "You'll have to ask him that."

"Will do."

"Anything else?" he asked.

"No, I think that's all. Thanks."

Montanez got up to leave. He paused at the door. "You were in the 13th precinct, right?"

"Yeah."

"Why'd you leave? You're a little young for retirement."

"Old enough that I'll still draw a pension."

"How's the private investigation racket pay?"

"For me, not very well, but the hours are good. You interested in making a career change?"

"What do you think?" Montanez said as he walked out the door.

I headed north to pay Dan Morrow a visit. It was early afternoon, and I was a little less than three blocks away from the Fourth District station when I passed some budding young entrepreneurs in front of a two-story brownstone. They were skinny black kids with spider-thin limbs and heads that seemed too big for their bodies. One, a kid no older than fifteen, approached an old rusted red Ford. He wore a pair of baggy pants that hung precariously on bony hips, the crack of his ass exposed to the brisk winter air. The kid walked with an exaggerated swagger, his shoulders swaying from one side to the other with every step. He reached into one of his pockets and withdrew a baggy containing several small plastic pouches filled with what appeared to be heroin. A gaunt-looking woman leaned out the window and handed the kid her money. He passed her the drugs, and she drove off.

The scene left me scratching my head. I had seen more than my share of drug transactions, had broken up a few, even took part in a few during my more carefree high school years, but I had not seen a deal done so brazenly in years, if ever—let alone within mere blocks of a police station.

Most drug deals are a multi-person operation. One person collects the money, telling the customer to meet him somewhere nearby. That kid sends someone to an apartment in the vicinity to retrieve the drugs and deliver the product to the customer at a prearranged meeting spot. Dealers want to spread the risk among several people. If you're going to go down, it's best not to lose both the inventory and the profits, not when the man you're working for is the same guy you depend on to bail your ass out of jail. Drug lords don't look kindly upon carelessness and stupidity. Those are the kinds of character flaws that can get a man killed. And yet, here was this kid dealing, out in the open, money and supply all in the pockets of a single pair of oversized jeans. If that wasn't enough, there must've been six other kids just like him hanging out in front of the brownstone, each carrying on like my little fashion plate.

I wondered if drugs had become an afterthought in these post-9/11, War on Terror days. Were the cops too preoccupied with lefty potlucks and the specter of Arab bogeymen to arrest petty drug dealers, and if so, how would the prison industry survive?

I continued on to the Fourth District police station. It was in a newish brick building with round windows and was less busy than Belmont Avenue.

An old white-haired man sat behind a Plexiglas window at the front desk. He was a frail-looking character that seemed better suited for night watchman duty in some quiet downtown office building. I approached to find him drifting off. His eyes struggled to stay open, and his breath came in gusty sighs that swept through a bushy mustache, the thicket of hair swaying like blades of grass in the wind. He watched me under heavy eyelids, and it took him a while to register that someone was standing before him, someone in need of service, someone clearing his throat to catch his attention.

My presence finally hit him, and he straightened in his seat. "Can I help you?"

I told Gramps who I was and asked for Captain Morrow. The old man shuffled off down the hall, and a few minutes later, he returned, followed by what appeared to be a load-bearing wall with legs. The guy was around six foot eight, broad-shouldered, with hands the size of tennis rackets and a head like a statue on Easter Island.

"Mr. Wozniak," the behemoth said in a deep baritone. "I'm Captain Morrow." He motioned to the old man. "Leonard here says you wanted to speak to me about Bill Bertram."

"Yes, I'm a private investigator, and a man named Edgar Marsh hired me to find his daughter Alison. Bill Bertram met Miss Marsh on his most recent assignment, and I have reason to believe his disappearance is related to the case I'm working on."

Morrow drew a bloodless bottom lip from between his teeth and motioned with one of his gigantic mitts in the direction from which he had just come. "Let's have a seat in my office."

Morrow led me to a stuffy, disorganized little room. Stacks of files and loose papers covered his desk. A photo of a matronly woman and two teenage girls that I figured to be his wife and kids sat on a messy credenza behind him. Their faces peered out over the stacks of files as if curious to see how their old man spent his day.

Morrow ducked as he entered the office. He took a seat and folded his legs, his right ankle resting on his left knee. He leaned back in his chair in an exaggerated posture of casualness. "How can I help you, Mr. Wozniak?" he said.

I removed my coat and took a seat in the visitor's chair. "I was hoping you could tell me more about Detective Bertram."

"I'll be glad to, but I'm curious why you think his disappearance has anything to do with your client's case."

"Bertram was working undercover at the anti-war group that Alison Marsh belonged to, and his disappearance coincides with hers. Also, several people mentioned her spending a lot of time with a man named Scott Richter, which is the name Bertram assumed for his undercover assignment, and Miss Marsh's roommate overheard her talking to a married man she called Bill."

"She called him Bill?"

"That's what her roommate said."

"So, he blew his cover to her."

"It would appear so."

The captain smiled to himself, as if amused by this information.

"You don't seem too surprised," I said.

"I am, but I'm not. Bill hasn't been himself the last few months."

"That's why I am here. Could you tell me what kind of cop Bill was?"

"Bill? He was a terrific detective. He made a lot of good arrests and took a lot of drugs off the street. Unfortunately, the stuff comes in quicker than we can remove it. You can arrest one of these kids in the morning, and he'll be back out on the streets by noon, and if not him, it'll be someone else. There's no shortage of cannon fodder in the war on drugs."

"And Bertram couldn't cope anymore."

"No, but it wasn't your typical case of burnout. Something happened."

"What?"

"A girl named Stephanie Landau. The Landaus lived across the street from Bill. He had known Stephanie since she was a little girl, watched her grow up. She had started running with the wrong crowd and developed a heroin addiction. A few months ago, she overdosed, leaving her a vegetable."

"So, Bill took it pretty hard?"

"Yeah, he's not been the same since. He felt he should've done more to stop it."

"What could he do?"

"Nothing. Nothing at all. That's why I volunteered him for the Joint Terrorism Task Force. He was no good to me in that state, and I thought it would help for him to get away and work on something else."

"What about his partner, George Wesley?"

Morrow shifted in his seat. "What about him?"

"Do you know where I can find him?"

"No, I told him to take some time off to clear his head, perhaps go away somewhere."

"He was in town as of a couple of days ago."

"He was?"

"Yes, I attended a meeting of the International League of Spartacists—the anti-war group Bill was assigned to—and George was hanging around outside. He tried tailing me after the meeting."

"It sounds like he's doing a little investigation of his own. I know he's been beside himself with worry. I can have him call you."

"Thanks, I'd appreciate that." I left Morrow my card on the way out.

Something told me I wouldn't hear from George anytime soon, at least not voluntarily. I had another visit to make, and I wasn't looking forward to it. Talking to Bill's partner was bound to be an emotional minefield.

I stopped by the front desk on the way out.

"Where's a good place to grab a drink around here?" I asked.

"Oh, I don't know," said the old man. "I don't really touch the stuff these days, doctor's orders. I mean, I might sneak a beer once in a while." He paused for a moment before adding with a wink, "Don't tell the wife. She'd kill me if she found out."

I could tell he was looking for an ear to bend, and I wasn't in the mood for his life story. "Okay, thanks," I said, heading for the door.

"Wait," the old man called after me.

"Yeah?"

"I know some of the guys are partial to Sal's Lounge. It's a couple of blocks east of here on Devon."

"Thanks."

"Don't mention it," he said. "Just stay out of trouble."

I smiled. "That's the plan."

SEVEN

Sal's was a throwback, the kind of cop bar I remembered going to when I first joined the force. It was a dive with a dirty tile floor and faux-wood paneling on the walls. A permanent haze seemed to hover about the rectangular fluorescent lights hung from the ceiling as though the place had an atmosphere all its own.

It was late afternoon, and a few grim-faced old men in shabby dress drank their beers. A couple of them looked as if they had been there since morning. They teetered on their stools, threatening to tip over like a pair of tops reaching their final revolutions.

The bartender was a gruff-looking character, squat with short, wavy hair and a face like a bulldog. I ordered a drink. The bartender poured it with a heavy hand, serving me a rocks glass more than half full of whiskey. Three large ice cubes rested in the red-brown liquor like a pixilated U turned on its side. They clinked in the glass as the bulldog set my drink on the bar. I downed it and ordered another.

"Hey, you get a lot of cops in here, right?" I asked.

"Does a bear shit in the woods?" the bartender said.

"Did a cop named George Wesley ever come in here?"

"Who wants to know?"

I slid my card across the bar to him. He eyed it with suspicion before looking up at me. "He was here yesterday," he grunted. "He'll probably be here tonight." He paused before adding, "And tomorrow and the day after that."

"He's pretty regular."

"About as regular as they come. You stick around long enough; you're bound to run into him."

I considered putting that theory to the test. I downed a couple more drinks in an hour with no sign of Wesley and decided it was best to move on before the siren song of binge drinking lured me off the job for good. I dropped a few dollars on the bar.

"Do you want me to have George call you when I see him?" the bartender asked.

"No, that's okay. I'm sure we'll run into each other before then. Sal, is it?"

"No, I'm Art. Sal works the night shift."

"Thanks, Art. I might be back in later on if I don't have any luck."

I headed for the door and was halfway there when I caught myself. "Hey, one more thing."

Art was washing a glass. He submerged it in a plastic tub filled with some kind of disinfectant before rinsing it in a second container of water. He lifted his head from his work and looked at me as if he was seeing me for the first time, his eyes narrowing into little slits and his nose crinkling. In fact, his entire face puckered like a large piece of dried fruit.

"Yeah," he said.

"George's partner, Bill, he ever come in here?"

"Sure, though it's been a while. He's usually more of a night customer, George, too, until the last week or so. He must be on vacation or lost his day job."

"When was the last time you saw Bill?"

"God, it's been a few weeks. He's not allowed in here anymore."

"Why's that?"

"On account, he got into a minor scuffle with one of the brothers."

"Brothers?"

Art leaned forward and spoke in a hushed tone. "You know, one of the black guys who are always hanging around down the block."

"No, I don't know. What are these guys like?"

"Gangbangers, drug dealers. There's a group of them that are always hanging out down the block from here. We've tried to get the cops to do something about them, but I guess they keep things quiet enough to stay out of trouble.

Anyway, one of them was in here one night, and Bill must've had a problem with the guy. They got in a nasty fight, and Sal told Bill not to come in here anymore, which is saying a lot because the old man's never dared stand up to a cop before. It's usually not a good idea, but I guess Bill's buddies knew he took things too far. There has been no trouble since banning him."

"Do you remember the name of the guy Bill scuffled with?"

"No, I just know that it was one of the brothers from the neighborhood. Sal might know. He was here the night it happened."

I left the bar and took a quick drive over to Wesley's building. This time I rang the bell. After a few minutes, I heard a door open somewhere inside the building and not long after saw George coming down the stairs. He wore an expression of resignation on his face, as if my visit were one he expected but dreaded. He opened the door and flashed a meager smile.

"Hi, Glenn," he said.

"You remember me?"

"It took me a second, but yeah. Dan called and said you wanted to talk. It's cold down here. Let's go upstairs."

I followed Wesley up to his apartment. The place was what I would call cozy if I were being charitable, small if I was being honest. The front entrance opened onto a narrow foyer. To the left sat an eat-in kitchen with a living room to the right. Beyond that was another hallway that led to the bedroom and a bathroom. I followed Wesley into the living room. A desk with a PC occupied one corner. A sofa and a coffee table sat across from a big-screen TV, an older model, the size of a compact sedan, which dominated the room. I took a seat on the couch. Wesley pulled up the desk chair and sat with his back to me.

A daytime talk show was on. The host, a long, lean man with salt-and-pepper news-anchor hair, berated a black kid with sleepy eyes about a paternity test. He chided his guest about being an adult and taking responsibility for his baby. All the while, the kid tried to suppress a smile as the audience jeered at him.

Wesley looked tired. His eyes were glassy and lined underneath with a pair of purple, crescent-shaped bags. A dark muzzle of scruffy hair covered his chin. He almost seemed oblivious to my presence, as if I were an old friend who had popped over out of the blue and he was too exhausted to entertain.

"What can I do for you, Glenn?"

"I guess we should get this out of the way now. I know you tried to tail me last night."

George rubbed his eyes. "Yeah?"

"You've got a dim right headlight. You should get it fixed if you're going to be following people. You stuck out like a sore thumb."

"I'll take that into account."

We both fell silent for a moment. "So, you got anything you want to tell me?"

"What do you want me to say? Bill's my partner. He's like a brother to me. I've been keeping tabs on the investigation, making sure that everything that can be done is being done to find him. I've been paying close attention to those anti-war hippies because that was the last case he worked on before he disappeared. And when I saw you talking to them, it caught my attention because you looked familiar and, at the time, I couldn't place how I knew you."

"And you decided to see what I was up to?"

"Exactly."

"Okay, fair enough. So tell me about your partner."

"I don't know, man. What do you want me to tell you?"

"I was wondering if he had been acting strange or given any signs he might skip town."

Wesley pursed his lips, a pained expression on his face. "Bill and I didn't talk too much after his transfer. Believe me, I wouldn't feel this lousy if I knew where he was."

"Did he ever mention an Alison Marsh?"

Wesley paused for a moment before answering: "Yeah, he said he had met some girl at those meetings and that they were seeing each other. Bill was never one for monogamy. He had several girls that he saw on the side: cocktail waitresses, strippers, even a couple of female officers."

Wesley snatched a package of Marlboros off the coffee table. He lit a cigarette with trembling hands and turned to watch the TV program. A teenage girl with big, bleached blonde hair was in a hallway somewhere offstage. She sat on the floor sobbing and hugging her knees to her chest while her mother, who looked too young to have a teenage daughter, tried to console her. The host stood over them, imploring the girl to return to the stage.

"Did Bill say anything else about Alison?"

Wesley shook his head. "Nothing that I remember. I don't know. He might've."

Wesley didn't look at me, his eyes glued to the absurd paternity test free-for-all unfolding on the oversized screen, the players larger than life. He didn't so much watch the TV as look through it, his mind a million miles away. Who knows what was going on in his head. I wasn't going to get much more out of him, not in this state, or at least that's what I told myself. To be honest, I couldn't wait to make my escape. The sadness there was palpable. It choked the air out of the room, and I just wanted to get back outside into the cold where I could breathe again.

I dropped one of my cards on the coffee table. "All right, George, I should get going. It was nice seeing you. I'm sorry it was under such lousy circumstances."

Wesley escorted me to the door. He had not quite closed it when something occurred to me. "One more question."

"Yeah?"

"Did Bill have a temper?"

George shook his head. "No, I wouldn't say that. At least, no more than anyone else. Why?"

"Alison's boss overhead her fighting with someone on the phone. He heard her tell this person that she didn't want to see him anymore. The call shook her up enough that she asked him to escort her home. I was wondering if she had been talking to Bill."

"Could be, but I've never known him to be violent towards women. It just wasn't his style. What are you getting at?"

"Just a theory: Bill starts an affair with an attractive, younger woman. He gets a little too clingy, and the girl, only wanting to have some fun or perhaps feeling guilty about messing around with a married man, decides to cut things off. Bill refuses to accept that it's over. He calls her at home, on her cell phone, at work, and each time she reiterates that they're through. Of course, Bill's a big guy, a cop with a gun. He could cause her some trouble. She becomes afraid and..."

"And she decides to run off."

"Or he does something rash and has to skip town."

"Something rash? You mean killed her?"

"Or kidnapped her. I don't know. It's as good an explanation as any."

Wesley leaned in the doorway, propping himself up with one hand on the frame. He ran the other hand through his hair and shook his head. "No, Bill had changed, but he wasn't a monster."

"Sure, it's just a theory. I heard there was an incident over at Sal's Lounge and it got me thinking. I guess Bill beat some guy up pretty bad there, bad enough to get banned from the bar."

I paused to read his reaction, only there wasn't one, his face a blank slate. "Anything you can tell me about that?" I asked.

"No, nothing. I don't know anything about it."

Somehow, I doubted that. "Nothing at all?"

"That's what I said."

"It's just that I know you two and other members of your unit spend a lot of time there, so I would've thought you would have heard something."

"I don't know anything about it," George said.

I didn't want to push it any further. "Okay, if you do hear anything, let me know."

"I'll do that."

I turned to the stairs. I was halfway down the first flight when George called out to me, "Hey, Wozniak!"

I looked up to see him peering over the railing. "Yeah?"

"What next?"

"Bill's wife."

"That's what I thought. Be gentle with her. She's not doing too well right now."

"I'll keep that in mind."

George nodded before stepping away from the railing and out of view. I heard a door close and resumed my descent, exiting the building. It was a frigid night, and I could see my breath as it twisted upwards into a steel blue sky. I stopped and lit a cigarette between cupped hands. The dull orange glow of the lighter illuminated the ridges of my palms. I pressed on, feeling eyes on me as I neared the front gate. I turned and looked back at the building. For just a moment, I saw the faint image of a pale face in Wesley's window, like the moon reflecting off murky water.

I reached the Bertrams' house a little after six. They lived in a quaint yellow-brick bungalow. A lawn gnome stood watch near the front door, overlooking a stretch of bare dirt that was probably a flowerbed in warmer months. I rang the bell, and a few moments later, a short blonde answered.

Denise Bertram was a buxom girl with substantial hips, a round middle, and full breasts that strained against the tight brown velvet blouse she was wearing.

"Hi, Mrs. Bertram, my name is Glenn Wozniak."

"I know," she said. "George called and said you'd be coming by."

She looked spent. Her round face sagged with the weight of her troubles.

I heard the scampering feet of a child behind her. A moment later, a small boy appeared. He clung to his mother's legs, and his little hands looked delicate and fair against the dark fabric of her pants, like those of a porcelain doll. The child couldn't have been more than four years old. He peered up at me with a wide-eyed expression somewhere between wonder and apprehension.

"Go in the living room, honey," Denise told the boy. "I need to speak to this man."

The kid backed up a couple of steps before turning and scampering away, his bare feet slapping on the hardwood floor.

"C'mon in," Denise said.

It was a warm, pleasant house, the kind of place a couple could grow old in. There were knick-knacks and lace curtains. Plants hung in the windows. I glanced into the living room as we walked past. The little boy sat playing with a toy convertible on a scarlet and cobalt Persian rug.

Denise led me to the kitchen. Along the way, I passed a photo of the couple during happier times, Bill's arm around his wife's shoulder. He was a fair-skinned, broad-shouldered man with the simple corn-fed look of a Midwestern farm boy.

The kitchen was a bright room with canary yellow wallpaper, light seeming to emanate from every direction. We took a seat at the table, and I began with the usual inquiries: When did you last see your husband? What was he wearing? Can you tell me the make, model, and license of his car? What was his behavior like in the days leading up to his disappearance?

Denise didn't share anything too revelatory. Bill went through his normal routine in the days leading up to his disappearance. That morning he had a cup of coffee and a bowl of cereal for breakfast. He kissed her and the boy goodbye before departing, and that was the last she'd seen of him. He left no evidence that he had been planning to go away. Their luggage remained in the closet upstairs. He didn't even pack a razor.

"I'm sorry, but I don't see what my husband has to do with this Marsh girl you're investigating."

"Bill knew Alison Marsh. He met her while on assignment for the Joint Terrorism Task Force, and they disappeared on the same date."

Denise slumped in her seat. She stared down at the table, shaking her head. "What are you saying?"

"I'm saying I have reason to believe their disappearances are related."

She looked up at me. "You think he was sleeping with her?"

Not knowing what to say, I kept my mouth shut.

"It wouldn't be the first time he's been unfaithful," Denise said.

We sat in silence for a while. "You know what? The cheating wasn't the worst of it. It was the worrying. I don't know how many nights I spent waiting up for him, scared to death something had happened to him, only to discover he was off fucking another woman."

I heard a gasp behind me. It was a small voice, the boy's. The child stood in the entryway to the kitchen, his mouth agape, a look of surprise on his face. "Mom, you swore," he said.

"I know. Mommy said a bad word."

"You're going to have to wash your mouth out with soap," the child said, a mischievous smile on his face. At that moment, I could see the resemblance between the boy and his father. They had the same doughy face, the same wholesome look in their eyes.

"Billy, do you want to watch Elmo?" his mother asked.

"Okay," the boy replied as he scampered off into the living room.

Denise followed him, returning a few moments later. "Thank goodness for videotapes," she said. "TV's a godsend when you're raising a child by yourself."

Again, I found myself at a loss for words. I looked at her, the dulled clockwork in my head grinding along, struggling to figure out how to get through the interview with as little discomfort as possible.

Denise took a seat across from me. She stared at her hands and spoke in a low voice. "I caught him before. Twice. The first time was before Billy was born. I found a phone number for a girl named Leslie. One day I checked his cell phone bill, and sure enough, there were several calls made to that same number, many of them coinciding with nights when he had come home late. I called her. She seemed like a nice enough girl. Younger, but nice. Apparently, Bill neglected to mention that he was married. She was as upset as I was, or at least she claimed to be. Who knows, right?"

I shook my head, still struggling for words.

"Anyway, I went back home to my parents. Bill kept calling me. He'd send me roses and little notes. It took a while, a few months, but he wore me down. We'd been together since we were kids. I couldn't imagine life without him. I don't know. Maybe I'm just a sucker."

"No, that's understandable. You had a history together."

"Right," Denise said.

"What about the last time?"

"That was with a woman officer. I told him I was going to leave him, and he'd never see his son again."

"And?"

"He begged me to stay. He promised it would never happen again, that he would change. He said that it was the job—that it had hardened him, and he had trouble with intimacy. That's why he slept around. He said casual sex was easy. He told me he loved Billy and me and wanted to change. And again, like a sucker, I gave him another chance. He changed for a while. He stopped staying out so late, and spent more time with Billy and me. Things were good."

"I take it they haven't been so good of late."

"No," Denise said, her voice cracking. She turned her head up towards the bright kitchen lights and strained to hold back the tears. "He started coming home late again. We stopped having sex. We haven't had sex in almost four months." Denise stopped, tears in her eyes. She stood up and walked out of the room for a moment, returning with a tissue. She dabbed at her eyes. "I'm sorry to bother you with all this. I've been under a lot of stress."

"Of course, no need to apologize," I said, unable to look at her. Another few minutes and I'd be stuck giving her a shoulder to cry on, a job I was never any good at.

"I think I've got all that I need," I said, rising to my feet.

I pulled a business card out of my coat pocket and handed it to her. "Call me if you think of anything else."

Denise glanced at the card before laying it on the kitchen table. She walked me to the door, and we passed the living room again. Billy was sitting Indian-style on the floor, just a couple of feet from the TV. Elmo was on the screen, laughing and waving his noodle arms in the air.

I noticed another photo on the wall. Denise stood flanked by Bill and George on the deck of a boat, the cops dressed in colorful Hawaiian shirts and the Chicago skyline visible in the background. Bill and Denise looked straight ahead, George at Denise.

There was something in the way he looked at her.

"Do you have an extra photo of Bill I might have?" I asked.

"Sure, one second." Denise went upstairs, returning a few minutes later with a picture of her husband. It was a professional photo, the type you might get at a mall. Bill sat in front of a sky-blue background, half-smiling like he just wanted to finish the shoot and get on with his day.

"Thanks, this is helpful," I said, standing in the doorway, the cool night air at my back. "Let me know if you think of anything else or need anything from me."

"I will," she said.

Billy came to the door. "Bye," he said, waving at me.

"Bye," I said, smiling and waving back.

The temperature was dropping, and the wind had picked up. I hurried to the car. Once inside, I slumped into the driver's seat. Frost covered the windows. I looked in the rearview mirror. The street lamps reflected red, green, and blue through the prism of the snow crystals. I started my car and let it warm up. Light emanated from the rows of bungalows on either side of the street like pale eyes watching me; the neighborhood watch.

I felt drained. Too much sadness. Too much loss. This was one of the things that drove me from police work in the first place. I couldn't take all those stories of loss. Lost friends. Lost family. Lost faith. Every case a reminder that nothing lasts.

I pulled away and headed south towards home. It was still early, and sleep was the furthest thing from my mind. I pulled up to an intersection, which gave me a second to think. But I didn't want to think. I wanted to shut down for a moment, get to that almost unconscious state where my thoughts are little more than white noise, and nothing more challenging than determining my next meal or drink. No such luck. All I could think of was Maya. By the time the light turned to green, I could almost see her face, smell the vanilla scent wafting off her warm, freshly washed body. I made a U-turn and headed north.

EIGHT

It was almost ten, and I probably should've called before going over. I sat in my car gazing up at Maya's building and conjuring her image in my head. I pictured her dressed the same as when we met, just a T-shirt and panties, the lighting just right—dark enough to set the mood, but light enough that I could see every inch of bare flesh.

I replayed the scene a few times, taking multiple takes as in a movie. I'd change the emphasis placed on certain words, concocting various motives for her attraction. In one version, I reminded her of her first crush. In another, I made her feel safe. And in still another, she had a thing for private investigators.

"I was hoping you'd return," she'd say. "I couldn't stop thinking about you."

"I know," I'd reply confidently before taking her in my arms.

At some point, she'd say something about how she likes a man with a little meat on his bones, something to grab onto during sex, or perhaps she'd praise me for leaving the rat race to be my own man. "You're such a risk-taker. I find that sexy."

I spent a good ten minutes sitting in my car mulling these scenarios before finally heading over to her building. I rang the doorbell, and a few moments later, the buzzer sounded. My heart raced as I clambered up the stairs, my footfalls sounding loud and clumsy. Maya greeted me at the door. This time she wore a pair of worn blue jeans and a black baby T-shirt. Her feet were bare, and she looked cold standing in the doorway. "Ever hear of a phone?" she asked.

"I'm sorry; I was in the area, and I realized there were a couple of things I forgot to ask you about the case."

Maya gazed down at her feet and sighed. "Well, don't just stand there," she said, shaking her head. "Come in."

I already regretted the visit, and yet, oddly, I found her more attractive like this. Perhaps it was because she seemed unattainable. I've always had an appetite for futile pursuits and their attendant humiliations. Maya's frown and furrowed brow carried a lot of potential. They could inspire me to commit a hundred stupid acts, and right about then, I was at my most vulnerable: tired, bored, and horny.

Maya closed the door behind me. She brushed past me on the way to the living room. I stayed where I was, with my coat on, and watched her from the foyer.

"I can come back if this is a bad time," I shouted.

"No, that's okay. What did you want to know?"

I entered the living room. Maya had taken a seat on the sofa, the TV on. I racked my brain for a plausible reason to visit, some way to get out of there with my dignity intact. Just then, it hit me.

"Alison's cell phone bills," I said.

"Alison's cell phone bills?"

"Yes, Alison had a cell phone, right?"

"Well, duh, it's the 21st century."

"I was wondering if I might see her cell phone bills. I'd like to see who she had been talking to in the days leading up to her disappearance."

Maya furrowed her brow.

"Sorry, I should've asked for them the last time I was here."

"Sure, whatever," Maya said after a long pause.

I motioned with my head toward Alison's room.

"That's probably the best place to look."

I made my escape. Once inside Alison's bedroom, I half-heartedly searched through drawers I had looked in just a couple of days ago.

"I found these in the kitchen," Maya said from behind me.

I jumped at the sound of her voice.

"Sorry, I didn't mean to startle you," she said, handing me a small stack of cell phone bills.

"Thanks." I stared at the pieces of paper, unable to face her. I still had my coat on, and it felt like a hundred degrees in there. A radiator sat about two feet away from me, just beneath the room's only window, heat emanating from it. Beads of sweat formed on my scalp and ran down the back of my head.

"Is that all you need?" Maya asked.

"I guess so," I said.

Maya stood with a hand on her hip. "I don't think it is."

"What do you mean?"

"I mean, I think you came here for something else."

She was on to me. "I don't know what you're talking about. I came for the cell phone bills."

Maya's eyes turned a shade darker, a few degrees colder. "Well then, you got what you were looking for. Why don't you leave?"

"Are you upset with me?"

She sighed. "No, I'm just tired. Give me a call if you need anything else."

"Okay."

I made for the door, but Maya barely moved. She turned her shoulder, giving me about a centimeter more room, and I squeezed past her, my wrist brushing against her arm. She felt warm and soft and smelled nice, clean as if I had just caught her coming out of the shower again.

I paused for a moment, trying to think of the right thing to say. "Look, I just wanted to see you again." I cleared my throat. "And I thought you might've wanted to see me."

"What made you think that?"

"I thought you might have been giving off some signals the last time I was here."

"Signals? What kind of signals?"

"Never mind, I must've been imagining things."

"No, tell me. What signals? I want to know."

"Well, you answered the door half-naked and didn't put any clothes on the entire time I was here."

"So? It's my apartment, and I'm comfortable with my body. What's wrong with that?"

"Nothing, you have a nice body."

"You think so?"

"Yes."

"I wish my breasts were bigger."

"I think they're fine."

"Fine?"

"They're nice. I mean, I haven't actually seen them or anything, but they look like nice breasts as far as I can tell."

She laughed. "Thank you. What other signals?"

"Look, I ought to get going."

"What other signals?" she insisted, moving closer.

"That's it."

"You said signals, plural. That means more than one."

"Okay, you said you were into older men."

"And you're an older man."

"Right."

I stopped, unsure of what to add. "These are helpful, thanks," I said, waving the stack of cell phone bills in my hand.

Maya stared at me. "So, you came here thinking I'd fuck you."

"No! No, I thought I'd ask you out on a date or something."

"I'm not interested in dating."

"Okay, sorry. I'll get going."

"I'm not asking you to leave."

"No?"

"No. Look, I'm not looking for anything complicated. I just got out of a relationship."

"Okay."

"I just want to have some fun."

"That works for me."

"But just because I sleep with you, it doesn't mean I'm your girlfriend."

"Of course."

"And you're not my boyfriend."

"Gotcha."

"And you can't just pop by out of the blue whenever you feel like it. Call first. Is that so hard?"

"No, sorry, I don't know what I was thinking."

She took my hand. "Come with me."

She led me to her bedroom. We took a seat at the edge of the bed. She kissed me, her tongue entering my mouth, probing for mine. We stopped, and she removed her shirt, revealing a pair of small, firm breasts with light brown nipples.

"Do you have any protection?" I asked. "I don't have anything on me."

"Hold on," Maya said. She opened her nightstand, and there must've been a couple dozen condoms inside.

"Here," she said, handing me one.

We started kissing again. My mind lingered on that drawer full of condoms for a while before I decided to just let it go and enjoy the moment—her kiss, her scent, her touch. Afterward, we lay quietly in bed. The room was humid with body heat and sweat; the air tinged with sex. I felt drowsy, but sensing she wanted to talk, I strained to stay awake.

"You know what's funny?" she said after a while.

"What?"

"Alison and I weren't close, and yet I feel like I've lost a little piece of my world since she disappeared."

"That's understandable," I said, stifling a yawn. "She was a part of your life. You lived among her stuff, shared a bathroom, negotiated refrigerator space. Your relationship was kind of intimate, in its way."

Maya stared at the ceiling, her jaw tense and her lower lip quivering. "I haven't been sleeping. I don't feel safe, Glenn. I've lived in this city my whole life, and this is the first time I haven't felt safe. I don't know why. I grew up in a rough neighborhood. I've seen some shit, but for some reason, this frightens me. The funny thing is, I think it's because she was a rich white girl. I mean, if someone like Alison isn't safe, then who is?"

"There's no reason to be afraid. First of all, we don't know that anything has happened to her. For all we know, she ran off with her boyfriend." I rolled over on my side, facing her. "Besides, I won't let anything happen to you."

We fell silent and listened to each other's breathing and the ambient noise of the city outside. Maya seemed to relax, the tension in her face fading away, her eyes becoming glassy under heavy lids. "So did you ever find out who this Bill guy is?" she asked, yawning.

"As a matter of fact, I did. He's a cop named Bill Bertram."

"A cop? That doesn't sound like someone Alison would date."

"I know. I thought the same thing. Bill met her on assignment. He was working undercover to investigate her anti-war group."

"So she didn't know he was a cop?"

"No, she knew. He used an alias, Scott Richter, but Alison knew his real name. At least, that's what you told me the other day. You did say she called him Bill?"

"Uh-huh."

"Right, so unless she was talking to someone else, she was in on Bertram's little charade, or he blew his cover."

"So what'd this guy look like?"

"He was the big, beefy type, older than you, but younger than me."

Maya nudged me in the ribs. "Hmmm, sounds cute. You'll have to show me some pictures."

"I just might. You said you'd met some of her friends from the group, right?"

"Uh-huh."

"Any men?"

"A couple, but nobody named Scott or Bill."

"Okay, then never mind."

Maya turned on her side and regarded me with a look of mock seriousness. "No, honey, I still want to see that picture."

"Aren't I enough?"

"I don't know the meaning of enough."

Cute, but I feared she meant it, and for a second, I felt a little jealous. Just then, something occurred to me. "You never met Bill, right?"

"That's what I've been trying to tell you. That's why I need a picture of this boy."

"Did Alison ever bring any boyfriends here?"

"No. At least not when I was at home."

"Okay, so assuming they weren't stealing a moment here and there while you were out, where were they meeting? It sure as hell wasn't at his place, not with a wife and kid at home."

Maya's face lit up. "I see what you're getting at."

"I think the two of them must've spent some time in a motel. At least it's something worth looking into."

Maya rolled over and nestled her head against my chest. "I hope she's okay."

"Me too, but let's not think about it right now."

"Tomorrow," she said, her eyes fluttering closed. A few minutes later, she was snoring.

I had a hard time falling asleep, preoccupied with thoughts of motels and undercover cops and jealous boyfriends. They scurried through my mind like rodents in a Habitrail. Eventually, I drifted off into a fitful slumber, my troubled thoughts turning into obsessive dreams.

I awoke lying on my side, facing a delicate white wicker chair with a large stuffed puppy dog on it. The plush animal sat hunched forward, its wide-eyed look of joy belied by a slumped posture. A hazy gray morning light trickled through the sides of the blinds.

It took a while for me to process that I was not at home. I felt behind me on the bed, and finding no one there, I sat up and looked around the room. My clothes sat neatly folded on the dresser. I got up and padded into the kitchen. A half-pot of coffee sat on the counter, and there was a note on the table: "I had to go to work. Give me a call later. Good luck motel hunting. Love, Maya."

I poured myself a cup of coffee and plotted my day. I checked Alison's cell phone bills. Hopefully, I'd come across Bill's number and get some dates of when they may have met. I could then hit some motels in the area and see if anyone matching their description checked in on those dates. It was a simple matter of doing the work, and that's why I spent a good hour and a half in Maya's apartment drinking coffee, thumbing through the paper and just plain staring off into space.

It was almost ten in the morning by the time I got dressed. I studied the cell phone bills, recognizing the number Tim had given me for Bill's alias, Scott Richter. Sure enough, Alison had made several calls to him on the day of her disappearance, one coming shortly before she had called in sick to work. I grabbed Maya's yellow pages and compiled a list of motels in the area, figuring that I would start closest to where they lived and fan out from there.

This wouldn't be easy. The far north side of the city was lousy with motels. There was a time when they did robust business. They were inexpensive places where families from Wisconsin and Iowa stayed while visiting the city on vacation. Now, they served mostly transients and adulterers with a smattering of criminals thrown in for good measure. Prostitutes plied their trade in these rooms. Drunks flopped there. Desperate men with debts to the wrong people hid in them. They were dingy little rooms filled with desperation and regret.

I must've hit a dozen of these places with no luck. Each one seemed to employ the same desk clerk, a thin, elderly man with skin the color of a nicotine stain and the musty smell of stagnant water. I half expected these guys to disintegrate before my eyes. I had shown them all Alison and Bill's photos without luck. Two clerks told me to check back with the night clerk, a prospect I didn't relish.

I drove west to the border of Chicago and Lincolnwood. The next stop was a place called the Stardust Motel. These dumps all sported romantic names like The Spa or The Shangri-La.

The Stardust was a two-story, L-shaped structure with all the charm of a bomb shelter. Metal staircases, one at each end, led up to the second floor. The rooms had dented metal doors that I imagined were once bright red but had faded to a dull auburn. Dirty curtains with abstract patterns prevalent in the sixties hung in the windows. It was like every other dump I had visited that day. The only distinguishing characteristics were a giant black crater in the center of the building and a tangle of yellow crime scene tape blocking the stairway.

I got out of my car and surveyed the damage. The second floor had collapsed onto the first floor. An enormous pile of charred debris sat on the lower level. The crime scene tape flapped in the wind like a death rattle.

For some reason, I thought about Iraq. I imagined there were hundreds of burned-out buildings just like this throughout the country, places suspected of housing weaponry or something the U.S. deemed of strategic importance. I had read that Saddam often hid weapons in schools and hospitals. Was that a deterrent? Did that stop the bombs? I hoped so. That's the problem with nations: they're so freaking big, they often don't know when they've crushed a ten-year-old boy with a case of appendicitis.

The office door was ajar, and I could see the beam of a flashlight probing the darkness inside. I lit a cigarette and stood outside watching, all the while, wondering if I should leave before I got myself into trouble. The door opened, revealing a short man with a moon-shaped face, pudgy red cheeks, and colorless lips. A messy tousle of greasy hair sat atop his head. He stopped, frozen, a look of panic on his ruddy face, and regarded me with moist eyes. So much for finding trouble on the other side of the door.

He held out his hands, a framed black-and-white photo of a chubby, round-faced couple in one of them. "I know I'm not supposed to be here, but I swear I didn't disturb anything. I just came for my parents' photo."

"Okay," I said.

"I won't do it again. I promise."

"Okay."

"Wait, you're not with the fire department?"

"No."

"The police?"

"No, I'm a private investigator."

"The insurance company sent you?"

"No."

The man exhaled and laughed. "That's a relief. I thought you were an arson investigator. I'm not supposed to be on the premises on account of its being a crime scene."

"I'm not here about the fire. I'm working on a missing person case."

The man exhaled. "I see."

"I'm looking for a girl named Alison Marsh. She was having an affair with a married man, and I thought they might've frequented one of the area motels."

"Makes sense. We used to get a lot of that here. The Stardust wasn't fancy, but I always kept a clean hotel. It's not a bad place to take a woman, all things considered."

"You're the owner?"

"Yup, Gerry Lombardo."

"Glenn Wozniak," I said, handing him my card.

He studied it for a moment. "What was that girl's name again?"

"Alison Marsh."

"Doesn't sound familiar. I'd show you the registry, but the arson investigator confiscated all my records."

"So, they suspect arson?"

"They don't suspect. It *was* arson. The fire started in Room 203. Someone doused the place with gasoline—the floors, walls, the bedding. It went up like a match." The little guy paused for a moment and rubbed his eyes. "I rented the room out to a young couple. I wish I could find them. They disappeared without a trace."

"Do you remember their names?"

"The guy's name was Scott Richter."

"Scott Richter?"

"Yup, you know him?"

"I've heard of him."

"You have? You mind telling the arson investigators? As far as they're concerned, the guy doesn't exist."

"When did this happen?"

"It was January 29th, a Thursday."

That was the same day Alison and Bill disappeared. I showed him a picture of Alison. "Recognize this girl?"

Gerry studied the photo. He squinted, his small, dark eyes reduced to mere slits. "Yes, I think so," he said, looking up and nodding his head. "You've got a picture of the boyfriend?"

I showed him a photo of Bill Bertram, and his face lit up. "Yup, that's him," he said. "That's Scott Richter. Big guy. Drives a black Pontiac, a late nineties model. I didn't get as good a look at the girl because she would stay in the car when he checked in, but I'm sure it's her. Those two have been coming to the Stardust about once or twice a week for the last couple of months."

"What time did they check in on the 29th?"

"Around three o'clock."

"And around what time did the fire start?"

"It was around 10:30, 11:00 PM."

"You say there were people in the adjoining rooms?"

"Yes."

"Did anyone hear or see anything out of the ordinary?"

"No, I asked. Not a thing until the fire broke out. There was one strange thing I noticed that night. I had a guy who used to clean the rooms and do some odd jobs around the building for money off his rent. His name's Larry. Not the most reliable guy, but I believe in giving folks a chance. Anyway, about a week before the fire, he went on a bender, and a ring of keys to the rooms went missing. We tore the place up looking for it, but no luck until the night of the fire. That night I found it just lying out in the parking lot."

"What did the arson investigators say?"

"Not much. I don't think they believed me."

"What do you mean, like you planted it there?"

"Uh-huh. The cops think I started the fire. I mean, they haven't come right out and said so, but they've been asking me a lot of questions about the business and my insurance. I know they're just doing their jobs, but the hotel was my life. My father opened it. I grew up around this place. Setting it on fire would be akin to spitting on my parents' graves. I'd as soon set fire to my home. I knew most of the folks who lived here. I cared about them, and I wouldn't do anything that would put someone's life at risk. There were folks in each of the adjoining rooms. Thankfully, everyone got out okay, or I wouldn't be able to live with myself. There was an old couple, Bud and Doris, who lived in the room directly below. Thank God they were out getting a cocktail when the fire occurred, or they might've been killed. The second floor caved in onto their room. The two lived at my motel for close to a year. They were frequently late with the rent, but I never once threatened to evict them. I floated them time and time again—did the same for about a dozen other folks. I never cared about the money."

"I hear ya," I said.

"Anyway, I hope you find them. They disappeared without a trace—the car, everything, gone. Trust me; I've looked. If they don't turn up, it'll be my ass. I've called the DMV, City Hall, the police, and no one's been able to verify the existence of anyone named Scott Richter. It's like he never existed."

I shouldn't have gotten involved, but I felt sorry for the guy. "That's because Richter is an alias," I said. "The guy's real name is Bill Bertram. He's a cop."

Gerry's eyes widened. "A cop? No kidding."

"No kidding. Look, give the police a call. Tell them that Officer Bill Bertram checked into your motel under the alias of Scott Richter and that the fire started in his room. Tell them to ask Captain Montanez about Scott Richter if they give you any trouble. That should straighten out any problems you're having with the police."

"Who's Captain Montanez?"

"He's someone who can verify Richter's true identity. I'm afraid that's all I can tell you. In fact, I've probably said too much as it is."

This was my good deed for the day, and it was bound to bite me in the ass. I could just imagine Captain Montanez's face after Lombardo's call. He'd demand my head on a spit, perhaps turn my name over to one of his buddies at the FBI. After all, I had just outed someone working undercover for the government.

NINE

Sal's was a little livelier than the last time I visited. It was six in the evening, and the professional drinkers had cleared out, with cops in their place. A frail man with white hair manned the bar. I tabbed him as Sal.

The old guy looked worn out. I didn't envy him. There are certain benefits to owning a cop bar. You don't get many visits from the liquor commission or the board of health or the fire inspector or the building inspector or any other city department specializing in shakedowns, except one, and they're your customers. Cops never pay full price, and in a business where the margins are thin, you have to sell a lot of beer to make ends meet.

A Journey song played on the jukebox, and a cop was singing along in a nasal south side whine, belting out the words with the kind of conviction that only comes from mixing Irish whiskey and beer. A couple more cops played darts near the back of the bar. Just beyond them, a burly foursome shot pool. One of them leaned over the table to make a shot, his belly resting on the green felt.

I scanned the room for George Wesley or Captain Morrow, finding no sign of either. I squeezed my way between a couple of customers along the bar and made eye contact with the bartender.

"What'll you have?" he asked, his eyes scanning the bar, already planning his next move.

"I'll have a Pabst," I said.

The bartender had my beer on the bar so fast, I would've sworn he had been hiding it up his sleeve. I handed him a five. He spun around and keyed the transaction into the register, returning seconds later with my change.

"Keep it," I said.

The bartender raised his eyebrows in surprise. "Hey, thanks!" he said, smiling.

"No problem. Are you Sal?"

The guy raised an index finger, motioning that it would be a moment. He walked down to the other end of the bar and served one of the heavyset pool players, a large, red-faced guy who had sweated through his shirt. He watered down the great athlete and returned in just over a minute.

"What'd you say?" he asked.

"I asked if you were Sal."

"I'm him. Who're you?"

I handed him my card. "My name is Glenn Wozniak. I'm a private investigator, and I'm looking for a missing girl by the name of Alison Marsh."

Sal chuckled. "We don't get many girls in here. Maybe the occasional lady cop, but that's about it."

"Actually, I was wondering what you could tell me about a guy named Bill Bertram. He come in here much?"

"Bill? Used to, but not anymore. I told him to stay away. He was causing too much trouble." Another customer caught his attention. "Hold on a second."

He returned a little later, just as I was polishing off my beer. I ordered another.

Sal leaned halfway across the bar and motioned for me to come closer. He whispered in my ear. "I think Bill was mixed up in some shady business, he and his partner."

"Wesley? What makes you say that?"

"One day, I overheard them arguing. They were over at the table right behind you, and Bill said something along the lines of, 'I'm tired of covering for these assholes.'"

"What'd George say?"

"I don't know. That's all I heard. 'I'm tired of covering for these assholes.' What assholes? I don't know, but it didn't sound good."

"What do you mean?"

"Look, I've been around these guys long enough to know that every guy who breaks the law is an asshole. A burglar's an asshole. A drug dealer's an asshole. They're all assholes. That's just how cops talk. So, what am I supposed to think when I hear Bill say he's tired of covering for these assholes?"

"You think they were taking kickbacks?"

Sal shrugged. "Who knows? Look, I'm just saying."

"Okay, so tell me about the fight Bill was involved in."

"Who told you about that?"

"Art."

"Oh, it was nothing special, just your typical bar fight. This black guy named Dantrell Miles came into the bar and got into it with Bill."

The old man noticed some cops eyeing him impatiently at the other end of the bar and put his story on hold. He served four people and rang them up in less than five minutes.

"Sorry about that," he said. "Where was I?"

"You were telling me about Dantrell Miles."

"Oh, yeah; I don't know the guy too well. I've seen him around the neighborhood, but we haven't talked much. I've heard rumors that he was dealing drugs, but who knows."

"How old is he?"

"I don't know. Late twenties, early thirties."

"How would you describe him? Any distinguishing features?"

"He's tall, dark complexion, muscular build. He has a deep voice, kind of like that singer, what's his face."

"Barry White?"

"Yes, Barry White. He has a voice like Barry White."

"Okay, so Dantrell comes into the bar, and then what?"

"Almost immediately, Bill is in his face telling him to stay away from here and that if he catches him anywhere near this place again, he's going to blow his head off."

"Did Dantrell say or do anything to provoke him?"

"Not that I can tell. Bill was on him from almost the second he entered the bar."

"So what did Miles do?"

"At first, he tried to play it cool, but Bill kept getting angrier and angrier. Next thing I know, the two of them are shoving each other. His partner, George, and some other cops tried to separate them."

"George split them up?"

"Tried to. He kept telling Bill to take it easy, but there was no calming him down. It must've taken six cops to hold him back. Anyway, Bill got some good licks in. He bloodied the guy's nose."

Wesley had lied to me, but that wasn't all that was bothering me. "I'm sorry, but something's not right. You're telling me some gangbanger comes into the bar, pisses a cop off and the cop's buddies try to protect the gangbanger?"

"I know it's weird, but that's how it happened. Anyway, the two started threatening each other. Miles told Bill that he was fucking with the wrong nigger, his words exactly. Bill told him he was going to kick his teeth in. It was your typical pissing match, only both these guys are a little out there, if you know what I mean, especially this Miles character."

"What do you mean?"

"From what I hear, he once knifed his own mother and her boyfriend."

I raised an eyebrow at that. I heard these kinds of stories from time to time: legendary bad men, rejects from the Old West. If half the stories I heard were true, I'd be safer packing up and moving to Afghanistan.

"So then what?"

"At that point, I'd had enough. I told George to get them out of there and that neither one was allowed back in the bar. George told Miles to get lost and gave him a head start. A few minutes later, he and a couple of the boys escorted Bill to his car. That was the last I'd seen of either of them."

"Any idea where I might find this Miles guy?"

Sal shook his head. "No idea."

Some thirsty cops beckoned from the other end of the bar, and the old man scurried away to serve them. I downed my drink and stood up to leave.

"Hey, hold up," Sal said. "You leaving already?"

"Yeah, I should get going. I've had a long day, and I still need to call my client." That couldn't be more true after my last conversation with Marsh.

"Aw, c'mon, stay for one more, on me."

The old man had a face I couldn't say no to—a sad, pasty face with big brown puppy dog eyes. I felt for the guy. The old man was in a nickel-and-dime racket serving guys who wouldn't think twice about nickel and diming him. For some reason, he had taken a shine to me. It must've been the tip. I'm sure the rest of these guys had dropped little more than pocket change on the bar for a single round. The cheap bastards.

I ordered another Pabst and settled in. From time to time, I can stop at one or two drinks, but after that, I'm in trouble. My drinking has a momentum to it, and a third drink is like stepping off a precipice. I could no more stop at three drinks than violate the law of gravity.

Sal stepped away to serve some other customers. I put a twenty on the counter. If Sal charged me cop rates, I'd be there for another six beers and still be able to leave an okay tip.

The volume rose throughout the night as more and more officers poured into the bar. They were short, stocky cops and long, lean cops. They were white, black, and Latino—plainclothes and in uniform. They all seemed to speak at once. They talked loudly and at length about the job, nothing but the job: war stories and horror stories. If my experience was even the least bit characteristic of the profession, they had all heard each other's tales a hundred times before. They laughed and clapped each other on the back, chided each other and exchanged knowing been-there, done-that looks.

I'm not an angry drunk, but on this night, my patience wore a little thinner with every drink. I jostled with overzealous patrons jockeying for position at the bar, throwing elbows and dirty looks. I was buying more than drinks. I was buying trouble. One cop—a tall, lanky troll with thinning red hair, freckles and a bulbous nose—appeared ready to show me how my evening could rival his mug in ugliness. He leaned over me to put in his order, invading my personal space without so much as an excuse me. I spun on my bar stool with my elbow bent at a right angle, planting it into his ribs. I then did it again, and once more when he didn't notice the first two times. Nothing seemed to faze him until I took things a little too far and jostled him as he was accepting a couple of beers from Sal. The beer splashed on his forearms, wasting, by my estimation, an eighth of a cup per glass. That was enough to set him off.

"You got a problem?" the troll asked, setting the glasses on the bar.

"Yeah, I seem to have a large, ugly growth coming out of my back, and it appears to be secreting some kind of amber liquid." It was the kind of thing I only said to guys who were bigger than me because my brain doesn't function quite right and seems hell-bent on using my mouth to kill me.

The troll regarded me with a mixture of disgust and surprise, as if he had just discovered dog shit on the bottom of his shoes. He had pale, jagged lips like scars. They curled into a smirk.

"Oh, a smart guy," he said.

The troll reached into his back pocket and retrieved his badge. "You see that?"

I nodded, unimpressed.

"That's a license to kick your ass, no questions asked. It means I can make you my bitch."

"No, it means you can try."

I cringed the second the words left my mouth.

The troll smiled, a thin, tight-lipped smile that looked like it would be more at home on a reptile. He turned as if to collect his beers off the bar and leave, but I could tell he had no intention of going, not just yet. In a moment, he would turn around and plant his fist in my face, perhaps blacken an eye or shatter my nose. I knew it, but I was in no condition to do anything more than brace for the attack. Luckily, Sal saw it coming a mile away. He put a hand on the guy's shoulder.

"Take it easy, Lenny," the old man said. "Let me buy you and the boys some shots. I'll run 'em over to your table."

Lenny put his order in, collected his beers, and walked away. He gave me a hard look before returning to his seat.

The place took on a funhouse quality after that. Everything appeared warped, and no one looked friendly. Everything about Sal's seemed sinister, everything but Sal himself, and he couldn't help me. He was up to his neck in thirsty, demanding patrons. I was just another face in the crowd, another slurred voice ordering drinks.

At one point, I thought I noticed George Wesley. He sat alone, drinking a beer and glaring at me over the top of his glass. I scanned the room for Lenny but couldn't locate him. I left a few more dollars on the bar and headed for the exit. The din of the cops' voices seemed to grow louder as I neared the door only to die in the silence of a cold winter night.

I walked on unsteady legs to my car, half expecting Lenny or George or some other cop from the bar to ambush me. I braced for it, preparing myself for a quick fall and some kicks to the ribs, but nothing happened. I got in my car and started it up. It groaned to life, struggling against the cold. I waited a couple of minutes for it to warm up before pulling away from the curb and heading for home. I drove slowly, carefully, leaning forward in my seat with my hands glued to the steering wheel. Somewhere among the monotony of the passing street lamps, darkened storefronts, and a cold, dry road stained white by a winter's worth of salting, the tension of the bar dissipated, and the warmth of an evening's alcohol consumption washed over me, putting me at ease. That sense of well-being stuck with me almost the entire trip, interrupted only by my car jumping the curb and plowing into a tree, followed by the painful thud of my head striking the steering wheel and darkness.

TEN

I awoke in the front seat of my car with my head resting against the steering wheel. My watch read a quarter to seven in the morning. I sat up and peered through the windshield. Large snowflakes drifted to earth like tufts of down and settled on the hood of my car. A slowly rising mound of white collected on my windshield, and a dull winter morning sun shone through the frosted glass. It was almost dreamlike except for one key detail: my head ached, and not in the way it usually does after a night of drinking. There was a sharp pain above my right eyebrow. I put a hand to my temple and felt an open wound. There was blood on the steering wheel where my head had come to rest.

I stretched upright in my seat and peered over the mound of snow collecting on my car's hood. A tree seemed to project out of the front bumper. It was a young sapling with a thin trunk.

I didn't even know where I was at first. I peered out the frost-covered windows and scanned my surroundings. It must've been a couple of minutes before it hit me: I was on Wolcott Avenue, just a block from my building. I exited the car and surveyed the damage. It wasn't too bad. The front bumper had a nasty knock in it from the tree, but otherwise, the car was fine. I looked up to see a man watching me with his arms folded.

"That tree's going to die," he said.

"Excuse me?"

"The tree. You killed it. It'll never survive after the damage it sustained."

The tree had seen better days, its bark chipped and splintered about a quarter of the way up.

"Yeah, well..." I began before realizing I didn't have a response.

The guy looked familiar. He was tall and slender with pale skin and dark spiky hair that made his already long face seem even longer.

"Hey, what can I say?" I said. "I fucked up. I had a little too much to drink last night and did a really shitty job of parking."

He regarded me with a look bordering on disgust. "You're lucky to be alive."

I wished this guy would mind his own business and leave me alone. I thought about telling him that, but I wasn't in the mood for a confrontation.

"I hear ya," I said. "You won't get any arguments out of me. I shouldn't drink and drive."

"The next time, you might not be so lucky."

"I know."

"You could've killed yourself or someone else. The next time, it might not be a tree. It might be a person. You might plow into a mother of two and orphan her kids."

The kid sure was laying it on thick.

"I know," I said. "I know. I shouldn't have gotten behind the wheel last night." I tried to maintain eye contact, to let him know I was sincere, but he was unmoved. He just stood there staring at me, his eyes tearing up for the poor tree I had so callously murdered. It was then it hit me where I'd seen him before.

"Hey, I remember you," I said. "You were at that anti-war meeting the other night."

The kid's expression remained the same.

"You live around here?" I asked.

"No," he said.

"Just passing through?"

No answer. We just stood in silence for a moment, enjoying the cold.

"That was nice of you, giving the group all that money," I said.

"I wanted to help. They're good people. They care."

"Definitely," I said, nodding. "I agree 100 percent."

"You don't care," the kid scoffed.

"Excuse me?"

"You're not like them. You don't care. You don't care about anyone but yourself. You drink and drive, putting other people's lives at risk. You go around killing trees. Do you ever stop to think about how your actions affect others?"

"Look, man—" I began.

"People like you make me sick," the kid said, storming off before I could offer anything in my defense. Not that I had one.

"Nice talking to you," I muttered before hopping back inside my car. I turned the ignition, and the vehicle struggled to life. I backed off the curb, the front tires hitting the street with a thud, and parallel parked, this time sparing the surrounding vegetation any further damage.

I headed up to my apartment and checked my voicemail: three messages from Edgar Marsh, each one more unpleasant than the last. I should've called right then, just done it and gotten it over with like pulling off a bandage, but I did nothing of the kind. I went to my freezer and retrieved an ice tray. I put half the tray in a Ziploc baggie and the rest in a rocks glass. I then added vodka to the glass, took a seat on the sofa, and placed the baggie on my forehead. I sat with my feet on the coffee table, or to be more exact, with my feet on top of a pile of newspapers and magazines sitting atop the coffee table, and drank my vodka. A few minutes later, I nodded off when my cell phone rang.

It was Marsh. "Wozniak, what the fuck is going on? I don't know what you have been up to, but I'd like to know if you're going to work this job. My daughter's life is on the line. Did I or did I not tell you to—"

"Shut up," I said, the words startling even myself.

"Pardon me?"

"I said, Shut up. Look, you paid me to investigate your daughter's disappearance, and that's what I'm doing. This is how I work. This is how fast I work. This is how often I report to the client. This is how I talk to the client. If you don't like it, I'll be happy to refund your money minus the time I've spent on the case thus far. It's up to you."

Marsh stammered and harrumphed, failing to emit any noises that could possibly be mistaken for words. Tired of listening to gibberish, I hung up. A moment later, the phone rang again. "Yeah," I answered.

"Look, I didn't mean to question how you do your job, it's just that—"

Feeling bold, I cut him off. "Mr. Marsh, unless you're calling to tell me I'm fired and where to send your refund, we've got nothing else to talk about."

"Mr. Wozniak," Marsh began before pausing. "If I don't start seeing some progress on my daughter's case, you will receive just such a phone call."

He hung up. I reclined in my seat. There was just one more good-sized gulp left in my glass. I downed it. A few minutes later, I drifted off, waking a little before noon. I showered, changed my clothes, and fixed myself a sandwich. I then called Todd to tell him I'd scored with Maya and ask him about Dantrell Miles. He was not interested in either subject but agreed to help me with the latter if I said no more about the former. He called back about an hour later with Miles' life story.

Dantrell worked for Curtis Bledsoe, a high-powered drug dealer on the far north side of the city. At 33, he was older than most in the trade and had a relatively clean rap sheet. His only felony: a single count of manslaughter.

An argument with his mother's boyfriend, a man named Grady Bingham, got out of hand, and Dantrell stabbed him in the chest. Grady was beating Miles' mother, and Dantrell pulled a knife to scare him off. The boyfriend rushed him, they scuffled, and Dantrell accidentally stabbed him in the chest. The prosecution agreed to a plea deal, and Miles wound up getting seven years in Joliet. He got out after three. Since then, his mother passed of a stroke, and he had moved in with a girlfriend near the Chicago/Evanston border, a woman named Wanda Briggs.

I decided to pay her a visit.

I headed north again, this time to a three-story apartment complex in Evanston. Wanda lived on the second floor. I knocked on her door and a few seconds later heard scampering feet followed by a woman shouting at someone.

"No, you go in the other room like I told you!"

The door opened a crack, drawing the security chain taut. An eye peered through the opening. "Who are you?" the woman asked.

"I'm sorry to bother you," I said. "My name is Glenn Wozniak, and I was looking for Wanda Briggs."

"Are you with the police?"

"No, ma'am, I'm not. Are you Wanda Briggs?"

"What do you want?"

"I'm a private investigator. I'm looking for Dantrell Miles."

"He ain't here."

She tried to close the door, but I slapped an open palm against it, holding it open.

Wanda continued pushing on the door. I leaned into it, my weight resisting her. "When do you expect him back?"

"I don't expect him back."

"Wanda, could you open the door for a second? I just want to ask a couple of questions, and then I'll be out of your hair."

"Oh, hell no! I don't know you. I ain't opening shit."

I tried to pass her a card through the narrow opening, but as I did, she threw her weight against the door, slamming it on my fingers.

"Son of a bitch!" I cried. "Wanda, open the door! Open the fucking door! You're crushing my fingers!"

Wanda wasn't listening. She kept pushing, the door grinding into my flesh. I slammed all my weight against it, knocking Wanda back and pulling the security chain out of the frame. I could now see her in full. She was a short, light-skinned woman dressed in a pink terry-cloth robe and shaped like a beach ball. I held my wounded hand, my head cloudy from the pain.

Wanda backed away, moving slowly, deliberately, toward the living room. I felt vulnerable. It's never smart to barge into a home in a rough area where the law is ineffective. Too many people carry weapons, and they are more than willing to use them. I slipped my aching right hand inside my coat as if going for a gun.

"Hold it right there," I said. "Don't even think about it."

"Think about what?"

"Just stay where you are."

"Listen, motherfucker, Dantrell doesn't live here. I ain't seen him in weeks, so why don't you take your sorry, fake-cop ass out of here before I call up the real police."

I stood my ground, and for a while, neither one of us said anything. Wanda gave me a hard look. I gave her one back. This wasn't going well. Most likely, she could tell that the wheels in my head were spinning, through mud, trying to figure out how I could get her to talk to me.

I should've lied from the start and said I was a cop. Then I would've had the threat of repercussions on my side. She'd still be hostile and tightlipped, but she would've at least opened the door. Now I had backed myself into a corner. I was little better than a criminal, a home invader. There's no law saying that anyone needs to cooperate with a guy like me. There was one against breaking and entering.

I remained in the doorway. There were about ten feet between us. The apartment was small and dingy. To the left stood a small kitchen. Beyond that, I could see part of the living room. A TV played cartoons, the volume on high. Hot Wheels cars and assorted action figures lay scattered about on the floor.

The small, round head of a little boy appeared behind Wanda. He clutched the pink terry cloth of her robe with one small hand. The boy couldn't have been older than four or five. He had chubby cheeks, and his complexion was darker than Wanda's—his like onyx, hers more like mocha. He wore nothing but jockey shorts and a T-shirt covered in stains. The boy studied me for a moment before turning away.

"Malcolm, go in the other room," Wanda said.

The terry cloth slid from the boy's grip. He backed away, his eyes shifting from me to Wanda to the floor.

"Hold on a second, buddy," I said, taking another step inside the apartment. "Don't go away."

Malcolm stopped and looked up at his mother.

"You heard what I said," Wanda snapped. "Get in the other room now!"

Malcolm scampered away. Wanda's eyes narrowed into tiny slits. She hunched her shoulders, crooked her arms, and clenched her fists. She looked like a linebacker, and I half expected her to charge me, but we just stood there, glaring at each other.

"Dantrell's?" I asked.

"What?"

"The boy. Is he Dantrell's?"

"Where do you get off asking me something like that? Do you ask white women who fathered their children?"

She had me there. I considered apologizing, probably should have, but I didn't say a word. Neither of us did. At an impasse, we stood and stared some more until we were tired of looking at each other.

"Perhaps the boy will talk," I said. Wanda was about to protest, but I cut her off. "Malcolm!"

The boy appeared behind his mother, with a quizzical but shy expression on his face.

"Come here," I said. "I want to ask you about your daddy."

The kid approached, and Wanda shook her head. "Oh no, fuck that. Malcolm, what'd I tell you?"

The boy stopped midway between us. He looked up at his mother, his bottom lip protruding in a pout and his eyes moist with tears.

I glanced inside the kitchen. There I noticed a scale and several small plastic baggies laid out on a card table. I looked down at Malcolm and smiled. “It’s cool, Malcolm. Listen to your mother.”

The boy ran to Wanda and buried his face in her robe. She caressed the back of his head, watching me with a resentful expression on her face.

“Whatcha got going on in there?” I said, motioning with my chin at the card table.

Wanda smirked. “I have no idea what you’re talking about.”

“It looks like you’re running a drug operation out of your kitchen.”

Denise tried to play it cool. She shrugged, avoiding eye contact, careful to keep her mouth shut. Curtis Bledsoe would’ve been proud.

I reached into my coat and retrieved my cell phone. “I bet DCFS would like to have a look around. This doesn’t seem like a suitable environment for a child.”

“Perhaps I oughta call the police and let them know how you forced your way into my apartment.”

“You do that, Wanda. You let the cops in here. It’ll give them a chance to look around. I’m sure Curtis Bledsoe will have no problem with you inviting law enforcement into one of his stash houses."

Wanda didn't respond. She just glared at me, her lips pursed.

"In fact, why don't I call them," I said. I held the phone in my palm and dialed nine. I looked up to check Wanda's expression. It hadn't changed, so I dialed one.

"What do you want?" Wanda said.

"Pardon me?"

"What do you want?"

"You know what I want."

Wanda tilted her head to one side and rolled her eyes at me. "I told you I ain't seen that faggot-ass motherfucker."

"You're going to have to give me something. It's me or the police. You decide." I raised the phone and poised my index finger above the one to show her I meant business.

"What am I supposed to give you? I don't know nothing."

"How about an address?"

Wanda paused for a moment. "If I give you that, will you go away and leave me alone?"

"I might."

"He lives over on Lunt."

"Where on Lunt?"

"1536 West Lunt Avenue."

"Great, I'll be on my way." I turned to leave, stopping just outside the door. "If it's any consolation, I don't mean Dantrell any harm."

Wanda laughed. "Like I give a shit. Fuck Dantrell."

I closed the door, glimpsing Malcolm peering up at me as I did. There was a strange sadness in his eyes, one that was far too world-weary for a child of his age. I felt a pang in my gut, and that familiar urge to quit, to run away, crept back into my thoughts, taking residence in my mind like a restless spirit.

Dantrell lived in a run-down two-flat just south of the Morse El-stop. Some faded gang graffiti, ornate script surrounding the rough sketch of a crown, adorned the front door. There were a pair of mailboxes to its right, and just beneath those a pair of doorbells. The first was labeled Hernandez, the second left blank. I rang the second but got no answer and took a walk around to the back. A rickety-looking wooden staircase enclosed in white, partially rusted corrugated metal led to the second floor.

I picked the backdoor lock and went up the stairs. I peered in the first-floor rear window. An older Mexican woman sat at the kitchen table, watching what appeared to be a Spanish-language soap opera. A rugged caballero in an ornate cowboy getup was on the screen. He argued with an attractive brunette. The woman blurted out something, cringed, and turned away from him. In a nice dramatic touch, she bit the knuckle of her right index finger, tears welling up in her eyes as she faced the camera just before a fade.

I continued my ascent. The light had burned out on the second-floor porch, and only the slightest illumination trickled in through a single small window. I felt my way to the kitchen door and peered inside. The apartment was pitch-black. I picked the lock and entered.

This was hardly the first place I'd broken into. I'd busted into several homes and offices while on the job, either to plant surveillance equipment or snag an incriminating piece of evidence. Break-ins are not for the faint of heart, every sound amplified—every breath, heartbeat, and creaking floorboard. The key is to remember that no place is ever completely silent. Background noise is always present and most often goes unheard. If you pay too much attention to the creaks of the floorboards or the sound of your breathing, you will panic, and that's when mistakes happen. That's when you trip or upend some furniture.

I switched on the lights. The kitchen was impeccable. There were no dishes in the sink, and I could practically see myself in the tile floor. A food processor and microwave were visible on the counter. A wooden table and four chairs occupied the center of the room. I peered in the cupboards and drawers: not much in the way of food.

I made my way into the living room, turning off the kitchen light behind me. A wicker chair sat in one corner of the room. To the left of that were a loveseat and an end table. A round beechwood coffee table sat in front of the sofa across from a cheap-looking entertainment center made of pine. The unit carried little more than a modestly sized television, a DVD player, and a combination cassette player/CD console stereo.

I shut off the lights and headed into the bedroom. It had a closet with shuttered doors. I looked inside—just a few silk shirts in primary colors, one suit (purple), and some oversized blue jeans and sweats. There was a queen-size sleigh bed in the center of the room. To its right sat an antique nightstand with a red ceramic reading lamp on it. A large dresser with an attached round mirror lay opposite the bed, and to its right was a white cabinet. A TV and a VCR sat on top of it.

I opened the cabinet doors and found a couple of stacks of VHS tapes. Half were standard mainstream fare, mostly guy flicks: *Scarface* (the DePalma version), *Dolomite*, *The Godfather I* and *II*, *Cooley High*. The other half was porn, each tape featuring an all-male cast. I picked up one of them, titled *Undercover Brothers*. The cover showed a large black man wearing a fedora and the tattered remnants of a suit. The pants were cutoffs, the shirt and jacket sleeveless, revealing some rather large, muscular arms. He was cuffing a nude, even more muscular black man.

I returned the tape to the cabinet and continued my search. I checked the dresser drawers hoping to find something, anything that might carry the occupant's name. No luck. I shut off the lights in the bedroom and ducked into the bathroom. I searched the medicine cabinet for prescription drug bottles. Again, no luck. While in there, I noticed a couple of stains on the tile floor, each copper-colored and no larger than a dime. The droplets were under the sink. I bent down and took a closer look: dried blood.

I shut off the lights and headed for the back exit. Halfway across the living room, I heard the creak of the kitchen door opening followed by the voices of two men. I ducked into the bedroom and weighed the pros and cons of two lousy hiding places: under the bed and in the closet. The cons for both were the same: They are among the first places anyone looks. I was in a full-fledged panic, turning from the bed to the closet and back while standing just inside the darkened bedroom. I settled on the closet, reasoning that the bed left me in a more vulnerable, prone position. I hid inside, pushing all the way to the back. My heartbeat sounded like a bass drum inside my head, and it felt like a thousand tiny wings were fluttering against the inside of my ribcage. I crawled on my knees to the front of the closet and peered through the door's horizontal slats. It was too dark to see anything.

"I'm tellin' ya, he's not coming back here," said a familiar-sounding man.

"Yeah, but I want to take a look just in case," said the other. Another familiar voice. This one sounded monotonous and distracted, like someone fatigued and drained of emotion.

I peered out again and could see their backlit shapes. They were standing in the living room, just outside the bedroom door. One of them leaned inside and slid a hand along the wall. The bedroom lights turned on, making my heart jump. Light poured through the slats, and my eyes blinked, trying to adjust.

I could see the two men now. The tired-sounding cop was George Wesley. The other was Lenny, the freckled troll I almost came to blows with at Sal's.

George mumbled to himself. "Fuckin' shit."

"What's a matter?" asked Lenny.

"Nothing, I was just thinking about Bill."

"I know. I can't stop thinking about him either."

"Man, I get my hands on that son of a bitch Miles, and I swear..."

Lenny shook his head. "He's gonna pay. That's for damn sure, the piece of shit. Though I must say, the guy knows how to handle himself."

"What, you mean T-Bone and Watkins? That's what Bledsoe gets for sending a couple of punk kids to do a man's job. I mean, we're practically dealing with a wild animal here."

"Yeah, but he fucked those boys up."

"He won't be hurting anyone else when I get through with him."

George left the room. Lenny took a couple of steps towards the closet, casting a shadow across the door. I slid a hand inside my coat pocket and felt for my gun, only I wasn't carrying. I rarely did. Tailing adulterers and insurance frauds is not exactly the most dangerous work. I sat there helpless with my back pressed against the rear wall of the closet, and my knees pulled up to my chest.

Peering out from behind Miles' purple suit, I could see Lenny reach for the closet door. The elongated shadows of his fingers jutted towards me, looking sharp, like the shears on a pair of hedge clippers. I held my breath. The purple suit pants brushed against my face, the wool catching on my stubble, and the sensation made me shudder. I shut my eyes tightly as if wishing Lenny away to some never-never land. His hand stopped just short of the door. He turned, head cocked to one side. Something on the other side of the room caught his attention. I scooted to the front of the closet and peered out. I had left the cabinet door ajar. Lenny hunched down and looked inside. He reached in, retrieving a tape.

I could hear him chuckling to himself. "Oh, I've got to see this," he said.

He put the tape in the VCR and turned on the TV. A moment later, I could hear some generic techno music playing and the sound of a door opening.

"Find anything interesting, detective?" said one of the porno actors.

"Yes, but I'm going to have to take a closer look," replied his costar.

"Be my guest."

A fly unzipped. "Just what I thought, a big black cock."

"And it's loaded."

"Be careful with that thing."

"I'm calling the shots here. Now on your knees, detective."

At that, Lenny burst out laughing. "Oh my God! George, get in here! You've got to see this shit!"

"What is it?"

"Just come here and look."

"All right; hold on." Moments later, George entered the room. "What?" he asked, and then seeing what was on the TV, "Oh for fuck's sake, turn that shit off."

"Hilarious, right?" Lenny said. "Man, I wouldn't have taken Miles for a fag."

"Nothing surprises me anymore."

Lenny shut off the TV. "So, what'd you find?"

"I'm pretty sure our boy came here after his run-in with T-Bone and Watkins. I found some blood on the bathroom floor. He must've stopped back to clean up and grab some clothes."

The two stood silently for a moment.

"Are we done here?" Lenny asked.

"Yeah, let's go."

They headed out of the room, shutting off the lights behind them. Moments later, I heard the back door close. I waited a while longer before coming out of hiding. My legs were sore from crouching, and they creaked as I stood up.

Three names: T-Bone, Watkins, and Bledsoe. I wrote them down. Bledsoe I knew, and if I heard George and his friend correctly, Dantrell was no longer in the man's good graces. That's where T-Bone and Watkins came in. Bledsoe sent them to take Miles out, but they couldn't finish the job. I doubted he'd be so lucky if Lenny and George got their hands on him. That's why I had to find him first.

ELEVEN

There are hundreds of guys like Dantrell Miles on the streets of Chicago. They are men living on borrowed time, men stalked by debt or who've made enemies of the wrong people—refugees of the drug trade. You can see it in their faces, in their uneasy demeanor, somewhere between panic and resignation. That's if you see them at all. More often than not, they just dissolve into the shadows and fade away.

That was Dantrell Miles. He was like an apparition. You might catch a trace of him for the briefest of seconds before he'd disappear. But where? Where does a guy like Dantrell hide? How can a man like him, a man who'd spent his whole life slinging dope for Curtis Bledsoe, go anywhere without being discovered? It would be one thing if Bledsoe were the only one looking for him, but Dantrell had George Wesley and the Chicago Police Department on his trail.

Where could he go? Dantrell didn't have any family left, and even if he did, he wouldn't be safe with them. That's the first place Bledsoe would look. Dantrell's friends were most likely other gang members, and no matter how close they might be, they weren't about to risk their necks crossing the boss to hide him. If he turned to a friend, it would have to be someone outside his usual circle. There was only one place I could imagine him meeting such a person: the Stateville Correctional Center.

I called Howie Jensen the following morning. Howie was a Stateville corrections officer. He was a big, awkward-looking goon, 6'4" with a lean but imposing build and the freakishly long wingspan of an NBA power forward.

I'm not exactly sure why, but Howie liked me. I'd visited Stateville often as a homicide detective. I'd stop by and play 'Let's Make a Deal' with the occasional inmate, a few years off a guy's sentence for information that would help increase the prison population. In all that time, I don't remember anything but the most superficial interactions between us. *How's the weather? You catch the game last weekend? The Bears have got to get themselves a quarterback someday*, and so on. Howie would just nod, a faraway look on his face. I'm not even sure why I continued trying to converse with him. I suppose the silence and his imposing presence made me nervous, and I used all the chatter to mask my discomfort. Still, the guy warmed to me.

One day he asked me to join him for lunch, and I suffered through a half-hour of silence punctuated by awkward attempts to spur some semblance of a conversation. He must have thought it went well because from then on, he'd go out of his way to say hi whenever I visited, often suggesting a few beers and a game of pool after work. I suppose just saying a kind word or two was enough to set me apart from everyone else.

Howie said he remembered Dantrell and, luckily enough, Miles' old cellmate was still working off some years for armed robbery. I hopped in my car and made the long drive south. I took Highway 55 down past all the numbered streets, past several high-rise ghettos, and past forests of smokestacks spitting dark streams of poison into a blue-gray sky. I grazed the few well-off southern suburbs, their affluence passing in a blur before giving way to industrial ghost towns and trailer parks.

It was late afternoon when I reached the prison. From the outside, the place had the look of a fortress. A 25-foot-high fence ran the complex's length, a loose coil of razor wire sprouting from the top like thorny vegetation. Inside the gates, it looked much like your run-of-the-mill industrial campus with its extensive collection of cinderblock buildings.

I met Howie in the visitor's waiting area, and we headed down a long corridor to an interrogation room. A metal table sat in the center, bolted to the floor and surrounded by four orange plastic chairs. A fluorescent light fixture hummed overhead.

"Have a seat," Howie said.

I sat down. Howie towered over me like a shady tree. He dropped a manila envelope on the table. "That's the guy's file."

"Thanks," I said. "I appreciate the help."

Howie stared at his giant shoes, a goofy grin on his face. "I'll be right back."

I smiled and nodded in reply. Howie lurched off, turning to take one last look at me before closing the door behind him.

I thumbed through the file. Dantrell Miles' former cellmate was a guy named Freddy Baxter, a petty drug dealer four years into a seven-year sentence for possession with intent.

Howie returned a few minutes later with a chubby black kid in an orange prison jumpsuit. Freddy had shackles on his wrists and ankles and a blue do-rag on his head. The kid kept his eyes on the floor as he entered. Howie placed one of his giant mitts on the convict's shoulder and guided him into the chair across from me. I leaned forward, resting a forearm on the Formica tabletop, and smiled. The kid reclined in his chair, a defiant expression on his face. He tried to fold his arms, but the handcuffs got in the way, ruining the whole casual, don't-give-a-fuck vibe he was trying to pull off.

"Glenn Wozniak, this is Freddy Baxter," Howie said.

Baxter regarded me with disdain, his head tilted to one side, and his eyes narrowed into slits. His tongue probed the inside of his cheek, forming a lump on the right side of his face. He sucked his teeth. It was a full-on tough-guy routine. I guess the teeth sucking and the like were my cues to break him. I didn't want to disappoint, but was out of practice and played good cop instead.

"Hey, Howie, you think you might be able to remove the cuffs and give us some time alone?" I asked.

Howie shot Baxter a look that told him he better behave and unlocked the restraints.

"I'll be just outside the door," he said. "Holler if you need me."

Howie ducked as he went out the door. I watched him and smiled. There was nothing particularly pleasant about watching Howie lumber about like a grizzly bear on its hind legs, but smiling gave my face something to do.

It was now just the two of us, and Baxter grew more charming by the minute. He spat on the floor and then gazed up at the ceiling, smirking.

"Did Howie tell you why I was here?"

"I don't know, something about Dantrell. I ain't seen him. He hasn't been to visit, and I sure as hell ain't been outside these walls."

"Did Dantrell have any friends in here? Someone who's been released recently?"

Freddy shrugged, smirked, the usual.

I leaned forward in my seat and flashed a halfhearted smile. "All right, here's the deal, Freddy. I'm working for a wealthy man, one of the richest men in the city. If you cooperate, I'm sure I can pull a few strings, make life a little easier for you in here."

"You're sure?" he said. "I don't want to hear you're sure. I want a deal."

"What do you want?"

"I want up outta this motherfucker. I want some years off my sentence."

There wasn't a thing I could do about his sentence, not without going to the DA and turning the case over to the police. Marsh wouldn't like that.

"How long have you got left?" I asked.

Freddy held up three fingers. His hand was small, delicate, like a child's.

"Sure, not a problem," I lied, forcing myself to nod as I spoke the words.

"Cool, but I'm not saying shit until I get something in writing."

I was losing my patience with him. "There's no time for that, and you're not getting shit unless this info is useful," I said. "I'm not fucking around, Freddy. Those are your years to do, and you can do them all, for all I care."

Freddy pursed his lips and leaned forward in his seat. I could smell the musty scent of his prison uniform. It reminded me of church, apropos considering I was about to hear the gospel according to Freddy. "I might look young, but I ain't stupid. You show me something in writing, and I'll talk. Otherwise, don't waste my time. I can do my years. That ain't no problem, but I ain't giving you a thing without getting something in return. Ya' feel me?"

Freddy rested his small, childlike hands in front of him on the table. I wondered how he'd survived the last four years. The kid was in over his head. For all I knew, Miles raped him nightly when they were cellmates.

Freddy hunched his shoulders and looked at me with his head cocked to one side. I stared back at him.

"Why are you in here?" I asked after a while.

"Man, you know damn well why I'm in here." He then motioned with his head at the manila folder now nestled under my right forearm, saying, "Shit, that's my file right there."

"It says here you were caught with what? A couple of ounces of weed?"

"That's right, and it was only my second offense. The judge was a hard-ass giving me all these years for some trifling bullshit like that."

"And where were you living?"

"What?"

"Where were you living when you got arrested?"

"In Englewood, bitch. That shit's no joke."

"No doubt. Englewood's a rough area, but I think you meant to say you were living in Englewood with your mom."

"What?"

"Your file says you were living with your mom."

"So? What are you saying?"

"Nothing. Just it must be hard, a young kid like yourself in here with all these hard gangsters and psychopaths."

"You best believe I'm carrying myself like a man up in here."

"C'mon, Freddy, how many guys punk you a week in here? Five? Ten? I bet Dantrell made good use of your black ass. I know he sure liked to swing that way."

Freddy clenched his fists. "You want to try me, bitch?"

That's right, Freddy. Get mad. Lose your cool. Just give the word, and the rest of the story writes itself. I'll take care of the bad man for you. I'll make sure he gets what's coming to him. Just tell me how to find him.

"There's nothing to be ashamed of," I said. "Dantrell's an imposing figure. There's no shame in someone of your ..." I paused for a moment, trying to find the right words, before continuing, "Youth and slight stature getting overpowered. Just say it. Dantrell raped you."

Freddy was on the edge of his seat, hatred in his eyes. “Fuck you!” he screamed, lunging at me.

The light orange chair skidded away, striking the back wall before tipping over on its side. The sound echoed inside the room. Seconds later, Howie came bursting through the door, cuffs in hand, just in time to see Freddy grab my collar. The guard’s entrance distracted my assailant, and in that instant, I sucker-punched him.

“It’s all right, Howie,” I said. “Everything’s under control.”

Freddy lay on the floor panting, his bottom lip swollen and bloodied. I stood over him, and he looked up at me. A little of the hard edge had disappeared. Either that or he was biding his time until Howie left the room. I took my chances and asked the big guy to go. He lingered in the doorway, clutching the cuffs with one hand, his other poised above the holster of his billy club.

“It’s cool, Howie.”

I offered Freddy a hand, but he waved it off, deciding to get up on his own like a big boy.

“We’re cool, right, Freddy?”

“Yeah, we’re cool,” he said.

We returned to our seats, and Howie exited the room. “I’m letting him off the leash the next time you touch me,” I said, motioning towards the door and the enormous man who stood just outside it.

Freddy said nothing. I didn't either for a while. We just sat there and looked at each other. Freddy looked away and mumbled something into his chest.

"What's that?" I asked.

"I said Dantrell was cool."

"Is that right? How so?"

"He looked out for me. And you know what? He didn't have to. I don't run with those Bledsoe boys, ya' know what I'm saying?"

I nodded.

"But Dantrell took care of me."

Freddy fell silent again. His hunched figure cast a large shadow across the table. He balled his hands into fists, his fingers digging into his palms. I tried to look him in the eyes, but he turned his head.

"Freddy, if Dantrell was cool, then help me. He's in a lot of trouble. There are people on the outside who not only want him dead but want him to suffer. I need to reach him and warn him."

Freddy thought for a moment. "If you're trying to help, then what was all that Dantrell raped you bullshit about?"

"It was just that," I said. "Bullshit. I was trying to get you to talk."

Freddy rubbed his eyes and shook his head. "I don't know."

"Dantrell is in trouble, and he's running out of time. That's the honest-to-God truth. If he took care of you, then don't you think you ought to repay the favor?"

"All right," Freddy said, sighing. "Dantrell used to kick it with this boy Julius when he was in here."

"You got a last name?"

"Meeks. Julius Meeks."

"Thanks, Freddy. You done good, and I'm sorry about the bloody lip."

"Bitch, you sucker-punched me, and you know it."

"You're right. Sorry about that."

I put out my hand, tried to make peace, but Freddy left me hanging. I called for Howie, and he took the kid away. When he came back, I asked him to check Meeks' last known address.

"Wait here," Howie said before leaving the room. So I waited. Time drags in prison, even when you're not an inmate. I waited for almost half an hour, but it felt longer, and I felt relieved when he returned.

"Hey," he said, nodding as if we had just run into each other for the first time that day.

"Hey."

"So you want to maybe hang out tonight, grab some beers and catch a movie?"

I tried my best to conceal my irritation. "Did you find anything on Meeks?"

"Oh, right, sorry, I forgot. I need to give you this."

Howie held out a yellow Post-it note. He'd printed the name Julius Meeks on it in big childlike letters. Beneath that was an address: 1245 South Karlov Avenue.

"Thanks," I said.

"Julius got out of prison three months ago. This was his mother's place. She passed away while he was inside and left him the house."

"What was this guy in for?"

"Assault and battery. I guess he robbed some old fag that was paying him for sex."

"Thanks, this helps."

"So how 'bout that drink?"

"I'll give you a call when I'm done visiting this Meeks character."

Howie nodded his enormous head, and we said our goodbyes. He looked sullen, more so than usual, like he didn't expect to see me ever again. I wondered if he knew something I didn't.

TWELVE

I made a brief stop at my office to retrieve the .357 Magnum I kept in the top drawer of my desk, and drove west, taking Madison Avenue, the revolver stashed underneath the passenger's seat.

Stores and apartments gave way to abandoned buildings with boarded-up windows. Tattered awnings swayed in the wind, their colors dulled. Faded store signs alluded to more prosperous days, days so long ago few remembered them. There were once businesses on this street: offices, taverns, pool halls, and restaurants. Now there were just ads for board-up services in the windows of empty storefronts.

The scene grew bleaker the farther west I traveled, with the buildings in progressively advanced stages of disrepair, some partially burned to the ground. This was Dresden or Hiroshima on the west side of Chicago.

Once upon a time, desperate, frustrated people set fire to this area, angry about the assassination of Martin Luther King. Thirty-five years later, little had changed. Those days' tragic results were still evident—each burned-out building serving as a monument to neglect.

Not far from my destination, a group of young men with tired eyes stood on a street corner. They wore the collars of their coats upturned, obscuring their faces. Some warmed themselves around trash-can fires. A few others huddled in a doorway as if hiding from something.

I turned off Madison onto a street filled with decrepit old wood-framed houses. Julius Meeks' home stood at the end of the block. It was a gray, two-story A-frame house. The paint was chipping, and a long, deep crack meandered up the concrete staircase leading to the front door. I parked the car about a block east of the house. It was late afternoon, twilight at this time of year, and waves of dark clouds rolled over the pitched roof of the house. The structure seemed to move, making the clouds look like billowing jets of exhaust. All the lights appeared to be out, and the shades were drawn.

I snapped up the gun from underneath the passenger seat and tucked it in the waistband of my pants. The weapon made me uneasy. The last time I fired a gun on the job was a good two years before I retired from the force. I was apprehending the murderer of a convenience store clerk in Humboldt Park.

The perpetrator was a kid in his early twenties named Raoul Pinto. He was robbing a convenience store when, suffering from a case of nerves, he inadvertently fired his gun, putting a bullet in the store clerk's neck. Hardly an old pro, Pinto fled without even taking the money from the cash register. I found him hiding at a relative's house, close to the scene of the crime.

Raoul had made a run for it. He snuck out the rear window as I entered through the front. I caught sight of him scaling the backyard fence and pursued him on foot. He tried to lose me in the basement of a nearby building and might've gotten away if he hadn't put a nasty gash in his leg climbing that fence.

I tracked his droplets of blood from the alley through the backyard and down the stairs to the basement where he was hiding. Cornered, he shot at me, the bullet just missing my head. I returned fire but flinched, blowing a hole in a window about five feet to the right of him. Had I just missed, Raoul would've fired back instantly, and I wouldn't be alive today, but I was so wide of the mark, he just had to stop and marvel at my terrible aim. We both did. We stared at the blown-out basement window—a look of amusement on his face, one of shame on mine. Then, remembering the gravity of the situation, I fired off another shot. This time I fared better, striking Raoul in his right hand. I was aiming for his knees, but it didn't matter. The shot did the trick, knocking the gun from Raoul's hand. He surrendered and spent the next couple of days in the hospital, telling anyone who would listen about my dreadful shooting. My failed marksmanship became the stuff of legends down at the precinct, never failing to get a laugh from my colleagues.

No, guns were not my friend, but my close call with George and Lenny reminded me I was dealing with some dangerous characters and could use a little protection.

I headed around to the back of the house, just barely clearing a short chain-link fence along the way. I landed awkwardly, the balls of my feet absorbing most of the shock. My momentum carried me forward a couple of extra steps, but I managed to keep from falling.

The Meeks had a small backyard. A large shade tree took up one corner, a dense network of branches stretching overhead. A laundry line extended between two metal poles, and just beyond that was a small detached garage. I peered through its window. The garage was empty, most likely cleared out a long time ago, the door kicked in, leaving an opening that even I could get through at the bottom.

I approached the house and peered through the kitchen window. It was like a museum, the appliances all circa 1960. The stove was small and white with oversized plastic knobs and four burners arranged in a tight cluster on top. The refrigerator was a massive brown monolith. There was a built-in hutch with glass doors along one wall that held old lady Meeks' dishes. It was almost empty: just a few plates, a couple of bowls, and some coffee mugs. The rest were dirty and unceremoniously stacked in the sink. Someone had clearly been here not too long ago.

I walked back to the side of the building. There, I found two small frosted windows leading into the basement. A piece of cardboard covered a hole no bigger than a baseball in one of them. I pressed on it and could feel it give. I took out my gun and struck it with the butt. The cardboard separated from the window, leaving a gummy tape residue behind. I peered inside, but couldn't see anything, the basement pitch dark. I felt for the window latch, extending my arm as far as I could until I was pressed flush against the building, my cheek resting against the wood exterior. My cold, stiff fingers located the latch and turned it. I gripped the window and pulled, opening it about two inches. I slid the tips of my fingers inside the small space beneath the window and lifted. It resisted at first before opening with a loud rattle that echoed throughout the basement.

I entered facing the window, giving any potential assailants a good long look at my backside. A stray nail in the frame caught my coat and pulled it up around my neck. I tried to jiggle the fabric free. When that failed, I unfastened the buttons and squirmed out of it, first freeing my right arm and then the left. I continued my descent into the basement.

Once inside, I tried again to free my coat. Standing on tiptoes, I reached for it, gripping a handful of fabric, and attempted to wrest it away from the snag without luck. I made another attempt, this time shifting the material to the left and then to the right. Another failure. Throwing caution to the wind, I yanked the coat free. There was a loud tearing sound that made me cringe, and the motion jarred the window loose. It slammed shut with a rush, the impact reverberating in the darkness. I stopped breathing for a moment, frozen to the spot where I stood.

The reverberations faded, and all was silent. I looked up through the hole in the frosted glass at an early evening sky. The evening air chilled my face. Perhaps it was just my unease at a less-than-discreet entrance, but I sensed I was not alone. I felt eyes on my back and turned around, finding only darkness.

The place was not much different from most basements. There was a damp chill in the air and a cloying, musty odor. I put my coat on, retrieved my flashlight from its inside pocket, and drew my gun. The grip felt cold and heavy in my hand. A wooden staircase lay at the other end of the room, its steps ascending into darkness. I climbed them, trying not to make much noise. At the top, I found a door. It was solid, made of oak, with an oval brass knob. I turned it, and the door, to my relief, opened quietly onto a foyer. There was the kitchen to my right and to my left, the front door. A living room full of old-lady furniture and knick-knacks stretched in front of me. A faded rag-weave rug sat in its center. There was a floral-print couch with thin wooden armrests of a dark cherry color.

I imagined old lady Meeks had kept it covered in plastic and would be mortified to see it exposed to the elements. An antique lamp sat next to a mustard-colored easy chair with matching ottoman, by far the most comfortable-looking furniture in the house. A cabinet with glass doors held a series of ceramic figurines, cherubic black children engaging in the most wholesome activities. One chubby-cheeked little boy held a baseball bat. Another carried a sled. A boy in a red baseball cap hugged a young girl, her hair in pigtails. They were like scenes out of a Norman Rockwell painting—simple, clean, and wholesome.

I took a quick look around the room but found nothing out of the ordinary and moved on to the kitchen. Assorted papers covered the counter—mostly bills and bank statements; some addressed to Julius, others to his grandmother, Johanna Meeks.

I checked the kitchen drawers, finding little of interest, and made my way upstairs. A floorboard creaked out of rhythm with my steps as I neared the top of the staircase. I stopped and listened for a moment. Hearing nothing, I peeked around the corner at the top of the stairs.

On the second floor, I found a bathroom and two bedrooms: one opposite the stairs, the other at the end of the hall. The first bedroom was a tiny cubicle. It held a twin bed, a dresser, a nightstand, and a stereo system. The stereo was an older model with a turntable and a dual cassette player but no CD. A couple of milk cartons sat on the floor next to it, one filled with records, the other with cassettes. They were mostly disco albums with some house, funk, and soul mixed in—Donna Summer; Frankie Knuckles; Earth, Wind and Fire; Isaac Hayes.

A small closet, its door slightly ajar, sat opposite the bed. I looked inside. It was filled to bursting with men's clothes. I checked the dresser drawers, nothing too unusual, just socks, underwear, and shirts. A wool blanket hung off an unmade bed. The nightstand was bare except for a digital clock radio and the empty wrapper of a Trojan condom. The package's metallic interior dully reflected the red light of the clock face.

Though considerably larger, the other bedroom was so crammed full of stuff there was little room to move. Old lady Meeks was a packrat. Several cardboard boxes sat piled against one wall, each filled to bursting with books, magazines, newspaper clippings, bills, and photos. She even kept expired coupons, some dating back to the Nixon administration. Many were for stores that no longer existed: Goldblatt's, Chas. A. Stevens, and a wig shop called the House of Boris (buy one wig, get a second wig half off).

I found an old picture of her grandson on the nightstand turned face down. The photo appeared to be from the 80s, when Julius was a teenager. He had a box cut and wore parachute pants and a baby blue mesh shirt.

Still no sign of Dantrell Miles. I checked everywhere, finding nothing but more boxes and more junk. The closet was the worst. Old Lady Meeks packed it from floor to ceiling with paperbacks, old newspapers, clothes, shoes, photo albums, and a colorful array of Sunday hats for church.

The search was going nowhere. I turned around and headed for the door, taking a couple of steps before stopping. There was something different about the room, a strange scent, sweet yet musky. A couple more steps and a floorboard creaked. I stopped and listened, uncertain whether the sound came from me or someone else. All I could hear was the hum of the refrigerator downstairs and the blood coursing through my head. Otherwise, all was silent.

I exited the bedroom and made for the stairs. The scent grew stronger. I turned the corner, my eyes meeting another pair of brown eyes, opened wide. I raised my gun. Someone screamed, and I felt hot breath on the back of my neck and heard a loud crack, like thunder. There was a flash of brilliant, blinding light followed by darkness and a long descent. I fell and fell but didn't hit bottom, like a feather dropped into the abyss.

THIRTEEN

I remember feeling a sharp pain shoot through my skull and down my spine. There was a brief flash of brilliant light, and then nothing but the sensation of falling forward and the anticipation of hitting bottom. But I didn't hit bottom. Nothing followed, and after that, more nothing. It was as if I were floating weightless in outer space.

The sensation didn't last.

I'm not sure how long I was out. A few minutes? A couple of hours? It's hard to say. My head throbbed as I returned to consciousness. It was a jarring experience, like a child entering the world. My hair was cold and slicked with blood. I could feel my feet on the floor and something hard pressed against my back. My entire body ached. I tried to open my eyes, but they wouldn't cooperate.

I heard a voice somewhere in the distance. The speaker was but a shadow, and his words sounded like they were coming from the other end of a deep tunnel. It was a man's voice, high-pitched with a slight nasal whine.

"So Miss Thang says Grandma promised her them figurines upstairs," he said.

"What'd you say?" asked another voice. This one was deeper, a bass, low but not guttural, smooth. His words seemed to ooze as though delivered in tablespoons of honey.

"Me? Nothing," said the nasal voice. "She left this shit on my voicemail. I've been avoiding the bitch. Grandma left me the house and everything in it. Shit, I was the one who took care of her when she was sick. Besides, Rolanda don't need no money. She's got a job doing accounting or something for ComEd. I bet she makes forty, fifty grand. Shit, that bitch be wanting everything."

None of this made any sense to me. I wondered if I had dreamed my visit to the Meeks' home. Perhaps I had fallen asleep in front of the TV after a few good belts of whiskey.

I tried to open my eyes again. The other man spoke. His voice was almost like the purring of a big cat: a lion or a tiger. I couldn't make out what he was saying. He sounded far away, farther away than before. I was drifting off. A tingling sensation that began in the back of my head swept in a wave across my body. I felt like I was suspended in mid-air, floating through a field of television static, my flesh bombarded by black and white particles.

The voices faded once more into oblivion, and the tingling sensation ceased. I still felt a dull throbbing in my temples and the top of my head, but otherwise, I had gone numb.

I'm not sure how long I remained in that state. After a while, the pain in my head grew worse, and the sweet musky scent I had smelled before returned, this time mixed with a stale odor like mothballs.

I heard voices, the same as before: one high-pitched and nasal, the other deep and velvety. Shapes appeared, dark and fuzzy as in a smudged charcoal drawing.

"I think he's coming to," said the bass.

"Shit, about time," drawled the nasal-sounding man.

The bass shouted in my ear, "Hey!"

I tried to speak, but my mouth wouldn't cooperate. My lips felt as though they had been injected with Novocaine. All I could manage were infantile gurgling noises. I heard a loud crack that coincided with a sharp pain in my right cheek. One of them had struck me.

I then heard a voice mumble, "What the fuck?" That was me speaking.

"Wake up, motherfucker," the bass said.

I opened my eyes. The shadows came into focus, my eyes distinguishing between light and dark again. I was in a dimly lit room with cinderblock walls and a concrete floor. Frosted windows floated high above, the evening sky appearing a cold dark blue behind them. Pipes and exposed woodwork lined the ceiling. A utility sink sat in the corner of the room. I missed these details the first time I passed through the basement. I had missed little. The place was light on charm, but it had a certain ambiance: terror tinged with desperation.

I could tell I was in bad shape. I was sitting with my feet bound to the chair's legs and my hands tied behind me. My head and neck ached. My eyes were puffy and swollen. That I could see was a miracle in and of itself.

I faced the staircase. Two men sat across from me. One was short and slight of build with a light complexion. He wore his hair closely cropped, and a thin wisp of a mustache covered his top lip. He sat on the second stair, oblivious to me, his eyes riveted to the other man in the room.

The second man was tall and muscular, with skin as dark as onyx. He wore his hair in cornrows, and his eyes were like two dark, cold marbles. He sat across from me in a chair turned around so that the back was facing front.

"Who are you?" he asked in that deep cat's purr I had heard somewhere between unconsciousness and this waking nightmare.

I looked up at him and studied his face through swollen eyes. This was the guy, Dantrell Miles. His friend: Julius Meeks.

Dantrell stared back at me, his mouth twisted into a snarl. "Well?" he asked.

"Glenn Wozniak. My name is Glenn Wozniak."

Dantrell stood up. He stepped around the chair where he had been sitting and reached into his pants pocket. He retrieved a beat-up black leather wallet. My beat-up black leather wallet. He tossed it at me. The wallet struck me square in the chest and fell to the floor, making a slapping sound. I stared at it lying between my feet.

"I got that much," Dantrell said. He regarded me with his head cocked to one side, his mouth twisted into a sneer. "But who are you?"

I stared dumbly at him, not sure what he wanted and feeling wholly unprepared for a philosophical discussion of being and identity. I looked up at Dantrell's companion on the stairs, hoping he might clue me in.

Julius seemed almost bored by the proceedings. Had Dantrell killed others down here? Was that why he was so nonchalant? I could see my gun jammed down the front of Dantrell's pants, the grip pressed against his abdomen. How long before he pulled it?

I'd found plenty of kids killed in much the same manner when I was in homicide—gangland slayings, execution style. If they weren't tied to a chair, they were on their knees, hunched forward, ready to accept a bullet to the back of the head. Most had pissed themselves beforehand. That's what's so bad about dying this way. The suspense is almost unbearable, every second pregnant with an overwhelming poignancy and yet routine enough to be utterly banal, a reminder that life in this town, this state, this country is both precious and cheap. I imagined most of those kids went out the same way they came into the world, crying for their mommies.

"He wants to know what you're doing here," Julius said. "Who sent your stupid ass here to get killed?"

"I'm a private investigator," I mumbled, my eyes on the floor. "A man named Edgar Marsh hired me to find his daughter. Her name's Alison Marsh."

Dantrell spun his chair around and took a seat. He cocked his head to one side and studied me. "What's that got to do with me?"

"Alison was having an affair with a cop named Bill Bertram. You may know him."

Dantrell laughed. "I may?" He turned around and looked at Julius. His friend shook his head. Dantrell turned to face me again. "Man, you know I know him. That's why you're here, right? Quit fucking around. Who really sent you?"

"Edgar Marsh," I said.

"You sure it wasn't Curtis Bledsoe or George Wesley or Dan Morrow?"

Morrow? What did he have to do with this?

"A man named Edgar Marsh hired me to find his daughter," I said. "That's the truth. I have nothing to do with any of those people. Shit, I never even heard of Bill Bertram before this case."

Julius Meeks got up and stood by Dantrell's side. He rested a forearm on his friend's shoulder. "Let's kill this guy and get it over with already," he said. "I don't want to be up all night with this bullshit."

Dantrell waved him off. Julius sighed and returned to his seat on the stairs.

"What makes you think I have anything to do with any of this?" Dantrell asked.

I told him what I had learned thus far—that Bill Bertram had met Alison while working undercover spying on anti-war activists, that they had begun an affair and were last seen checking into a motel room on January 29th. I told him how I had heard about his altercation with Bertram, and about my visits to Wanda Briggs' place and his apartment.

"Wesley and another cop were there," I said. "It looks like a lot of people are looking for you."

"They better hope they don't find me," Dantrell said.

Julius nodded his head in agreement behind him, and I thought about T-Bone and Watkins.

Dantrell studied me, looking for a reaction, with that same hard look on his face. His expression softened. "That Marsh girl is dead," he said. "She never made it out of that motel room alive. The same with Bertram."

I figured as much, and yet my heart sank at the news.

"How do you know?"

"Curtis. Curtis told me Bertram and the girl were killed at the Stardust Motel. Someone shot them. He asked me if I had anything to do with their murders. Can you believe that shit? I mean, I've done some things for Curtis, ugly things. Ya' know what I'm saying? But I'm a soldier. I follow orders. I don't go off on my own settling scores. That's not my style. I'm a professional. Ya' feel me? Curtis of all people should know that by now, after all we've been through."

"So, where were you that night?"

"He was right here," Julius said before Dantrell could answer.

Dantrell nodded. "But that's not what I told Curtis. I said I was at home asleep."

"He's ashamed of me," Julius said.

"I am not. I just don't like folks knowing my business."

Julius rolled his eyes.

"Don't worry about me," I said. "I already knew about you two."

"Knew what?" Dantrell asked.

"You know."

"No, I don't. What are you trying to say?"

"He's calling you a cocksucker," Julius said.

Dantrell glared at him and then at me.

This wasn't going well. It was cold in the basement, no more than fifty degrees, and yet I was sweating. I changed the subject. "So, what happened between you and Bertram?"

Dantrell laughed. "Man, that motherfucker's crazy. I was at Sal's Lounge picking up some smokes, and he comes up to me asking me what I'm doing in there, so I says, 'Nothin', just buying some smokes.' And he tells me that Sal's is a cop bar and I don't belong there. So I'm all like 'Hey, take it easy. We're all brothers now.' But that just sets him off, and he says something like he may have to tolerate me in his district, but he never wants to see me in his bar again. Can you believe that shit? This motherfucker's getting rich off my work and he's dissing me. Anyway, I don't want any trouble, but I can't let this bitch talk that trash without saying something back, so I says, 'You got to tolerate it as long as you're on Curtis' payroll, motherfucker.' I then turn and head out the door, not realizing that Bertram's right behind me. He sucker-punches me square in the back of the head, so we start to go at it, but Wesley and some other cops break it up. Now, just because of that bullshit, I've got Curtis and all these cops giving me a hard time for something I didn't do."

"Why does Bledsoe even care?" I asked. "I mean, what's it to him if you did kill some cop?"

"Man, weren't you listening when I said Bertram was on the payroll? He was one of ours. Bill Bertram worked for Dan Morrow, and Morrow has an agreement with Curtis.

He leaves us alone, and he and his boys get a cut of the profits. Not only that, but we let his unit know whenever some off-brand niggers move into the area. Morrow's boys come in and make the arrest—no shootings, no dead honor students caught in the crossfire, just a quick, easy arrest. Morrow looks good. We don't have to worry about the cops or turf battles, and the neighborhood stays nice and quiet. The shit works out good for everyone. Folks' property rates are going up. Developers are building new houses and condos, which makes the alderman happy because those developers are greasing palms in search of licenses and shit. It's a good deal all around, including for me. You think I want to fuck things up by killing some cop we already bought and paid for?"

"No, but Bledsoe obviously did, and I know George Wesley thinks you did."

"Yeah, well, fuck them. I didn't do shit."

Dantrell folded his arms across his chest and watched me. The look was a threat. He was daring me to say another word, daring me with his eyes and that scowl.

I should've shut up. I had touched a nerve, but I wanted to know. I needed to know. "You can see why Curtis suspects you. I mean, you threatened Bertram, and you have something of a reputation."

"What kind of reputation?"

"You've got a bit of a temper."

"I do?"

"Well, yeah, you know, like that whole incident with your mother's boyfriend."

I half expected Dantrell to lose it, but the tension faded from his face. He almost smiled, his mouth curling up on one side.

Julius hopped off his perch. "Man, that's some bullshit."

"Shut up, Julius," Dantrell said.

"No, it's about time someone heard the truth."

Dantrell leaned forward in his seat, hung his head, and sighed.

Julius continued, "You see, Dantrell's momma was dating this fine-looking brother who liked to sleep with men on the down-low from time to time. So, he and Dantrell started kicking it when Moms wasn't around. One day she came home from work early and caught them together. Moms flips out, goes to the kitchen and grabs a big-ass knife. In the meantime, Dantrell and this brother are getting dressed. I mean, they're throwing their clothes on. This guy, he's swearing up and down that it's not what it looks like and shit, but Dantrell's mom ain't buying it. She comes rushing into the room just as he's about to put his pants on and stabs him in the chest."

Dantrell winced as though he were there watching it happen again. "It was my fault. I shouldn't have been with him."

"Nigga, please," Julius said. "You *done* your time. The way I see it, you more than paid her back. Fuck, I would've let Moms go to jail, but that's just me."

"That's right," Dantrell said. "That's just you. I never should've put my mom in that position. That shit's on me, regardless of the time I served."

Julius turned to me. "You see that? Dantrell's not some fucked-up psychopath. He's a good man. Shit, he been taking care of that fat bitch Wanda's boy even though we all know that child ain't his." Then, turning back to Dantrell, "Right?"

Dantrell didn't answer. He hopped from his chair and withdrew my gun from the front of his pants. "Man, fuck this shit," he said, jamming the barrel against my forehead.

I squeezed my eyes shut, waiting for the blast, and when it didn't come, I opened them again. Dantrell was breathing heavily, a pained expression on his face, the gun still pointed at my head.

"Look, I believe you," I said in a rush. "I don't think you killed the girl or the cop, and I want to find out who did as badly as you do."

Dantrell lowered the gun, which didn't put me any more at ease, because now he was pointing it at my crotch.

"I can help you," I said. "I'm a former homicide investigator. I have experience in solving these kinds of cases. I find out who did this and you're in the clear."

I didn't believe that for a second. Dantrell would never have his old life back, not after T-Bone and Watkins. Bledsoe would be too afraid he'd want revenge, but some things are better left unsaid.

"Man, why should I trust you?" Dantrell said.

"What other choice do you have? You can kill me, but that won't change anything. If I'm legit, you've got someone on the street looking into this case, trying to clear your name. If I'm not, you're no worse off than before. If I found you, they certainly will. You could run, but what kind of life is that? You let me go, and you at least have a fighting chance."

Dantrell looked at Julius. He shrugged. "Don't look at me. If I were you, I'd put a bullet in his head and forget about it, but you do what you think is best."

"All right," Dantrell said at last. "I hope you're playing straight with me, for your sake."

"Don't worry. The only way you'll get any trouble from me is if I find out you lied about Bertram and the girl. Otherwise, I don't care what you do."

Dantrell untied me, emptied the bullets from my gun and gave it back to me. A few minutes later, the feeling returned to my arms and legs. We headed upstairs. It was a little before seven AM, and a burnt-orange sun struggled to shine through the thick cloud cover of an overcast winter morning. Dantrell glanced over at the sink, noticed the dirty dishes, and flashed Julius a disapproving look.

"Relax, I'll clean up after you finish getting played for a chump by this white boy," Julius said.

Dantrell let that slide. He saw me out through the back. Before I left, he jotted down a number and pressed it into my palm. "This is my pager. Call me if you hear anything."

"I will."

Dantrell reached inside one of his pants pockets and withdrew my business card. "I got this from your wallet, so I know where I can find you if anything funny happens, understood?"

"Understood."

We shook on it, and I headed out into the cold, still feeling phantom ropes about my wrists and ankles.

FOURTEEN

I drove back to Rogers Park, taking Lake Shore Drive north. I opened the window, winter air pounding my face. "Mother of Pearl" by Roxy Music came on the radio. I turned it up full blast. I did this to stay awake, to jolt myself into feeling something, anything.

It was another gray March day. Melting sheets of ice bobbed atop the waters of Lake Michigan. Lines of bare trees sped past my window on either side of the expressway, looking like skeletal limbs. Here and there, I passed pedestrians walking into a frigid winter wind, collars up and their chins tucked against their chests. They hunched their shoulders, becoming bigger like pigeons fluffing their feathers to combat the cold.

My cheeks turned numb from the blast of cold air streaming in my window, and my ears burned. I peered in the rearview mirror at a beet-red face with bloodshot eyes sunk deep in their orbits.

I drove back to the Stardust Motel and sat with the car idling in the parking lot, staring at the burned-out shell of a building. I pondered the events of January 29th. If Bill and Alison were killed at the Stardust, what happened to their remains? And what became of Bill's car? It had yet to turn up. I imagined the murderer killed Bill and Alison, destroyed the crime scene by setting fire to the motel room, and then disposed of the Pontiac with the bodies inside. It was a plausible enough theory, but where would he ditch the car? It would have to be somewhere close by. The killer wouldn't want to drive too far in a stolen car with a couple of corpses in the trunk.

I pulled out of the parking lot and headed east. I drove over a bridge, crossing the Chicago River. The brownish-green water undulated, rising and falling as though it were alive and breathing. Patches of snow covered the hard, frozen surface of the riverbank.

I spun the car around and parked at the entrance to a large park. This seemed like a good place to dispose of a vehicle. A chain-link fence separated the recreation area from the riverbank. I scaled it slowly and with great difficulty only to lose my footing when I got to the other side. I tumbled backward down the embankment towards the frigid water. My hands tried to grip the hard, frozen ground, the tips of my fingers scraped raw. I jammed a hand into a thicket of dried weeds and held on for dear life, stopping my descent.

A chill wind whistled in my ears as I lay prone on my back, staring up at a dull gray sky.

I climbed to my feet and walked north along the river, pushing my way through thin, switch-like branches and dried prairie vegetation. Burrs caught on my pants legs and shoelaces as I walked. The terrain was treacherous, and I almost slipped on a couple of occasions. Each time I righted myself by swinging my arms out like a trapeze artist balancing on the high wire. I made my way over felled trees and under graffiti-tagged viaducts. Occasionally, I would hear the sounds of cars whizzing by in the distance; the only reminders, aside from the graffiti, that I was still in the city.

I'm not sure how long I walked, but the farther north I went, the narrower the river became and the thicker the woods. Above me, the chain-link fence at the top of the embankment ended. There was nothing but trees—thin, spindly trees with thin, spindly branches that cast a shadowy mosaic on the ground.

I kept walking until I came across a spot near an abandoned factory. The building was made of brick painted white and looked like a giant pillar of salt, standing in stark contrast to the dark gray winter sky above. Its frosted windows opened inward, many of them busted out to reveal the darkness inside. A weathered sign hung above the front door. It read: Owens Manufacturing, Ltd.

The woods thinned out, and the embankment wasn't as steep. A couple of picnic tables sat at the top overlooking the water. There I noticed two long ruts running from the top of the embankment into the river. I took a closer look. Tire tracks.

I approached the river's edge. The water was shallow, ten feet deep at the most. There was something down there: a large, dark object. The image warped and shuddered beneath the water.

I looked around me. Many of the trees along the bank bore long gashes in their bark. One sported a slash of black paint. I clambered up the embankment, the trip leaving me breathless, and stood hunched over, my hands on my knees, and sucked cold air into my lungs.

I was in a field. It was a long stretch of prairie, which in the winter means patches of dried, wheat-colored reeds amongst a sea of cold, barren earth. To the north stood the abandoned factory; to the south, a road. The tracks I found running down the embankment into the water stretched all the way out to the road. I followed them across the field and walked along the roadside until I reached a gas station.

Time to put an anonymous tip into the police. I found a payphone and dialed 9-1-1.

A woman answered. "9-1-1, what's your emergency?"

"I want to report an accident. There's a car submerged in the river. It's by the old Owens Manufacturing plant on McCormick Road. Please send someone quick."

I hung up. It was a little after one in the afternoon. I went inside the gas station and bought a pack of Camel filters. The cashier, noticing the assorted bruises, cuts, and abrasions on my face, gave me the once-over. I conducted the transaction, eyes downcast, before heading back out into the cold.

I returned to the riverbank, taking a seat on a concrete barrier in the Owens Manufacturing parking lot. My back made a cracking sound as I sat. I lit a cigarette and waited. The sun peeked out from behind the clouds, didn't like what it saw, and went away again. My shadow stretched on the ground in front of me, pointing towards the river.

About a half-hour passed before a squad car and a tow truck arrived. I hid, peering from behind a corner of the building to watch the proceedings. The vehicles made their way across the field. They appeared as if in a fever dream, their progress so deliberate, it looked like they were hardly moving at all. The squad car led the way, with the tow truck following like a muscled goon. Its yellow mars lights spun, casting a pale intermittent beam into the trees along the embankment.

Two officers got out of the squad car and met the tow truck driver by the picnic tables. They were young beat cops. One was an Asian male of average height with thick, muscular arms, no neck, and a large head. The other officer was a tall black man, about 6‘2“, with a hunched posture. The tow truck driver got out of his vehicle. He was a squat, heavyset black man in gray pants and a navy-blue jacket that he wore unzipped. An old red, white and blue White Sox cap from the 80s sat perched atop his round head. The Asian cop gestured at the tire tracks, his finger tracing their path from the road to the embankment and down towards the river. His companions nodded. They descended the incline, disappearing from view. I stepped out a few paces from the building and craned my neck, searching for any sight of them. After what seemed like a long while, they reappeared. The black officer took a seat inside the car, one leg hanging out the driver's side door. He was radioing for assistance.

The tow truck driver returned to his vehicle and drove off. About an hour later, another larger tow truck arrived on the scene, driven by a different guy. A van full of people and special equipment joined him.

The scene resembled an archeological excavation—everyone milling about, surveying the landscape, and engaging in animated discussion. A couple of divers stood at the top of the embankment in wetsuits, holding their fins in their hands. One shifted his weight from foot to foot, looking cold and impatient. After a while, they headed down the embankment, disappearing from view. I hugged a corner of the building, popping behind it whenever anyone looked in my direction.

The operation dragged on. Men shouted instructions at each other. They hauled cables from the tow truck and ran them down the embankment. Machinery hummed in the background. I killed time smoking and pacing back and forth, out of sight below the broken windows of a factory that made God-knows-what once upon a time. It was cold and getting colder. I drew the collar of my coat up and tucked my chin into it. The tips of my fingers were numb, and it was all I could do to avoid dropping my cigarette.

I heard the loud groan of another machine and the whir of a cable retracting. I peered around the corner, one numb, rosy hand on the cold brick to brace myself. A hydraulic winch reeled in a thick cord that ran down the embankment, emitting a groaning noise as it strained to pull the vehicle. A group of cops appeared, backtracking up and away from the river's edge, followed by a black Pontiac. The car emerged trunk first, water streaming out the seams of the doors and windows. The winch continued retracting, pulling the vehicle up onto level ground.

"All right, that's good," a cop shouted to the driver.

The driver cut the power to the winch, and the car's backward progress drew to an abrupt halt. The cops huddled around the vehicle. One of them went to the van and returned with a crowbar. He worked his way through the crowd. The huddled mass of cops swallowed him. I couldn't see a thing. I even stepped out from the safety of my hiding place and craned my neck while standing on tiptoe. Still nothing.

The crowd parted, and I saw a cop pull a pair of large plastic garbage bags from the trunk. The officer laid them on the ground as a second cop approached. He was a plain-clothes officer, an older, gray-haired man in a rumpled suit. I recognized him at once. It was Doug Greshing, a former colleague from homicide.

Doug put on a pair of plastic gloves and got down on one knee. He tore open a bag, revealing a hand with only traces of gnarled, water-logged flesh clinging to it. The index finger pointed at the sky as if gesturing to the heavens above.

FIFTEEN

Later that night, I was at home on my couch, wrapped in a blanket, and watching the evening news. The discovery of the submerged car was the lead story. According to the report, the authorities had yet to determine the identities of the bodies.

There was a message from Edgar Marsh on my voicemail. "I've just heard from the police," he said. "They've positively ID'd Alison as one of the..." He couldn't finish. "Please call me," he said before hanging up, his voice little more than a soft rasp.

I shut off the TV and stared at its darkened screen, my figure reflected in the glass. The phone rang. This time it was Todd. "Hey, Glenn, I just checked in with the boys at the lab, and they ID'd the remains as Bill Bertram and Alison Marsh."

"So I heard. Edgar Marsh left me a message on my voicemail."

"They don't know much just yet. Those bodies had been down there for a long time. They had been shot multiple times, and the level of decomposition in that environment is consistent with the two being murdered on January 29th. Also, whoever did this caught Bertram by surprise. They found his service revolver in the trunk, and it hadn't been fired."

"Anything else?"

"Yes, do you know a guy named Gerry Lombardo?"

"Sure, I saw him a few days ago."

"That's what he says. He said you had shown him a photo of Bill Bertram, and he recognized him as a guy who had stayed at his motel on January 29, registering under the name of Scott Richter. A fire started in his room. I guess the arson investigator has been giving Lombardo a hard time. He was on the horn to the police the second you left him."

"I don't blame him."

"Neither do I, but you made yourself some enemies downtown when you told that guy Scott Richter was Bill Bertram. Captain Montanez is about ready to have you drawn and quartered. He says you compromised the work of the Joint Terrorism Task Force."

"I didn't say one word about what Bill was doing or the Joint Terrorism Task Force. I simply told Lombardo that Scott Richter was Bill Bertram's alias."

"Regardless, consider yourself number one with a bullet at the top of Montanez's shit list."

"Great."

"I'll try to smooth things over for you."

"Thanks, I appreciate it. Is that it?"

"Homicide's none too happy that you didn't tell them about the motel because they think it's where the murders occurred and that you're holding out on them."

"What can I say, client confidentiality. Anything I find out is for Edgar Marsh's ears and Edgar Marsh's ears only."

"So, why should you expect me to help you out?"

"I don't, but I appreciate it. Anything else?"

"No, just that Homicide notified the victims' next of kin, but you knew that."

"Yeah, I still need to call Mr. Marsh back. Who notified them?"

"Doug Greshing. Conrad turned the case over to homicide, and he was the catching detective. I imagine he'll be heading up the investigation from here on out."

At least they now had a competent detective on the case. Doug was my polar opposite, the epitome of a dedicated police officer. He had no life outside of the job—no wife, no children, not even a stray extracurricular activity or bad habit. Doug spent all his time thinking about dead strangers and the bad men who took their lives. That's the detective the Marshes deserved, not some half-assed drunk like me.

I hung up with Todd and dialed Maya's number. "Hello?" she answered, her voice sounding small and frightened.

"Maya?"

"Glenn?"

"Yeah."

"Could you hold on a second? I've got Alison's father on the other line. They've found Alison's body."

"I know. I just heard from a friend on the force. Give me a call back when you're done, but please don't tell Mr. Marsh that I called you. I still haven't spoken to him."

"My lips are sealed," Maya said.

About twenty minutes later, she called back. I must've been lost in my thoughts because the ringing made me jump, and I answered sounding out of breath.

"Are you okay?" Maya asked.

"I'm fine, just a little tired. How about you? How're you holding up?"

"I don't know. I kind of expected this, but it's still a shock. I feel so bad for Mr. Marsh."

"What'd he have to say?"

"He just wanted to let me know they found Alison. He's in pretty terrible shape. I guess his wife was taking it even worse than he. Her doctor has her on some kind of sedative."

"That's probably for the best."

We both fell silent for a moment.

"Why are you avoiding Mr. Marsh?" Maya asked.

"I don't know. I guess I'm burned out. In fact, I think I'm going to encourage Mr. Marsh to leave the case in the hands of the police. They're better equipped, and they have a much better man on the job now."

More silence. This time I broke it. "Are you okay over there? I mean, would you like some company?"

"Yes, it's kind of...I don't know. I just don't want to be alone right now."

I knew how she felt. I told her I'd be by later and hung up. Just one more call to go, one more and this would all be over with me only a little bit worse for wear. I'd be going back on my word to Miles, but fuck him. What's he ever done for me but knock me around and hold me hostage in some dank, freezing basement for a few hours? He could rot for all I cared.

I dialed the Marshes' number, feeling like a condemned man taking his last steps to the electric chair. Each number hurt, each ring was excruciating, and the jolt I felt when someone answered might as well have been a trillion kilowatts because it stung so much I could feel it in my bones.

One of the servants answered. "Hello?" she said.

"Hello, may I speak to Mr. Marsh?"

"I'm sorry, but Mr. Marsh is not taking any calls right now."

"I'm returning his call."

The woman paused for a moment. "Who, may I ask, is calling?"

"My name is Glenn Wozniak."

"Okay, hold on a moment."

Minutes later, Edgar's voice came on the line. He sounded terrible, like he had aged a thousand years since we last spoke, his voice little more than a dry rasp, like air seeping from a leaky tire. "Wozniak," he said.

"Mr. Marsh, I just heard. I'm so sorry. I know you hoped for a better outcome. We all did." I cringed as I spoke, expecting him to either break down in sobs or tear into me. But he remained silent. I waited for him to speak.

"What have you got for me?" he asked after what seemed like an eternity.

I didn't understand the question.

"What have you got for me?" he repeated, the impatience evident in his voice.

"I'm sorry," I said. "I'm not sure I'm following you."

"What the fuck have you learned about the case? Isn't that what I'm paying you for? To investigate, to learn what happened to my daughter and report back to me?"

"Yes, sir," I said. I went over everything I had learned since we last spoke. I told him about Bertram and his affair with Alison. I told him about the undercover operation Bill was working, his kickbacks from Bledsoe, his rendezvous with Alison at the Stardust, his run-in with Dantrell Miles, my run-in with Dantrell Miles, and how I discovered Bertram's abandoned Pontiac. I told him everything, barely taking a breath along the way, and I felt as though I was unburdening myself, as if I were confessing to a crime.

Edgar didn't say a word when I finished. I could hear him breathing heavily. "Mr. Marsh?"

"Yes," he said, his voice cracking. He sobbed heavily, the weight of his daughter's death pressing on his chest, squeezing the air out of him. He alternated between gasping for air and repeating, "My little girl," in a chilling wail. I waited for him to calm down. I waited for a long time. All the while, I could think of only one thing: Quit. Quit now while you still can.

Mr. Marsh, I'm afraid I am going to have to offer you my resignation. You don't need my services anymore. The Chicago Police Department has assigned an excellent detective to your daughter's case. Again, I'm sorry for your loss. I will send you a bill for all services rendered minus the advance you gave me. Good day.

That's what I wanted to say, what I would've said if given a chance.

"I can't talk right now," Marsh said, almost choking on the words. "Call me tomorrow."

He said it so fast, I had no time to react. Before I knew it, he had hung up. I thought about calling back but decided against it. The man had been through enough for one night. I'd call him in the morning.

I threw on some clothes and drove over to Maya's. She answered the door in a T-shirt and panties, just like the first time we met. The shirt had a wide neck, and a bare shoulder peeked out of it. I wanted her right then and there.

"You don't look so good," she said, studying my collection of injuries.

"I've had a rough night."

I eyed her hungrily, and by hungrily, I mean obviously, blatantly. I stopped just short of drooling.

Maya didn't return the sentiment. "Not tonight, Glenn," she said.

I felt the words in the pit of my stomach, like a punch to the gut.

"I just want some company. Is that okay?"

It was a stupid question. Of course, it wasn't okay. It was downright unconscionable for her to answer the door in next to nothing and give me the I-just-want-to-cuddle routine. I had taken a beating, spent a night tied to a chair in a cold basement, and had just completed a long day of wandering along the river bank. My only reward: an abandoned car with the severed remains of two bodies in the trunk. Not only was I still hopelessly, horribly employed by the Marshes, but I wasn't getting any sex either. Was that okay? No fucking way, sister.

Maya took a seat on the couch. After a few moments of coming to grips with my disappointment, I grabbed a spot on the opposite end of the sofa. She slid closer to me, lifting my right arm and wrapping it around herself. I didn't cooperate. My arm hung there still and limp like a dead fish. Maya nestled her head into my chest. I smelled her hair, and softening, wrapped my arms around her. Before long, we were both fast asleep.

I awoke a little before sunrise, the apartment dark, and Maya no longer in my arms.

"Maya?" I said, my voice strained and raspy.

No answer. I stood up. A light shone from down the hall. I heard a scream.

"Maya?!" I shouted.

"Glenn!" she answered from the direction of the light.

I ran down the hall to find Maya in Alison's old room. She was standing, a hand cupped over her mouth, facing an open closet door. She motioned with her head in its direction. I peered inside but saw nothing out of the ordinary, certainly nothing to merit a scream, just an empty closet.

"I don't get it."

"Look!" Maya insisted.

"I am looking. There's nothing there but some clothing and shoes. What's wrong?"

"Her paintings! Her paintings are gone, you stupid idiot! Someone took her paintings. They were in her closet, and now they're gone."

"When was the last time you saw them?"

Maya shivered, all the color drained from her face. I thought about putting an arm around her, but she didn't look like she wanted to be touched. She stared into the closet and shook her head. "I don't know, a couple of days ago, maybe. I don't know."

"Does anyone else have a key to the apartment?"

"Just the landlady."

"And no sign of a break-in?"

Maya shook her head. She didn't look at me. She directed her gaze towards a spot on the floor just before my feet. I followed her lead, saw nothing, and wondered if something else was missing, something that was supposed to occupy that spot. I put an arm around her, and she buried her face in my chest. I could feel warm tears seeping through the fabric of my shirt. "C'mon, there's nothing we can do about this tonight. Let's go to bed."

"No, I don't think I can sleep," she said. "You go ahead."

I shook my head. "No, I don't want to leave you alone. I'll make some coffee."

I brewed a pot, and we sat across from each other in silence, too tired to talk, staring into our mugs.

"Are you really going to quit the case?" Maya asked.

"Yes. I just don't think I'm up to it."

"Why?"

I rubbed my temples. "I don't know. It's not what I do, at least not anymore."

"Would you stay on if I asked you to?"

"How 'bout I move in for a while, so you're not alone? I could take care of you."

Maya's shoulders slumped. She hung her head, her chin touching her chest, and sighed.

Okay, scratch that idea.

"I won't feel safe until I know the person who did this can never harm another person again," she said.

I could sense my resolve slipping away. "The police have a good man on the case," I said. "A better man than me."

"I don't know him. I know you. I trust you."

I didn't look at her. I didn't want her to see the resentment that must've shown on my face. "Shit," I said after a long pause.

Maya smiled.

"Shit," I repeated.

SIXTEEN

The Bertram and Marsh families scheduled the victims' memorial services on consecutive days. Bill's was first. The family held it at a funeral home about two blocks from the police station where he once worked.

It was a tiny greystone building with a pitched roof. The interior smelled like a mixture of rose water and old paperbacks—perfume and decay.

The funeral home conducted services in two rooms that sat across from each other, separated by a reception area. Everyone congregated in the center room. They lingered there as if avoiding the service. Perhaps they feared the finality of it all.

Most milled about, exchanging hugs and uttering words of condolence. The cops in attendance traded war stories or anecdotes about Bill. These were cringe-inducing tales about drug busts and crack whores and queasy addicts getting sick in the back of the squad car and ODs found a few days too late. No one talked about the circumstances of Bill's death. The relatives were around, and it wasn't like Bill had fallen in the line of duty. This was a guy murdered while getting some young tail on the side, a giant elephant in the room that everyone did their best to ignore.

Dan Morrow noticed me. He nodded in my direction and flashed a half-hearted smile before approaching. "Hey, Wozniak, what brings you here?"

"I just wanted to pay my respects."

"Is that all? You sure you didn't come to scope things out, perhaps ask a couple of questions?"

I shrugged, not knowing what to say. "I suppose I might. I don't know."

Morrow clapped me on the back. "Skip it, I understand. A man's got to make a living. I would suggest you steer clear of Wesley, though. He's not quite himself, and I don't think he'd take too well to you snooping around here."

With that, he was off, gone before I could ask him a single question.

People kept filing in. A line of cops and other attendees formed to offer Denise their condolences. She looked pale and fragile in a black dress and jacket, her eyes hidden behind a pair of dark sunglasses and her hair tied back in a bun. Denise didn't break down. Tears flowed, but without heavy sobs or wailing. She spoke to each person with her head bowed, occasionally flashing a brief, tentative smile at the offering of some kind sentiment as if she were embarrassed by all the attention. George Wesley stood by her side, his eyes also obscured by sunglasses and his cheeks moist with tears.

I went to offer my condolences. Even without seeing George's eyes, I could tell he spotted me at once. His face tightened, the musculature forming two round lumps along his jawline. George leaned over and spoke in Denise's ear. She tensed and looked up at me, her mouth twisting into a frown. George put a hand on her shoulder and leaned in to say something else. She immediately composed herself as if nothing had happened.

"I'm sorry about your loss, Mrs. Bertram," I said, extending my hand.

Denise grasped it for a second and let go without saying a word. George stood as still as a Buckingham Palace guard, his head upright, one arm at his side, and the other still resting on Denise's shoulder. His face remained clenched. I didn't have the nerve to say anything else to either of them.

I headed over to the opposite side of the room and got a cup of coffee. I stiffened up my drink with some whiskey from a flask I carried in my inside coat pocket. The coffee and liquor went down smoothly, each warming me in its way. I was settling down and feeling a little more like myself.

An empty seat beckoned from across the room, the perfect vantage point for scoping out the scene, observing who spoke to whom and how they conducted themselves. I had just reached the chair and was about to sit when I felt a hand on my shoulder. It was a big, meaty paw with a vice-like grip. I turned around to find myself face to face with George Wesley. He had removed the sunglasses, revealing two bloodshot eyes. They bore into me like lasers, my nerves frying under the glare.

"What are you doing here?" he demanded.

"I came to pay my respects to a fellow officer."

"Bullshit, you're not a cop anymore, and from what I hear, you never cared too much for your brothers."

"Who does? But hey, family's family."

"What're you doing here?"

"I already told you."

"I know, and I call bullshit."

I sighed. "Look, it sounds like you already have an answer in mind, so why don't you tell me why I'm here?"

"This is neither the time nor the place for your poking around. Why don't you leave this to the police? They at least have the decency to let the family have this moment to themselves."

I should've left things as they were and taken my leave, but I was going through a phase where I had to do things the hard way.

"George, we both want the same thing," I said, putting an arm around the stocky cop. That didn't go over too well. He eyed my hand on his shoulder as if he were about to remove it with his teeth. I withdrew it and continued. "We both want to catch the man that killed your partner and my client's daughter. Now, there are many people here, people who might know something, who might help me, *us*, with this case. I know this is not the best time, but—"

"But nothing. I want you to leave. Now!"

George glared at me and pointed towards the door, but I held my ground.

"Get the fuck out," he said, enunciating each word for effect.

I didn't appreciate the tone.

"I'll go, but not until you give me a few minutes of your time."

George was about to speak, but I cut him off. "No, if you're so concerned about me disturbing Bill's family and friends, then take one for the team, because I'm not leaving until we talk."

Wesley relented. "All right, go ahead."

"What can you tell me about Dantrell Miles?"

"Doesn't ring a bell. What about him?"

"I heard he got into a scuffle with Bill at Sal's Lounge."

"And?"

"And I have a witness who says he saw you and another cop break up the fight. This was not long before your partner's disappearance."

"Who told you that?"

"Oh, it was all over Sal's. It was practically the fight of the century, the stuff of legends. From what I heard, this Miles guy threatened Bill. I'd remember something like that. I find it odd you didn't mention it the last time we spoke."

"It was a bar fight. So what? People say a lot of things in a bar fight."

"That's true. I bring him up because he works for a guy named Curtis Bledsoe, who just happens to be a big-time drug dealer in your beat. I'm wondering if there's any connection."

"Look, I don't know what to tell you. This Bledsoe character is barely on our radar these days."

"So, you've heard of him?"

"Heard of him? Yeah, I've heard of him, but he's been quiet for more than a year. I doubt there's any connection to Bill's murder. Now, if you don't mind, I've got to get back to Denise. I've asked you nicely, and this is the last time I'm going to ask. Please leave."

George pushed his way through a crowd of people to rejoin Denise. I turned and headed for the doorway, and a man brushed past me on the way out. I looked up and immediately recognized his pinched, freckled face. It was my old friend Lenny.

I hung around for a bit and watched the proceedings. I stepped inside the coatroom and scoped out the reception area. George noticed Lenny and crossed the room to greet him. They exchanged a few words and then looked around in search of me. Morrow joined them. He put an arm around George and led him into the room where the services were being held, Lenny tagging along behind them. I waited a minute before following, taking a seat in the back of the room. Denise Bertram sat in the front row with her son on her lap. Her father and mother sat on one side of her with George on the other.

The priest was tall and thin with a rosy complexion. According to the padre, Bill was a dedicated public servant, a loving husband and father, and a concerned citizen. This was a sanitized version of Bill's life, a litany of generalities that everyone could feel good about—everyone but me. I regretted coming. It was a bad idea. The attendees all likely fell into one of two camps: people who knew nothing about the case and people who did but would never betray a brother's trust, even one who was no longer living. I wasn't going to learn anything here. Not in a million years. I was just making people desperate for comfort uncomfortable.

I stood up and headed for the door. George glanced in my direction. His face tensed at the sight of me. Even his dark sunglasses seemed capable of expressing anger at that moment. I left the room and made my way to the exit.

It was another cold, late-winter evening, frigid air chilling me to the core. I had parked in the lot behind the funeral home. It was a secluded stretch of blacktop enclosed on three sides by a chain-link fence. I heard footsteps behind me and picked up my pace, too scared to look back. The footfalls were heavy, and I imagined an imposing figure behind me. I fumbled about in my pants pockets for my keys, finding them as I reached the car. The driver's side window reflected the figure of a man behind me. I didn't have time to brace myself. I felt a firm hand on my shoulder and spun around to see Lenny. He flashed a deranged smile before slugging me in the gut. I felt the wind go out of me and my knees buckle.

"George asked you to stay away," Lenny said, the words sounding muffled and distant. "I trust you'll listen next time."

I dropped to my knees and came to rest on all fours. The cold pavement felt abrasive against the palms of my hands, and I watched as my assailant disappeared inside the funeral home. I coughed and tasted blood on my lips.

SEVENTEEN

I attended Alison's memorial the following day, wearing the same suit, three days of stubble, and a pair of matching bags under my eyes. The family held the service at an art gallery owned by a family friend.

Galleria Pugliassi was in a two-story loft space in the Streeterville area. It was high end, a place where already established artists displayed their work. A sculpture by someone named Lee Bontecou sat in the center of the room—a Mobius strip made of a material that was flesh-like in appearance. Photos of Alison covered the walls.

I couldn't blend into the crowd like I did at Bill Bertram's service. I kept encountering people I had met during my investigation: Tim, Phillip, and Brenda from the ILS; professor Bradshaw from the Art Institute; Jeff Ledewski from the Metropolitan Café; as well as other friends and family members I had called upon over the last couple of days. It was a warm, sociable group. They hugged and cried as you would expect on such an occasion, but there were also jokes and laughter.

I met Margaret Marsh, Alison's mother, for the first time. She was a tall, attractive woman with cool blue eyes and long wavy dark hair streaked with gray. Edgar made the introduction.

"Thank you for attending to my daughter's case, Mr. Wozniak," she said before turning to speak with someone else.

It was a welcome dismissal. I wanted to spend as little time as possible with the Marshes.

I searched the room for Maya. Phillip stopped me, his eyes red from crying. He looked like he hadn't slept in days.

"Something's been bothering me, and I was hoping you could help," he said.

"I can try," I said. "What is it?"

"Did Alison know the truth about Scott or Bill, whatever his name was? Did she know he was a cop?"

This was the last thing I needed. My big mouth had gotten me in enough trouble with Captain Montanez as it was.

"All I know is she knew his real name, and she knew he was married," I said.

"So she knew."

"I think so, but from the looks of things, she was a bigger influence on him than he was on her."

"What do you mean?"

"I mean, Bill stopped reporting on your activities. I think she changed him."

Phillip flashed a faint smile, his eyes tearing up. "Thanks, that's good to hear. She always had a way of bringing out the best in people."

"I wish I'd had a chance to meet her."

Phillip pulled some Kleenex out of his jacket pocket and dabbed at his eyes. "Thanks again," he said. "I just needed a little closure."

"No problem. That's what we're here for, right?"

Phillip nodded.

"Hey, you wouldn't have happened to have seen Alison's roommate by any chance?" I said.

He shook his head.

"Okay, thanks."

I pushed through the crowd and continued my search for Maya. I stepped outside to phone her. The answering machine picked up. I left a message and headed back inside, running into Edgar.

"What's wrong?" he asked. "You look concerned."

"It's Maya. She's still not here, and I'm getting worried. Someone had been in the apartment and removed some of Alison's artwork a couple of days ago."

Edgar frowned. "My daughter's art? Why is this the first I'm hearing of it? I've asked you time and time again to keep me apprised of any developments in the case." He stopped himself. His voice choked off, the weight of the moment pressing on him. Darkness crept into his expression. "You don't know how hard this is for my wife and me. It's bad enough that people are talking about my Alison, my little girl, sleeping with a married man. They're saying ugly things about my daughter, about my family, and I don't like it."

"I'm afraid that kind of thing happens when the daughter of a high-profile family is found murdered. You shouldn't pay any attention. It's not important."

"It's not important? That's my family's name being dragged through the mud."

Edgar clenched his hands into two tight fists, his knuckles white and his nails digging into his palms. He glared at me, his eyes swollen with tears. I didn't know what to say. His daughter fucked a married cop in a sleazy motel. Those were the facts, and he couldn't change or bury them, no matter how much money or how many private investigators he threw at them.

"I'll do a better job of reporting my findings," I said.

"See that you do."

I excused myself before I could get into any more trouble. The crowd grew thicker, and I fought my way to the exit. The cold air outside felt nice. I reached into my coat pocket and retrieved my flask. Turning to face away from the street, I snuck a swig of whiskey. The liquor went down warm, and I chased it with a deep breath of cold air that chilled my lungs.

I felt a gentle poke in my back and turned around. A short, heavyset woman with big, dark hair stood before me. She wore a long, dark coat, open to reveal a low-cut black dress. Everything about her, from her red lips to the height of her hair, was overstated. She had a round face and flushed chubby cheeks like a Kewpie Doll. Her makeup contrasted with her otherwise pale skin like primary colors splashed on a stark white canvas.

"Can you spare a drink?" she asked with a smile.

"Sure," I said, handing her the flask.

She took a small sip and shuddered. "Oh, what was that?"

"Whiskey."

"I guess I should've asked before taking a sip."

"Probably."

The woman extended a small, gloved hand. "My name is Erica, Erica Whitcombe."

"Glenn Wozniak," I said, taking her hand and giving it a short, quick squeeze.

"So how do you know Alison?" she asked.

"Her father hired me to investigate her disappearance."

"No kidding? So, you're a private eye?"

"Uh-huh. How about you? How did you know Alison?"

"She's my cousin. Her father is my mother's brother. I used to spend every holiday with Alison. She was the only halfway sane person in the whole family."

Erica reached into her purse and withdrew a pack of cigarettes. She placed one in her small heart-shaped mouth and lit it, all the while shifting her weight from one foot to the other. She seemed to be in a state of constant agitation, her eyes darting about like those on a Kit-Kat clock.

"You wouldn't have happened to have met an older man by the name of Merrill in there, would you?" she asked. "He's about five-eight, five-nine, skinny with salt-and-pepper hair, has a cleft in his chin."

"No, I'm afraid not."

"Figures. We've been dating off and on. It's been more off as of late. He met Alison a few months ago, and they hit it off pretty well. I told him about the service, and he said he'd come by." Erica paused and took a deep drag off her cigarette. She placed a hand on her hip and rocked from side to side as she exhaled a thick cloud into the air. The cloud hung above us, crawling like a mass of tiny white spiders against the dark blue sky.

Erica eyed me, her head tilted to one side. Some smoke drifted into her eyes, making her squint. "So, what's being a private eye like?"

"It's dull. I spend a lot of time sitting in my car watching people and taking photos. I write the occasional report. I attend to my taxes and crap like that, just like any small business owner, nothing exciting."

"I see."

I lit a cigarette. We stood on the front steps of the building and smoked. Every so often, we'd shoot each other awkward glances and smile.

Erica stamped out her cigarette. "I should head in. The service starts soon."

"Sure, see you inside."

I finished my cigarette, took a swig from my flask, and lit another smoke. I kept an eye out for Maya, feeling hurt and angry.

What am I doing here? I wondered. I was going to quit a couple of days ago, but she talked me out of it. Why, if this was so important, wasn't she here paying her respects? I should be on a barstool right now, enjoying a beer and watching a Bulls game. I should be surfing the net for porn and beating off. I should be taking an early evening nap. I should be anywhere but here.

I flicked my cigarette butt onto the street. Its trajectory followed a long arc before landing with a bounce in the gutter, the tip spitting day-glow orange embers upon impact with the pavement.

I headed inside. The humid warmth and loud murmur of a crowded room greeted me as I opened the door. I headed towards a small stage with a podium and microphone. People gathered in anticipation of the service beginning.

Tim stepped up to the podium.

"Hey, everyone, can I have your attention?" he said. "We're about to start the service now."

The crowd continued to congregate around the stage. I noticed Erica standing to my right. She smiled at me, and I smiled back.

"We will begin with a vocal performance from one of Alison's oldest friends, Carrie Schwartz," Tim said.

Carrie was a petite young woman with warm olive-colored skin and delicate bird-like features. She ascended the stairs to the stage and took her place in front of the microphone. Her small, slender hands gripped the stand. "Thank you," she said. "Alison always loved the opera. I'm going to perform one of her favorite arias, "Signore, ascolta" from Giacomo Puccini's *Turandot*."

Carrie sang, her voice at first as small and fragile as the figure standing on the stage. It gradually swelled to fill the room, and I felt it in my chest. My eyes moistened. I closed them to stave off the impending rush of tears. My stomach tightened and pitched with every crescendo, dropped with every sonorous tone. Warm tears ran down my face. This happened without warning, and there was not a thing I could do about it. I crept away to the bathroom, finding a nice little stall to hide in and took a couple of good long pulls from my flask. I remained there for a while and could hear Alison eulogized in the other room, the audience laughing from time to time at a humorous anecdote, at foibles I didn't know nor ever could.

I washed my face and returned to the gallery just as the last speaker, Alison's uncle Harold, finished his eulogy. He was a stocky man with a pale, chubby face shaped like a dinner plate.

"Alison believed in community, and her idea of community was large and inclusive," he said. "To her, community meant the world, and Alison believed we bore a responsibility to each other as citizens of the earth. Right now, I think she would excuse us if we were to think and act locally today. We are here because we have lost someone dear to us, and I think Alison would encourage us to be kind to one another, to help each other during this difficult time. So, please remember to stay in contact, make yourselves available to comfort each other and seek comfort in each other. Goodbye, Alison. We will miss you and will always cherish the all-too-brief time you gave to us."

Harold descended from the stage. Several mourners gathered about the Marshes, offering words of comfort. The rest of the crowd dispersed into smaller clusters and, taking Harold's advice, exchanged hugs and warm sentiments.

I felt out of place but thought I should say my goodbyes to the Marshes before leaving. I waited for the crowd to thin out and passed the time by taking another look around. Alison's photos were the hardest to bear. They followed her from when she was a baby to the months leading up to her death, her pixie-like face staring out at me with large, dark eyes, a restrained yet sweet smile on her face.

I was particularly struck by a photo of her as a little girl. It was a black-and-white picture taken in the middle of winter on a snowy hill. Alison was on a sled. She couldn't be any older than five or six. She was a tiny girl with chubby cheeks and a big toothy smile on her face, an expression of pure joy. Sitting behind her was a boy. He was older, perhaps eleven or twelve—tall and thin with dark hair and skin so fair, he looked almost spectral. The boy wrapped Alison in his skinny pre-teen arms, a placid expression on his face.

I wondered where that little boy was and how he'd feel about Alison's death if he knew. I felt myself tearing up again. Time to leave. Go home and drink it off. Give yourself a night at the Foot perched on your favorite bar stool with a bottle of beer and a shot of whiskey.

I searched once more for Maya. Groups of three to four people dotted the room, huddling together, talking in hushed tones. A tall, dark-haired man in a navy suit disassembled the microphone. A young couple perused the regular artwork on display. Someone nudged me from behind. I turned to find Erica Whitcombe staring up at me, an awkward smile on her face. "Hey."

"Hey," I replied.

"It looks like I've been blown off."

"I know the feeling."

"Were you supposed to meet someone here?"

"There was someone I was expecting to see here, but she didn't show."

"What're you doing after this?"

"I think I'm going to get shit-faced."

"Mind if I tagged along?"

I hesitated for a moment, thinking about Maya.

"Never mind, I didn't mean to put you on the spot," Erica said.

Perhaps it was the whiskey or the lighting, but she didn't look as severe as she did when I first ran into her. "No, that's okay, I could use the company."

Erica smiled. "Great, Rush Street's not too far from here. We can go somewhere around there." She paused and moved a little closer, adding: "Or we could go to my place."

"Let's hit the bars first and take it from there," I said, already beginning to question my decision.

Erica grabbed her coat, and we headed over to Rush Street. Even in the dead of winter, the street was hopping. Young men and women dressed far too skimpy for the weather crowded the sidewalks, parading from one bar to another.

We stopped at a sports bar named McGinty's. The place was packed with husband-hunting girls in their twenties, thick-necked jocks, and golden-haired young business executives with alpha-male smirks on their faces. They clustered in packs—the males preening and posturing for their potential mates; the females alternating between playing coy and gyrating against each other to attract the boys' attention.

There was a large oak bar in the center. A big-screen TV took up one wall. On the opposite side of the bar were a video golf game and a jukebox. I fought my way to the bar and ordered a vodka and tonic for Erica and a beer and a shot of whiskey for me. Erica grabbed a spot in the corner near the washrooms. She set her coat on the floor and leaned against the wall. I downed my shot and joined her.

The music was too loud, and the place far too crowded for conversation. We people watched. I drank—a lot—trying to wash Alison, Maya, and the case out of my head. Erica's image doubled, and the little light in the bar appeared celestial about her round figure, an aura of soft glowing colors in alternating shades of red, green, and blue.

I was horny and drunk. I slid a hand around Erica's ample waist and pulled her close, feeling the heft of her breasts pressed against my chest. We kissed. I closed my eyes, and the floor seemed to drop out from underneath us. I pulled away from Erica and opened my eyes, my hands on her shoulders to brace myself.

She drew me close and spoke in my ear, her breath warm and moist. “Let’s go back to my apartment.”

Next thing I knew, I was struggling to put on my coat as we were heading out the door, back into the cold. We walked, turning down side street after side street. Everything appeared warped as if in a funhouse mirror and every sound muted as if coming to me through a long tunnel. All around me was a swirling blend of images, too many to process. I caught bits and pieces: blonde hair; blue jeans; baseball caps; khaki pants; button-down pastel shirts; knee-high, black leather boots; muscles; cleavage; taxicabs; slow-moving SUVs; laughing faces; angry faces; neon signs; a puddle of vomit (perhaps my own); shadows; and street lamps. I closed my eyes, bracing myself against a sensory overload, only to experience the sensation of falling and my stomach rising into my throat. Erica clutched my arm, and I felt propelled forward, my companion dragging me. We stumbled twice, catching ourselves just short of striking the pavement. Each time Erica laughed and quickened her pace. We walked east towards the lake, the wind growing in intensity with every step.

The frigid air seemed to sober me up. We arrived at a white high-rise building with balconies spanning the front like a series of scaffolding. The building had a doorman. He wore a burgundy uniform with yellow piping on his trousers and the pockets of his jacket.

"Good evening, Ms. Whitcombe," he said, opening the door for us.

"Good evening, Earle," Erica said. "This is my friend Glenn."

Earle tipped his cap to me. "Pleased to meet you, sir."

I bowed, for some reason, mumbling something that might've been hello or nice to meet you. I could've asked him his weight or told him his fortune, for all I know.

From that point on, the evening gets a little hazy. I remember taking the elevator up to Erica's apartment. The apartment was on the sixteenth floor, but I didn't figure that out until the following morning.

The last thing I remember, we were in her bedroom: more kissing, more groping, some undressing. The place spun like a top, and darkness beckoned from underneath heavy eyelids. I saw a naked breast, felt a tongue snake inside my mouth. I reclined on Erica's bed and sunk into it. My eyelids fluttered, and I saw the top of Erica's head descending between my legs just before everything went black.

EIGHTEEN

I awoke to find myself in a strange bed with my pants and underwear down around my knees. My bladder swelled with an evening's worth of overindulgence. Erica Whitcombe lay on her side with her back to me. She was naked except for a pair of beige satin panties, her broad shoulders rising and falling in time to her breathing.

I rose from the bed and pulled my pants up in a single motion. Blood rushed to my head, and I swooned for a moment before steadying myself. I tiptoed out of the bedroom, locating a bathroom down the hall. I relieved myself and sneaked back into the room, intending to make a quick getaway before she woke up. I crawled about on hands and knees in search of my shoes. My head ached. It was the kind of pain you felt in the back of your eyes. I took a seat on the edge of the bed and rubbed my temples. Erica sat up, bleary-eyed.

"Hey," I said with a nod.

"What time is it?" she asked.

I checked the clock on the nightstand. It was a little after ten AM. I told Erica the time, and she grunted as if to say that figures, before lying back down on her side.

"Hey, did we...?" I asked.

"Almost, but no," Erica replied.

"I'm sorry. I guess I had a little too much to drink."

"That's okay," Erica said, sitting up. "It happens."

"I wanted to. I really did."

"No need to explain."

"No, I mean it. I shouldn't have drunk so much. Things were just a little weird last night."

"That's my family for you. It wouldn't be a Marsh family gathering if it didn't make you uncomfortable to the point of wanting to drink yourself unconscious." Erica sighed and shook her head. "I'm sorry. I'm sure I bored you enough with this stuff last night."

"If you did, I don't remember."

She smiled. "You had a lot to drink. One moment you were groping me in the hallway, the next, you were out cold in my bed."

"Yeah, I'm a wild man."

We were silent for a moment, looking at each other with goofy grins on our faces. "You want some coffee?" Erica asked.

"I'd love some."

I found my coat spread out on the floor like the chalk outline of a homicide victim, my shoes tucked underneath. I reached inside and retrieved my flask.

"A little hair of the dog?" I said, jiggling the container.

"Whiskey, right?" she said with a wince.

I nodded, and she shook her head. "No, thanks."

"Okay, suit yourself."

I took a drink, and the whiskey washed away the sick, groggy feeling. I felt a little more human, a little more awake.

Erica threw on a robe and led me to the kitchen. She brewed a pot of coffee, and we talked about her family. According to Erica, the Marshes' relationship was distant and cold. Edgar dedicated all his time to various philanthropic activities—working as much, if not more than when he ran Marsh Enterprises—while Margaret struggled to fill her empty days. She dabbled in everything from antiquing to pottery to swing dance lessons, jumping from one interest to the next on an almost weekly basis. When Alison disappeared, she drowned her pain in liquor and sedatives—Edgar too preoccupied with trying to control the situation to provide her any comfort. His primary concern was keeping the story out of the papers.

No surprise there. Guys like Edgar fear scandal like regular people fear bankruptcy or terminal illness. They fear people talking about them. The thought of the unwashed masses reveling in his family's problems bothered Edgar Marsh to no end.

"He was the same way when his first wife died," Erica said.

"Wait, Edgar was married before?" I asked.

"Yeah, Aunt Margaret's his second wife. His first wife was a woman named Leslie. She was tall and pretty, kind of like Aunt Margaret, only blonde and fairer skinned. She died in a car accident. My mom says she was drunk. She ran a red light and slammed right into the driver's side door of another car, killing a mother of two. Uncle Ed paid a lot of money to make that go away, and now it's as if Aunt Leslie never even existed."

"I had no idea. So who is Alison's mother?"

"Aunt Margaret. God, Uncle Edgar would kill me if he knew I was telling you this." Erica lit a cigarette, exhaling a thick cloud of smoke that twisted towards the ceiling. "That's the kind of man my uncle is. It's like we're not even people, just potential embarrassments. I had a drug problem when I was in high school. I was doing a lot of coke. I sometimes wish I were still doing it. I've almost doubled in size since quitting, but that's neither here nor there. Anyway, one day I attended a function at a private club my uncle belonged to while high as a kite and had a few choice words with a stuffy old bitch in the ladies' room. I was smoking in there against club rules. One thing led to another, and I lost my temper. I wound up flicking my cigarette at the old bat's face, almost hitting her in the eye. Uncle Ed heard what I did and decided it was time to nip things in the bud. Granted, my behavior had gotten pretty bad at that point, so I can't blame him for wanting to put me away. What bothered me was that he had my parents send me out of the country for treatment, because he didn't want people to know that his niece had a drug problem. He was ashamed of me."

"Maybe he just wanted to make sure you got better, and this was the best place for treatment."

Erica rolled her eyes. "Yeah, right. Anyway, I spent the next year in the Spanish countryside. When I got back, he hired someone to watch me and make sure I remained clean. Amazing, huh? Lately, dear old Uncle Ed has taken to lecturing me about my drinking and all the weight I've put on."

Erica's face reddened, and her eyes narrowed into slits as thin and sharp as a razor. "I mean, who the fuck does he think he is? He's not my father. I told him as much a few months ago. I told him to stay the fuck out of my life. My mom and dad keep telling me I need to make up with that tight-ass jerk, but if you ask me, he's the one who should apologize."

Erica stood up and poured herself another cup of coffee. She leaned against the counter and shook her head, laughing to herself. "I'm not the least bit surprised he hired you. That's what he does. He buys people. He doesn't trust anyone who isn't on his payroll. I'm sure he's steaming about the news coverage."

Erica played the hothouse flower, pretending to swoon, the back of her hand pressed against her forehead. "Can you imagine what people are saying?" she said, fluttering her eyelashes. "Edgar Marsh's little girl sleeping with married men in sleazy motels! Oh, the disgrace!"

"Were you and Alison close?"

Erica leaned across the counter and cradled her chin in an open palm. "We were pretty close growing up. Alison was about the only cool person in the family. I'm going to miss her." She stood up straight and shook her head, her eyes moist with tears. "I'm sorry about laying all of this on you."

"Don't worry about it. I asked, didn't I?"

Erica sniffled and nodded. She grabbed a napkin out of one of the kitchen drawers and dabbed at her eyes.

We finished our coffee and got dressed. Erica walked me to the door. "Thanks for listening," she said.

"Thanks for giving me a place to crash."

She jotted down her phone number and pressed it into my palm. "Don't lose it."

"I won't."

She pulled me towards her and kissed me.

"Thanks," I said, turning to leave. I didn't look back, but I could sense Erica standing in the doorway watching me, watching as I pressed the down button, watching as I spent an awkward few seconds waiting for the elevator to arrive.

I made my way back to the art gallery and retrieved my car. The ride home was a long, hard slog through bumper-to-bumper traffic. My car inched along, stuck for most of the trip behind a white, rust-speckled van I couldn't see around. For all I knew, traffic was moving just fine on the other side of the hulking metal box, and the driver was unwilling to pick up the pace. I sat with the sun streaming in, making me squint, my furrowed brow aching, and my eyes straining to stay open.

I thought about home and bed. I just wanted to crawl under the covers and sink into the mattress, to let it engulf me. I wanted to roll up as if in a cocoon and hibernate until the Marshes, and any other responsibilities, left me for dead, just disappear for a while.

It was early afternoon when I got home, and just seeing my building filled me with a sense of relief. I climbed the stairs to my apartment two at a time, and when I opened the door, I discovered a horrific sight. My place looked as though a tornado had hit it. My furniture had been upturned, and my belongings strewn around the room. Broken glass covered the floor, and my living room walls bore a series of threats scrawled in red paint.

"Next time we'll visit when you're home," said one.

"Wozniak is one dead piece of shit," said another.

Then there was my favorite; a message etched into my door in rough, jagged letters like streaks of lightning against a midnight sky. "Why don't you call the police?" it read.

I imagined George and Lenny had a good hearty laugh as they wrote that one. I could picture their faces—fat, porcine cop faces wearing ear-to-ear grins, laughing as they trashed all that was dear to me.

These guys had a way with words...and furniture. The poet laureates trashed my coffee table. It sat tipped over, stripped of its legs, the piles of paper that had once covered it now scattered about the room. They kicked in my television screen. Dark cracks meandered from a hole in the tube's center, like the veins in a bloodshot eye. Books lay open, face down like dead birds, many of their covers torn or their spines broken. The mirrored surface of hundreds of CDs—some cracked, some shattered, few intact—sparkled like jewels in the wreckage. I stood stunned in the center of the room and surveyed the damage, my mouth hanging open.

"Motherfuckers!" I shouted.

I saw the dog-eared insert from a Stooges CD on the floor. It was their debut album. I picked it up. Iggy Pop, Dave Alexander, and the Asheton brothers stared back at me—young toughs, their faces the picture of defiance. I felt the loss, felt it in the pit of my stomach. These things—the music, the books, my television—weren't much, but they were mine.

I got down on my knees and searched the floor for intact CDs. My hand glided over the debris until a jagged shard of plastic, the remnants of another destroyed disc, sliced into my palm, drawing blood. Tiny droplets of scarlet dribbled from the cut, settling in the cracks of my hardwood floor. I picked up the offending fragment of plastic. The Stoo—, it read.

"Motherfuckers!"

I went to the bathroom in search of a bandage to dress my wound. There I found some more pleasantries written in red on the walls, these suggesting the vandals questioned my masculinity. The bathroom mirror lay in glittering shards upon the tiled floor, and the contents of my medicine cabinet, including the bandages, clogged my toilet.

I wrapped my hand in paper towels and put in a call to George Wesley. His voicemail picked up.

"I hope you can back up all the tough talk, asshole, because I'm on this case for good," I said. "Don't ever, ever fuck with a man's music collection."

I hung up, jamming my index finger against the End button. It wasn't as satisfying as slamming the receiver of a landline phone down, so I hurled the stupid little contraption against the wall. Seeing as the phone was one of my few remaining possessions, I regretted my outburst. I ran and retrieved the device, cradling it in cupped hands as if rescuing a small woodland creature. To my relief, it still worked. I headed for the front door.

Next thing I knew, I was driving due north, cursing the cops under my breath. Of course, the traffic was a nightmare—bumper-to-bumper, rage-inducing gridlock. Just the thing to feed my fury. I was red-faced and stringing together profanities in the most colorful and creative ways.

I took Ashland Avenue and headed north, not knowing what I would do once I got there. I just knew I had to canvass the area once more and find something, anything, to fuck those rat bastards with.

The traffic thinned out in Rogers Park. I passed through quiet, tree-lined side streets heading west past the Stardust. I drove past the park and the abandoned factory, the sun eating through the remaining frost and snow to reveal an expanse of grass the color of wheat. My rage subsided, leaving only fatigue and despair. I regretted the message I left on George's voicemail. As bad as things were, guys like him had a talent for making them worse and, all tough talk aside, I didn't need any more trouble.

My mission deteriorated into aimless wandering. I circled the neighborhood, passing all the same areas I had seen in the past few days. I tried to figure out if there were places I had neglected to visit, people I had forgotten to question, but nothing came to mind.

I headed home and passed the Stardust again on my way back south. My head ached, and my eyes grew heavy with sleep, the road ahead appearing like a shimmering mirage in the middle of a vast desert. I reached inside my coat pocket and retrieved my flask. I took a swig, tilting my head back to down the sweet, warming liquor. As I did so, I caught sight of a traffic camera perched atop one of the street lamps, its dark glass eye staring me straight in the face as I drank and drove. Figures. Oh well, my cop troubles couldn't get much worse. I lowered the flask and saluted the camera with my middle finger. The light turned green. I started and then immediately braked, my car stopping in the middle of the intersection. Brakes screeched, and horns blared behind me. The commotion sounded like it was a million miles away because all I could think about was what that camera might've captured one night three weeks ago.

NINETEEN

Barry Munroe was a short, chubby cream puff of a man. He looked disheveled, his thick, graying hair greasy and tousled, his clothes rumpled and a size too small. Nothing about him inspired anything even resembling confidence, and yet this was the man I was counting on to break my case wide open.

Barry performed camera surveillance for the city. He worked in a tiny, cluttered office that smelled of stale food. Stacks of papers covered every square inch of desk space, with some spilling onto the floor. The dog-eared corners of documents and manila folders protruded from overstuffed drawers. The file cabinet was just as bad, if not worse.

Barry looked like a pale yellow fungus growing out of the clutter accumulated on the floor. His white button-down shirt strained against his girth and bore copper stains in the armpits.

I met Todd at Barry's office. He made the introductions and explained the reason for our visit. Barry didn't look at me the entire time. He just mumbled, "Yes, yes, yes," as Todd spoke before giving me a quick, limp handshake. With that out of the way, he turned around to scan grainy, pixilated images of cars on his computer screen, his pale blue eyes peering through thick glasses in oversized plastic frames.

Todd ducked out of the room to get some chairs, leaving me alone with this odd little man.

"So, do you think you'll be able to help us?" I asked after a while.

Barry grunted, his eyes still trained on the screen. His work seemed to comprise clicking his mouse two or three times between brief flourishes of keystrokes. Every so often, he would lean forward in his seat so that his nose was just centimeters away from the screen, his pale eyes blinking behind Coke-bottle lenses.

Todd returned with a couple of chairs. "Do you think you can help us?" he asked, taking a seat.

"I was just telling your friend that I might," he said, adding, "No guarantees."

"Of course not," I said, trying to remember exactly when he said anything of the sort.

Barry explained that the cameras recorded digital images, which were then stored on the Chicago Police Department's server. He just needed to know the date, which intersection, and a time to search. That and what he was looking for.

"I'm afraid that may be a little tricky," I said. "I'm not sure what I'm looking for. I guess I'll know it when I see it."

Barry furrowed his brow, with an irritated look on his face. "You smell of alcohol," he said before turning around to face his computer.

Todd looked at me and raised his eyebrows as if to ask, what are you going to do?

I shrugged. What could I say? I did smell of alcohol.

I gave Barry the date and times to search. He hunkered down in front of the computer. I kept quiet and watched him work, listening to the soft plastic clacking of his chubby little fingers striking the keys. I pulled my chair up so that I could get a better view of what he was doing. Barry grimaced and wrinkled his nose at me. He opened the top drawer of his desk and retrieved a starlight mint wrapped in cellophane. "Please," he said, thrusting the candy at me.

I took it and scooted my chair back a couple of feet. Todd watched the entire exchange with an amused expression on his face. Meanwhile, Barry continued clacking away at his keyboard.

"Here you go," he said after a while. "This is the file for the 29th of January."

"Great, let's jump to around 3:00 PM," I said.

More clacking. "Okay."

I scooted my chair forward, just enough that I could see the screen over Barry's shoulder without crowding him. The images appeared in the center of the screen with a menu of icons underneath. Barry progressed through them by clicking on an arrow icon that pointed to the right. I watched cars pass through the intersection in all different directions, their herky-jerky progression like stop-motion animation. The images were grainy, but I could still make out license plates and some of the drivers' faces, each one a stranger.

"You see that sign in the background of every photo?" I said.

Barry squinted. "The Stardust Motel?"

"Uh-huh. Bertram and Marsh got a room there on the night of the murder. Not only were they there, but their room caught fire. Someone had doused the place in gasoline."

Barry stopped his clacking and spun around in his seat. "Any idea when this fire started?"

"It was around 11:00 PM. My theory is they were killed in the room, chopped up, and their remains moved before the fire was set. The victims were found dismembered in the trunk of a black '98 Pontiac. The murderer would need someplace private to cut up the bodies, so the motel seems like a good bet for the initial crime scene. I'm thinking sometime between when they checked in and around ten."

"I just asked for the time," Barry said.

Todd laughed, and I shot him a dirty look.

Barry spun around and returned to scanning the photos. "Let's confirm the check-in, and we'll go from there."

Twenty minutes later, we found it: a black '98 Pontiac. The image was grainy, but I could still make out Bill and Alison in the front seat.

Barry continued searching. One grainy image followed another until all I could see were pixelated masses in shades of black and gray. The photos grew darker, the Stardust's neon sign the most visible aspect, glowing in the background like a firefly in the night sky.

Barry kept at it for about an hour. He stopped and stood up. "Break time," he said.

Todd stood up and stretched, his hands almost touching the ceiling. "That's a good idea. I've got to hit the head."

The two left me alone. I sat facing the computer screen. Several minutes went by, and I started getting nervous. After all, I was in a police station, enemy territory now that goons like George and Lenny had decided to play hardball with me. I stood up and paced the room. Periodically, I'd hear voices in the hall outside, and I'd stop and listen for any mention of my name. I could discern the rhythmic throbbing of my heart in my head, feel the rush of blood, the dance beat of my pulse.

Get what you need and get out, I thought.

I took a seat at Barry's desk and resumed searching the photos. Cars of various makes and models, sizes and conditions headed east, headed west, headed God knows where. Strange faces flickered past on the screen. Every so often, I'd stop at a photo of someone I thought I recognized, only to study it closer and discover I was mistaken. I clicked the mouse repeatedly. Images flashed on the screen, the only constant, the neon sign in the background. Photo after photo, it appeared, sometimes on, sometimes off, a silhouette of the motel in the background. It was a dark building, with only a couple of windows lit, at least among those that were visible. Which room were they in? I wondered. A few more clicks and I had my answer. I located a dull orange glow emanating from one of the window, the beginnings of a fire.

I hunched forward in my seat, the computer screen centimeters from my nose, and continued clicking the mouse. I increased my pace, the images flashing across the screen. After a while, it appeared again, a black '98 Pontiac. The camera caught it emerging from the motel parking lot. I could see the driver's face but did not believe my eyes. I enlarged the image, zoomed in, and, sure enough, it was him. George Wesley.

Unbeknownst to me, Barry had entered the room. "What are you doing?" he said.

The sound of his voice made me start. I stood up to face him. "Nothing, I was just...nothing. Sorry."

He pushed past me and reclaimed his seat. Todd entered the room carrying a couple of vending machine coffees in small paper cups decorated like playing cards—the Jack of Clubs in the left hand, the Queen of Diamonds in the right.

"What's going on?" he asked.

"What's going on?" Barry said. "I'll tell you what's going on, *Todd*. I did you a favor by letting you bring a friend to my office and perform a special search without filling out any of the requisite paperwork, and your friend messed with my computer."

Todd shot me a nasty look. "I'm sorry," he said through gritted teeth. "I can assure you it won't happen again."

"Darn right, it won't happen again," Barry huffed. "I won't be helping you next time."

"I brought you a coffee," Todd said. He handed him one of the playing card cups.

"Hey, what's the deal with those things?" I asked.

"What things?" Todd said.

"The cups."

"The cups? What about them?"

"Why do they have playing cards on them? Are you supposed to collect them or something?"

"I don't know. I suppose."

"And then what?"

"I have no idea. Do we need to do this right now?"

"Are you supposed to play poker with them or something?"

Todd shook his head and sighed. "I don't know."

"It doesn't seem practical. I mean, how do you shuffle a stack of cups?"

"I don't know. I've never thought about it."

Barry watched us, a look of disbelief on his face. "Is this guy for real?"

Todd sighed again. "I don't know."

"Look, Barry, I'm sorry about using your computer," I said. "I was feeling a little anxious and needed something to do."

Barry's face turned red. "Needed something to do? Then read a book, take a walk, drink some more, you fucking lush! Just stay away from my computer."

"Any luck on the search?" Todd asked.

"Take a look," I said.

Todd leaned over Barry to study the screen, prompting the little guy to sigh.

"Relax, Barry," Todd said. "We'll be out of your hair in just a minute."

He examined the image, his eyes widening. "That's not...?"

"Uh-huh," I said, nodding. "George Wesley."

"What time was that taken?"

"After the fire started."

"It says 10:47 PM," Barry said.

"10:47," I repeated.

Todd clapped his hands and rubbed them together. "I guess that settles that," he said, reaching for the phone.

"Settles what?" I asked, interrupting him mid-dial.

"The case. You've got a photo of George Wesley driving the victim's vehicle away from the crime scene. The bodies were later discovered in the trunk of that same car. It looks to me like we just caught ourselves a murderer. You're off the hook, Glenn. No more case, no more Mr. Marsh. It's over."

I took a seat and glanced over at the photo once again. George Wesley's face peered back at me. It was the face of a guilty man, of a man traumatized by his actions. I could see it in the eyes. It was there clear as day, and yet I couldn't help thinking there was more to the story.

I turned to face Todd. He sat with one leg folded over the other, a satisfied look on his face.

"Who are you calling?" I asked.

"Greshing," Todd said. He motioned for me to be quiet. "Hey, Doug, this is Todd Burton. Call me back. I've got some information I wanted to share about one of your cases. Thanks." He left his number and hung up. "There."

I shook my head. "I don't know."

"Don't know what? What's your problem now?"

"Something's not right. I mean, what's the motive?"

"How the hell should I know? That's for Doug to find out. All I know is we've got some mighty compelling evidence here."

I thought about Captain Morrow's arrangement with Bledsoe and wondered how that played into all of this. I wasn't about to let Todd in on that part of the case. From there, it would go to internal affairs, and then the Fraternal Order of Police would get involved, slowing any inquiry to a crawl. In the meantime, anyone who knew anything, namely me, would somehow meet with an untimely accident, or so I assumed.

"I don't know," I repeated.

"Don't know what?"

"From everything I've heard, George and Bill were close, like brothers."

"People kill family members all the time."

"Okay, but even if George were to kill his partner, why do it when he'd have to take out the girl?"

"Glenn, I don't know, but those photos don't lie. He was there. He drove the car that the bodies were found in, and he drove it after that fire was set. What more do you want?"

"I know. You're right."

Todd clapped me on the back. "Darn right, I'm right. Man, this is the best thing that could've happened to you. There's almost enough right there to convict, and I'm sure once we point Greshing in the right direction, he'll find a lot more. It's over, Glenn. You're free. Now, why don't you go home and get some rest?"

Barry nodded in agreement. I left the police station. It was early evening, and dark clouds roiled and rolled overhead as if the sky had been brought to a boil. I got into the front seat. I can't remember what I was thinking or whether I was thinking at all. I just sat there for a while, staring ahead at nothing. It may have been minutes, it may have been hours, but when I came to, a profound sense of loneliness and loss swept over me. I felt it first in the pit of my stomach, a gnawing sensation like hunger pains.

I reached inside my coat and retrieved my phone, giving Maya a ring. Again she didn't answer, and I hung up without leaving a message. I then thought about Dantrell Miles. He'd be interested in finding out about the photos. I dialed his pager and entered my number.

I could see some cops standing outside the station. They were looking my way and motioning towards the car. I had been there long enough to arouse their suspicion. I inserted my key into the ignition, and the car rumbled to a start. Not wanting to go home, I drove to a diner near my house. I ordered coffee, black, and a Denver omelet that I ate while scanning a free newspaper I picked up near the entrance.

My phone sat idle next to my coffee cup. Every so often, I'd look at it, almost begging it to ring. I finished my meal, drank several cups of coffee, and read the newspaper from cover to cover, the phone remaining silent the entire time.

I paid my bill and headed back to my car. It was a little after nine, my usual drinking hour. I hopped in my car and headed towards Club Foot but drove past the bar without stopping. I continued past it and my house, heading west. I opened my glove compartment and retrieved the .357 Magnum. I stuffed it, business end first, down the front of my pants and headed towards North Lawndale, passing empty storefronts, burned-out buildings, and the occasional stray person lumbering down the street like the undead.

I was going to pay Dantrell and Julius another visit. Not exactly my first choice for company, but these were strange days, and they made for strange bedfellows.

TWENTY

The stretch of Karlov Avenue, where the Meeks lived, seemed as desolate as the moon. Even the street lamps had stopped functioning. My headlights cut through the shadows like a knife, my car even more conspicuous in the deep-space void of Chicago's west side.

I parked the vehicle and walked across the street to the house. It was a cold, breezy night. Bare winter trees swayed from side to side, their branches sweeping the evening sky. All the lights were out, the windows as black as obsidian. I checked the time. It was a little after ten, too early for Dantrell and Julius to have called it a night, or so I assumed.

I climbed the front steps and considered ringing the bell before thinking better of it. Something felt wrong. I headed around to the side of the house, locating the busted window I had entered on my previous visit. I lowered myself into the basement, and the moment my feet hit the ground, I smelled blood. It was a pungent, cloying odor that enveloped me, as omnipresent as the darkness, the two elements mingling to create a single dread entity. I could feel its weight pressing on my chest, stealing my breath, and I stood frozen, afraid to move for what seemed like a long time before finally coaxing my legs to work again.

My eyes strained to make out my surroundings in the darkness, finding only amorphous shadows against a moonlit background. When they adjusted, I saw I was not alone. A man sat in the center of the room. I trained my flashlight on him. He sat with his back to me, his head at an awkward angle, tilted forward and to one side. I approached, the scent of blood growing stronger with every step. A shiver ran through me like an electric current. I felt queasy, and my throat was dry. A draft blew through the open window, chilling the back of my neck. My feet moved as if I were knee deep in water. I shuddered, stopped, and contemplated retreating before pushing forward.

The beam of my flashlight fell on another figure, this one lying in a heap upon the cold, grimy basement floor. I crossed the room, stopping halfway between the two bodies. I raised the flashlight, the beam landing on the face of the figure sitting in the chair. It was a horrific sight, a twisted mass of torn flesh and shattered bone, the man's features so ravaged, he was almost unrecognizable. I stared at him, the unsteady illumination of the flashlight in my trembling hand alternately revealing and obscuring the horror.

I'm not sure how long I remained that way before it occurred to me that whoever had done this could still be in the room. The realization made my heart jump, and my knees buckled for a moment. I caught myself, spun about and swept the room with the flashlight, the beam finding nothing yet suggesting all sorts of horrors. Dark, menacing shapes formed and dissolved as if I were sculpting the darkness with a bright, gleaming blade. I went over the entire room, finding only a utility sink, a workbench, and the usual collection of tools and boxes found in any basement.

A short cord culminating in a small bell-shaped piece of aluminum dangled from the ceiling to the left of the figure on the floor. I pulled it, and a single light bulb flooded the room with pale illumination. In the light, I could better make out the second victim. He was Julius Meeks. Whoever killed him was a skilled shooter, dispatching him with one well-placed bullet to the forehead. A dark puddle of blood mushroomed from a hole between his eyes.

The more ravaged corpse belonged to Dantrell. Julius's death was quick and clean in comparison. Someone had blown Dantrell's kneecaps out. An assortment of cuts, bruises, and cigarette burns covered his chest, neck, and face. Both bodies were cold to the touch, but judging by the chill air of the basement, the murders could've been as recent as an hour ago.

The killer ambushed Dantrell as he was coming down the stairs. Blood covered the bottom three steps with knee-level splattering on the cinderblock walls. Two long streaks of scarlet cut through the grime on the floor from the staircase to the chair where he died.

Julius arrived later, the treads of his shoes leaving tracks in Dantrell's blood that ended abruptly where he took a bullet in the head. I could only imagine what went through his mind in those final seconds before he died, the horror he experienced seeing the man he loved rendered a quivering mass of gore and mangled flesh.

I stood there, surveying the carnage. The entire scene felt unreal, though not unlike ones I'd seen when I was on the force. At first, these kinds of crime scenes left me traumatized. I'd close my eyes for a moment and flash on a gunshot victim or some poor sap whose head had been caved in with a blunt object. As time went on, the trauma lessened, and by the time I left the force, it had gotten to where even the most gruesome act of cruelty left little aftertaste.

The last crime scene I witnessed before retiring was not much better than what I found in the basement. The victim was an old woman who had the misfortune of being home when a man named Joey Grudzielanek broke in to rob her. He caved in one side of the old woman's head with a baseball bat, pushing her right eye out of its socket. When I found her, the eyeball dangled from her face by long gray strands of nerve tissue. It was what would've given me bad dreams during my early years on the force, but by then, I didn't even think twice about it. That night I went home, fixed myself some dinner, and fell asleep on the couch watching TV.

What I was not used to was the smell. It had been a long time since I had been around this much blood, and the scent was overpowering. I felt queasy. My throat tightened, and I struggled to breathe. The walls seemed to close in around me. Part of me wanted to leave right then, shut off the basement light and climb back out the window. Another part of me wanted to look around and confront whoever might have done this. I suspected I'd have to, suspected that whoever did this would come for me next. Besides, exiting via the basement window would be far more complicated than entering, the opening a good eight feet off the floor.

I pulled my gun and headed upstairs. The first floor looked much as it did before with its antique furniture and cabinet full of knick-knacks. Old Lady Meeks' figurines smiled dumbly, blissfully unaware of a world where a man's kneecaps are blown off before being tortured and killed. They lived in a world of baseball and barbecue, sled rides, and Santa Claus, a million miles away from the horrors I found in the basement.

I took a look around, checking everything from the kitchen pantry to the bedrooms upstairs. Not a soul in sight or any trace of an intruder, but no matter where I went, the scent of blood followed. It permeated my clothes, trailing me like a ghostly presence. An overwhelming feeling of nausea and fatigue swept over me as I descended the second-floor stairs. Bile welled up in the back of my throat, and my legs buckled for a moment. I didn't want to get sick, and I certainly didn't want to leave a mess, not there with two dead bodies downstairs. I steadied myself, locating a bathroom on the first floor.

I flicked the light switch on using the barrel of my gun. Faded floral-print wallpaper covered the bathroom. I set my weapon down on the sink and turned on the faucet. My face looked pale and drawn in the mirror; my scalp, temples, and forehead slick with sweat. Even my collar was damp. I cupped my hands and placed them under the faucet, filling them with ice-cold water. I closed my eyes, bent forward, and splashed my face. My scalp tingled, and a wave of relief washed over me. I cupped my hands again, refilled them, and splashed my face a second time. I straightened up, my eyes still closed. Cold water ran down my face and dampened the front of my shirt. I opened my eyes, and for a moment they struggled to readjust to the light.

At first, I only half-saw the figure standing behind me, the face little more than a blur. I blinked twice, and everything came into focus. George Wesley's face peered back at me from the bathroom mirror, stone-cold and as expressionless as a mask. I saw one of his hands reach out and then felt it on the back of my head. It propelled me forward, my face meeting the mirror with a crash. I felt the sting of my nose breaking and shards of glass slicing into my skin. My teeth rattled with the impact, and I felt as though I was falling, consciousness surrendering to pain and shock. I was going under, almost out, when I felt George's hand grab my collar and pull me backward. My shirt tightened around my windpipe, choking me. Darkness ahead. Falling faster.

The void rushed up to meet me, a giant gaping maw that threatened to swallow me whole. Everything turned deep red. I could see the darkness ahead, the hole becoming clearer. Only it was not a void, nor even that large. It was little more than your standard toilet bowl. Cold water filled my mouth and nostrils, and I could feel my lungs flooding. They stung, and in a panic, I swung and reached for something to grab hold of—a life preserver.

Darkness beckoned again. The stinging subsided, all sounds, and sensations washed away with the water stirring about my head. No more case, no more pain, just silence and nothingness.

TWENTY-ONE

I woke up with a screaming headache, my body chilled. The morning sun peeked through the side of the blinds, and I could make out Maya's figure in the bed next to me. She lay on her side, facing away, wrapped up in her blanket as though in a cocoon.

She stirred and turned to face me. "Sorry, I must've stolen all the covers."

"What time is it?"

"Early. You should go back to sleep. You look like you could use it."

"I am tired," I said, the understatement of the century. I felt faint, queasy, and my head throbbed. "I might just close my eyes for a second."

"Okay, how 'bout I make you some breakfast? Steak and eggs sound good?"

"Yeah, sure, that sounds great."

Maya got out of bed. She was wearing a T-shirt and panties, like the first time I had seen her. "You've got a nasty shiner. You could use a steak for that eye."

"I don't think it's supposed to be a cooked steak," I said, but she didn't hear me. She had already left the room.

I pulled the covers over my head, wrapped myself up, and closed my eyes. The sounds of cabinets and drawers opening and closing came from the kitchen, followed by a sizzling sound I took to be my steak.

I opened my eyes and sat upright in bed. Something was amiss. I shouldn't be here, I thought. I looked around the room, overcome by an overwhelming sense of dread. I noticed something on top of Maya's dresser. A figurine of a chubby-cheeked, black child in a baseball uniform holding a bat, a huge smile on his face, beaming ear to ear. Just then it hit me: Old Lady Meeks' house. I was in Old Lady Meeks' house and now I'm here. But how?

The apartment had gone quiet. No sounds of cooking coming from the kitchen. Nothing. I called out to Maya. No answer. I got up and dressed.

"Maya?" I called again.

Still nothing.

I walked out into the hall. It was longer than I remembered, a long, narrow corridor ending at a large wooden door. A shaft of light radiated from underneath. I headed towards it and knocked.

"Maya?"

No answer.

I turned the knob and opened the door, entering a grand hall with marble floors. Paintings covered the walls. At the far end of the room stood two people. A sharp pain shot through my skull, and for a moment, I saw nothing but bright light. When it cleared, the two figures came into focus. It was Alison and Bill. At first, they seemed oblivious to my presence. I approached, and Bill acknowledged me. He waved and extended his hand.

"Hi, my name is Bill," he said.

"Pleased to meet you, Bill. Glenn Wozniak."

"Come join the tour. Alison here was showing me around. I don't know much about art."

"Me neither," I said.

"This piece is one of mine," Alison said, gesturing to a painting covered by a white sheet. "I hope you like it. You're its debut, Glenn."

She removed the sheet, unveiling a painting of dogs playing poker.

That wasn't hers. I had seen Alison's paintings, and this was nothing like her work. I stood looking up at it, wondering if I should say something.

Bill nudged me. "Need a match?"

I looked down to see a gas can in my right hand. The room filled with thick, dark smoke. I could feel it in my lungs, choking me. Everything went black, the place now scorching hot. Bill and Alison were gone. I was alone, and all was quiet.

Somewhere, a floorboard creaked. The sound cut through the silence. I drew air into my lungs, and a rush of sensations overwhelmed me. My nose burned with the scent of benzene, chemical yet almost sweet. I coughed. It was a hacking cough that came from deep in my chest. My back ached, and I felt an intense pressure on the sides of my skull as if it were being crushed in a vise.

I drifted off, my body floating through space. Off in the distance, I could make out a familiar face. It was Alison Marsh. Her image appeared hazy as if through a dense fog, but I could make out her delicate features, her pale skin, her raven hair, and dark brown eyes. She appeared to speak, her lips moving noiselessly.

"Don't leave me here," she mouthed.

I wanted to respond, but I could not speak. Thick, dark smoke enveloped Alison's features. A figure loomed behind her, an all-consuming shadow that stretched towards me. A pale hand gripped her shoulder and pulled her backward. She dissolved into the haze as everything faded to black. I wanted to call out, but no matter how hard I tried, my mouth couldn't form the words. A moment later, she was gone, and I was alone.

Another sharp sensation of pain. I opened my eyes. I was in the Meeks' home, lying on the bathroom floor, my head propped up against the wall at an awkward angle, my arms and legs akimbo. It was the standard chalk outline pose, my body sprawled out like a marionette released by its puppeteer.

The bathroom filled with smoke, casting everything in a haze. At first, I didn't stir. I lay motionless, gazing up at the smoke swirling above me. My face stung from numerous cuts and abrasions. I touched my cheek and felt a small piece of glass embedded in the flesh. I winced, and the movement of my facial muscles ground the small shard against my cheekbone. I gritted my teeth and removed it.

My shirt was damp, and my nose burned with that same chemical odor I smelled earlier. The scent was coming from me. I'd been doused in gasoline, and a fire raged outside the bathroom.

I could hear someone stirring somewhere near the back of the house. I struggled into a sitting position with my back propped up against the wall. My gun lay just inches away on the tiled floor in a light pink liquid: two parts water, one part blood. A harsh glare shone off the shards of broken mirror surrounding it. I reached for the gun. The tips of my fingers gripped the floor, and my hand moved like a spider towards the weapon. I felt the cold metal of the barrel and picked it up.

A door slammed, the sound coming from the rear of the house. I scrambled to my feet. Outside the bathroom, flames engulfed everything. All around me, the Meeks' home crackled and burned, fire crawling along the floors, walls, and ceiling, a roiling mass of red and orange and pitch. I could see a discarded gas can sitting on its side in the living room, blackening in the fire, and a second dark can-shaped husk in the kitchen. There was no way out. I retreated to the bathroom and closed the door. I soaked a couple of towels and jammed them under the door to keep out the smoke.

There was a small window above the bathtub. It would be a tight squeeze, but it was my only hope. I opened it and shimmied through, tumbling outside. Fresh air filled my lungs. I lay for a moment on my stomach and felt the cold ground against my face. Behind me, I could hear the fire crackling and smell acrid smoke pouring from every window. I was on the side of the house, near where I had first entered. I rose to my feet and drew my gun, creeping towards the backyard. There stood the dark figure of a tall, slender man. His hands gripped George Wesley by the collar, and he was dragging his limp, unconscious body behind him, the heels of the cop's shoes digging grooves in the frost-covered ground.

A car sat idling in the alley. The tall figure opened the trunk and dragged Wesley's body inside. George stirred for a moment. He reached up and tried to grasp the man's shirt.

The tall stranger brushed his hand away and slammed the trunk closed. He paused for a moment before turning and looking toward the house. I could see his face. It was as pale as his hair was black. The pallor mixed with his blank, expressionless eyes gave him the look of something straight out of a zombie movie. A jagged streak of blood ran across his right cheek like war paint.

I'd seen this man before. It was the kid from the anti-war meeting, the kid who had scolded me outside my home for drinking and driving. Here he was again. He'd saved my life, and yet he terrified me. Our eyes seemed to meet for a moment, and I retreated into the shadows, my hand clenching the .357 Magnum. His expression remained impassive. He turned and got in the car. I swayed from side to side, my legs unsteady, and watched him drive away.

Somewhere, a siren blared. Time to make my escape. I cut across the backyard and made my way down the alley. It was pitch black, lights out in North Lawndale. I felt my way in the darkness and headed back to Karlov Avenue. There I saw a fire truck in front of the house, its mars light cutting swaths of red in the night's fabric, seams that closed as quickly as they opened. I kept low, crouching out of sight, and ran to my car. I entered through the passenger side and crawled on my belly into the driver's seat. More sirens blared somewhere off in the distance. I turned my key in the ignition, and the car started with a roar. It was louder than I had ever remembered it sounding in the past. I winced and shrank in my seat. Fuck it; just go, I told myself. I slammed the accelerator to the floor and screeched away from the curb.

I headed east towards home, but I wasn't going home. There was nothing left for me there. I turned and headed north towards Rogers Park, the same trip I had made time and time again in recent days. My car pushed forward towards Dan Morrow's district, Curtis Bledsoe's turf, and the home of one solitary friend who had seemed to have disappeared into thin air.

I drove on, my mind a million miles from the road. I tried to add it all up, but the numbers didn't compute. I shouldn't be alive. I shouldn't be here in this car, feeling the steering wheel in my hands or the pain in my head. The realization brought tears to my eyes. I craved human contact. I wanted to see a kind face, to feel the warmth of another body pressed against mine. I thought about Maya and considered the possibility that she would not be there when I got to her place, that I might never see her again. It hurt. I felt the pain in my gut, an almost primordial, animal pain. I was lost and alone. I'd passed the point of no return. No going back.

TWENTY-TWO

I sat in my car, the engine idling and my cell phone in my lap. Off in the distance, the morning sun struggled against the last remnants of a frigid night, the horizon glowing as though the west side of the city was on fire. I peered up at Maya's building, spotting a light on in her apartment. I dialed her number, and she answered on the second ring, sounding startled. "Hello?"

"Maya?"

"Glenn? Is that you? I've been trying to reach you."

"You have?"

"Yes, where have you been?"

"I was going to ask you the same question."

She paused. "Where are you? We need to talk. Can you come over?"

"I'm right downstairs in my car."

"You're here? Why didn't you ring my bell?" she asked, to my astonishment.

Why? Because you fucking told me not to come by unannounced. You practically bit my head off the last time.

"I dunno," I said.

"Come up. We should talk."

I hung up and crossed the street, pausing outside her building. Part of me felt relieved to find her alive and well, but another part felt hurt and more than a little suspicious. I wondered where she had been and why she hadn't called. Perhaps Todd was right about her playing me. Who was Maya Garcia? Could I trust her? I have a hard enough time bedding women my own age, let alone girls in their twenties. My life supplied little to write Penthouse about. I was overweight and underemployed. I suppose a girl could do worse, but most would hold out for better. Maya wasted little time jumping in the sack with me, and I couldn't help but wonder why. Was she working some kind of angle? Had Bledsoe or one of the narco boys gotten to her? Perhaps the cops were holding something over her head. Drugs? Prostitution? A no-good relative who'd go to jail if she didn't cooperate?

I went over what I had shared with her in my head. What could she tell them? Aside from how I was in bed, not much.

I checked my voicemail, and sure enough, she had left several messages. I was feeling a little better.

Maya greeted me at the front door, dressed in jeans and a sweatshirt. She looked tired—her skin flushed and her eyes glassy. I could see stacks of boxes behind her, towering above us like hired muscle.

The Marshes must be collecting Alison's belongings, I thought.

Maya's eyes widened at the sight of me. "Oh my God, what happened to you?"

Before I could answer, she took my hand and led me into the living room. Inside, I could see that it wasn't just Alison's things in those boxes.

Was she fleeing town? My guard went up again.

Maya led me through a maze of boxes. She removed a couple from the sofa. "Here, have a seat," she said, shepherding me onto the couch. "What happened? You look like you were thrown under a freight train."

I peered up at her, a hurt and accusing look on my face. "Never mind that."

"You must be wondering about all this," she said, gesturing with her head at the boxes.

I nodded, my eyes downcast.

"Look, Glenn, I want you to know that I enjoyed the time we spent together. I really did, but Alison's death got me thinking about my life and living in this city and..." She stopped, unable to look at me.

"And?"

"And I'm leaving Chicago."

Her words hit me hard, my chest aching. "Where are you going?"

"Florida. Miami. I have a cousin who lives there. She owns a gift shop at a resort, and she said she had a job for me if I wanted it. I thought this might be a good time to start over."

I stared up at her, not saying anything.

"What?" she said.

"I'm just trying to figure out what happened between us."

Maya shut her eyes as if wincing in pain. When she opened them, her expression changed. She glared at me. "We fucked; that's what happened. I never promised you anything. In fact, I distinctly told you I didn't want a relationship."

I rose to my feet. "Fine, neither do I. I never asked you for one."

"Then what's with the third degree?"

"Third-degree! What third-degree? You're the one who thought you should explain yourself."

Maya looked as if she were about to say something but stopped herself. "You're right," she said. "I'm sorry."

"No, I'm sorry," I said, collapsing into my seat. "I don't have a lot of luck with women, and with all that's been going on, I started wondering if you were playing straight with me."

Maya took a seat on the couch. "I don't normally go to bed with guys I've just met if that's what you mean. I don't know what came over me that night. I was in a weird mood.

I'm not sure how to explain it. You ever get the urge to do something crazy?"

"I don't know," I said. "I guess."

"That's how I was feeling. I guess I just wanted to feel something. Besides, you're cute in a goofy kind of way."

I nodded, still not entirely sure that I believed her. "So, where've you been?"

"That's what I was about to tell you. The night of Alison's funeral, I was in the bathroom getting dressed when I had this terrible, sinking feeling. My heart was pounding. I couldn't breathe. I couldn't move. I think I might've been having a panic attack. At one point, the phone rang, and I just stood in front of the bathroom mirror, staring at myself with a wide-eyed look of terror on my face. It rang and rang, and I couldn't move."

"That might've been me. I called a few times that day. I thought I'd hear from you."

Maya put a hand on my forearm and gave it a little squeeze. "I'm sorry," she said.

"It's okay," I said, not looking at her, my eyes trained straight ahead on a stack of boxes. "Go on."

"Anyway, the phone stopped ringing, and a little while later, I calmed down enough that I could finish getting ready. To be honest, I still didn't want to go to the funeral and see Alison's family or anyone."

"Anyone?"

Maya nodded, and again, I felt a sharp pain, this time in the pit of my stomach. I was about to say something but thought better of it. She continued, unable to look at me, her eyes on her feet.

"I just wanted to go hide somewhere until all of this—the murder, the funeral—just went away. Then the phone rang again, and this time, against my better judgment, I answered." She paused for a moment. "It was my ex, Pedro."

"Pedro?"

She sighed. "It's funny. I can't stand the man. He's pushy, controlling, and totally regressive with women, but I was happy to hear from him. Here was someone who had nothing to do with my life, someone from my past. So..."

"So?"

"So, we got together."

She had mentioned her ex once before, and I never gave him a second thought. Now I wanted to know everything about him. I wondered how he looked and how I compared as a lover. I pictured a man around her age, handsome, in good shape, a man physically superior to me in every way.

"So then what?" I said.

"The next day, I went home and decided it was time for a change. Going over to Pedro's was the last straw. My cousin's been asking me to move out there and work for her, and I decided now was a good time to take her up on the offer. There's nothing keeping me here other than a few good friends that I'll miss, and they're always more than welcome to visit."

At that, she looked at me and smiled. If she were lying, I couldn't tell. To be honest, I didn't want to know. I was better off thinking she was one of the good ones. It hurt that she slept with her ex-boyfriend, and I was disappointed that she was leaving, but I needed a friend. I took her hand and cupped it between my own. It felt soft and warm.

"What happened to you?" she asked.

If she were working for the cops or Bledsoe, she was about to hit pay dirt. Right then and there, I craved a sympathetic ear more than anything in the world. I told her everything. I told her about the funerals and Erica Whitcombe, my run-ins with George and the tall, pale stranger at the Meeks house. To my disappointment, Maya didn't seem the least bit concerned about my spending the night with another woman. She didn't regard me with jealousy so much as pity, the kind generally reserved for orphans, refugees, and puppy mill dogs found in charity infomercials.

"I'm so sorry, Glenn," Maya said. "I'm sorry you had to go through all that. Are you going to be all right?"

"I think so."

We fell silent again. I didn't want to talk anymore. I looked around at all the boxes, and the case no longer seemed important. Maya was leaving, just one more in a series of losses.

I stood up. “It looks like you’re busy, so I guess I’ll be going.”

Maya said nothing. She just took my hand and led me back to the couch. That was all the encouragement I needed. I pulled her to me and leaned in to kiss her. She put a hand against my chest, stopping me. “No offense, but you smell like a tire fire.”

“I’ll go clean up.”

“Good idea.”

I awoke from a deep sleep, Maya lying at my side, her face turned towards me. She looked peaceful, content, and for a second, I let myself think that had something to do with me. My head still ached, and the slightest stir sent a jolt of pain through my body, from the base of my skull to the tips of my toes. I groaned, waking Maya.

She regarded me groggily and yawned. “You okay?”

“Yeah, just a little sore,” I whispered.

Maya rose on her pillow and looked at me, running a finger down my chest to just above my navel and back again. “What are you going to do now?”

“I don’t know. I guess I’ll finish things up with the case. I don’t know what else to do.”

Her expression changed. She looked sad.

"What's wrong?" I asked.

Maya shook her head. She then lay back down with her back to me.

"You can tell me if something is bothering you."

Maya didn't answer. Her shoulders rose and fell. I took her by the arm and turned her so she was facing me. She was crying.

I wiped away her tears. "Hey. Hey, what's wrong?"

"You wanted to quit the case when they found Alison's body, but I asked you to stay on, and you were almost killed."

She was right. I had stayed on for her, and now she was leaving me. I looked at her with no particular expression on my face, the sight of her tears leaving me cold.

"You hate me, don't you?"

Resented was more like it, but why split hairs?

"I don't blame you," Maya said. "But I never meant for you to get hurt."

At first, I didn't answer, but then I looked at her. She was young, so much younger than me, and still searching for herself. The last thing any twenty-something-year-old woman needed was a jaded, broken, middle-aged drunk smothering her dreams and ideals. I wasn't what she needed, and what kind of man would I be if I stood in her way?

"Look, don't worry about it," I said. "It's okay, really."

Maya curled up next to me. She laid her head on my chest, a few strands of hair fanning across my face, tickling my mouth and nose. “You don’t hate me?” she asked.

I shook my head. “No, Florida will be good for you.”

I felt her slide a hand between my legs. She climbed on top of me. I closed my eyes and tried to forget that she was leaving. I tried to pretend there was nothing else, just me and her, the outside world and all its horrors fading into oblivion, if only for a moment.

TWENTY-THREE

I left Maya's apartment a little after three in the afternoon and headed home for a fresh set of clothes. My apartment was just as I had left it: a disaster. I rummaged in the fridge for something cold to put on my bruises. The ice tray was empty, so I grabbed a bag of frozen peas and pressed it against my face. That provided some measure of relief. It wasn't a stiff drink, but it would have to do for the time being. I stumbled over to the couch, cleared a spot, and slumped into my seat. The room was dark. I considered turning on the lights, but I was too busy thinking about Maya and feeling sorry for myself.

Priorities.

The phone rang. I dispensed with any ceremony. "Yeah," I answered.

It was Todd. "I got some news about the case," he said.

I only half heard him, his words mere background noise for my pity party.

"Do you ever wonder what it's all about?" I said.

The line went silent.

"I mean, what's the point? Nothing lasts. You meet someone you like and think maybe you've got something special, and it just ends. You know what I mean?"

Still nothing, Todd obviously at a loss for words.

"You there?" I asked, unable to deal with the silence.

"I don't know what you want me to say. What are you talking about?"

"It's Maya. She's leaving."

"Maya?"

"The Marsh girl's roommate. I told you about her. She's moving to Florida. You were wrong about her. She wasn't playing me. Then again, I guess she toyed with my emotions and broke my heart, so maybe you had it right after all."

Todd cleared his throat. "Perhaps this isn't the best time."

"You ever think about death?"

"Yeah, this sounds like a bad time. Why don't we talk later?"

I wasn't listening. "Life's a fragile thing. I could die just like that, and who'd miss me? What have I done with my life?"

"You should get some sleep."

"No, I'm fine. What'd you want to tell me?"

"It can wait. I'm gonna—"

"No, tell me. What is it?"

"There's been a break in the case. Doug used those traffic photos to get a search warrant and had forensics give Wesley's place a careful once-over. They found trace amounts of Marsh and Bertram's blood on the premises. Wesley's cell phone records show several calls to and from Denise Bertram on the night of the murder and a few more in the days leading up to it. According to some of George's colleagues, he's always carried a torch for her. The theory going around is that Denise figured out Bill was sleeping with another woman and put George up to the murders. We tried to bring her in for questioning, but it looks like she's skipped town. She's cleared out her bank account and left the boy with her parents."

"That's interesting," I said, only half hearing him.

"So that's pretty much that. It looks like we got our guy."

"Yeah, I guess so."

"Oh, one other thing. You remember that guy Dantrell Miles you had me look into? He's dead. He was found murdered out in Lawndale. The fire department was responding to a house fire, and they discovered him and another guy shot to death in the basement. Looks like some kind of gang beef. Miles was tied to a chair and had been tortured before taking one to the back of the head."

"No kidding," I said, my mind drifting back to the scene at Meeks' house.

"Hey, what's wrong? You don't sound happy. I thought you'd be relieved. It's over. You're free."

"You're right. I'm just tired."

"Okay, I'll let you get some rest. It sounds like you could use it. And hey, you're a pain in the ass, but I'd miss you."

"Thanks, man. Right back at'cha. You're my brother from another mother."

"Okay, get some rest. Forget about this bullshit."

We hung up, and I dialed Edgar Marsh. A servant answered. "Just a moment," she said when I asked for her employer.

I waited longer than usual before Marsh's voice emerged on the line, sounding tired, almost sedate. "Mr. Wozniak, I'm glad you called. I've heard from the police, a Detective Greshing. It appears they've found my daughter's killer. If you send me a bill, I'll cut you a check as soon as possible."

That was my chance, my way out. I should've just taken the money and walked away, but something wouldn't let me.

"Mr. Marsh, I wouldn't get my hopes up just yet," I said. "There are still a lot of unanswered questions and—"

"And nothing," he shot, sounding a little more like his old self. "George Wesley murdered my daughter. I just hope the police find him and bring him to justice so my wife and I can get some closure."

"Mr. Marsh, I might have a lead on Wesley's whereabouts. I ran into him last night at a house on the west side of the city. I had gone there to see a couple of informants. When I got there, I found them both murdered. Wesley ambushed me and tried to kill me, but someone interfered, and I survived. It was dark, and I didn't get the best look at the guy, but he was tall with dark spiky hair and a pale complexion. He knocked Wesley unconscious and stuffed him in the trunk of his car. He took him somewhere. I've run into this guy before on a couple of occasions. Once at a meeting of your daughter's anti-war group, and then once near my home. I get the sense he's been following me and keeping tabs on the case. I don't know who he is or what his role is in all of this, but I intend to find out."

I paused for a moment, hoping that Mr. Marsh would interject, but there was only the labored sound of his breathing on the other end of the line.

"Mr. Marsh?"

"I think you should leave things to the police. It sounds like Detective Greshing has things under control at this point."

"Whatever happened to not letting the government handle your problems? If you want Wesley brought to justice, we're going to have to find this guy, because he has him."

"Please, enough already. Send me your bill. Your services are no longer needed."

Marsh hung up, leaving me to sit and stew. That should've been it. The case was closed if I wanted it to be, but I had to do things the hard way. Deep down, I knew there was no turning back.

I got in my car and drove back north to Rogers Park, my gun hidden under the passenger seat. There was a sense of inevitability to my journey, as though I was being propelled against my will. I stopped outside the police station on Clark Street, located Lenny's car and waited for him to appear. Like any stakeout, it was not long before boredom and fatigue set in. I developed an acute sense of time, each second passing as slow as a freight train blocking rush hour traffic.

To make matters worse, I was in no shape to be spending hours on end in a car. Every joint and muscle ached. It was enough to make me want to give up and go home. I tried to reignite the rage I had felt earlier. Somewhere amid the fatigue and despair, it smoldered. I just needed to reach down deep and fan the flames a bit. I tried to picture Lenny as he trashed my meager belongings, chortling with glee at my misfortune. That did the trick. I didn't want much: good drink, good food, good music, and the occasional lay. Was that too much to ask? I suppose it is when you get in the way of people with bigger appetites.

Lenny appeared a little before eight in the evening. By then, I was half unconscious, and his sudden appearance had an almost dreamlike quality. For a moment, I sat and stared at his lanky figure in the distance. He staggered to his car, taking swigs from a pint bottle of what appeared to be whiskey. I watched him get in the front seat and turn his key in the ignition. He pulled out of the police station parking lot. I followed a few car lengths behind, tailing him to a vacant two-flat near the Chicago-Evanston border. There he met a skinny kid who couldn't have been more than fifteen or sixteen years old, another child gangster. Lenny followed the kid inside, and moments later, he emerged carrying a small blue athletic bag.

He got back in his car and headed south. I tailed him to a bungalow just off of Peterson Avenue on the Lincolnwood border. He went inside, with the athletic bag in hand. I wasn't sure what to do next, so I waited. A few minutes later, he left the house. My first urge was to follow him, but then I thought better of it. I stuck around, and when he had been gone for an adequate amount of time, I went around to the back of the house and peered in the kitchen window. Finding all the lights out, I jimmied the lock and went inside.

If there were a Mrs. Lenny, she had no say whatsoever in the interior decorating. Lenny had covered the walls in cheaply framed sports posters and cheesecake prints, the furniture of the function over fashion variety. I must say, the house was neater than the average bachelor pad. There were no clothes on the floor or dishes in the sink, no musty smells emanating from the bathroom. Lenny seemed to be doing quite well for himself. He owned a big-screen TV, a top-of-the-line stereo system with quadraphonic sound, and a new laptop computer. A picture of an old white-haired biddy sat on a shelf next to the TV. Must be the mom.

I imagined she came by weekly and cleaned up after her not-so-little boy—the proud, doting mother unaware that junior had purchased all his expensive things with kickbacks from drug dealers.

I looked around, but no sign of the athletic bag. I made my way downstairs, finding a furnished, wood-paneled basement with a well-stocked bar. The bag sat on the counter with a good twenty grand inside.

I took a break and fixed myself a drink. Something caught my eye on the bar: a Zippo lighter adorned with a raised enamel eight ball. I had bought one just like it at a head shop in the Bahamas one winter while on vacation. Then it hit me. That ugly son of a bitch didn't just trash my place. He robbed me.

I jammed the lighter in my pants pocket and craned my head, searching for more of my possessions. "That motherfucker," I said. And then a little louder, "That fucking asshole!"

No sooner had those words left my mouth than I heard a door closing upstairs. I downed my drink and shut off the lights. I felt my way along the wall to the stairs and headed up. A floorboard creaked just outside the basement door. I stopped in my tracks, about halfway up the staircase, and listened. Nothing.

At first, I wondered if my mind was playing tricks on me, but then the sound of music broke the silence. ABBA's "Take a Chance on Me" blared from the speakers of Lenny's stereo system. A smile crept across my face as I realized the song would provide the perfect cover. For once, I'd get the upper hand. I took the last few stairs two at a time, no longer worrying about the sound, and burst through the door. I pulled my gun, my heart pounding, and made my way to the living room. There I found Lenny standing with his back to me. He held a candlestick in his hand and was lip-syncing to the song.

Now I'd had enough. The fucking asshole who smashed my CD collection was rocking out to ABBA! Lenny lumbered about, red-faced, mouthing the lyrics. He gestured to an imaginary audience, opening his arms plaintively. All the while, ABBA blared from four speakers mounted in each corner of the room, their voices bombarding me from every direction.

I raised my gun, and the weapon felt heavier, as if it had grown overnight. My hands trembled. I closed my eyes moments before squeezing the trigger, unable to watch, afraid I'd miss. To my surprise, my aim was dead on. The sound of the blast drowned out the music before the bullet's impact silenced it altogether. The stereo smoked and sizzled. A brief flowering of sparks shot from the top of the console, and a tinny reverberation filled the room.

Lenny started at the gunshot. He jumped and spun around, taking a few extra steps before coming to a stop. I noticed a glazed look in his eyes and smelled the whiskey on his breath. His expression went from shock to outrage to hurt to befuddlement, all in the span of a few seconds. He lumbered forward a couple of steps, his lips moving silently trying to form words to express a reality he still hadn't fully grasped. I raised my gun and fired at the ceiling. A brief shower of plaster and dust rained from above, coloring our hair white.

At last, Lenny verbalized what was on his mind: "What the fuck?"

"I'm sorry, Lenny. Does it upset you when people destroy your things?"

The befuddled expression returned. Lenny fumbled for words before resorting to an old standby, "What the fuck?"

"What the fuck? Is that the question? I'm not sure what you're asking, Lenny, but let me take a stab at it. You trashed my house, so this is partly payback. But that's not the only reason I am here. You have information that I want, and I intend to make you give it to me."

Lenny stared at me wild-eyed, sweat gathering on his trembling upper lip. "You shot my stereo," he whimpered.

"What was that, a Bose?"

Lenny nodded, his bottom lip protruding like a kid about to burst into tears.

"Those are nice," I said. "A bit rich for my blood, but I'm not in the lucrative police racket anymore. Big money in those civil service jobs, right, Lenny?"

Lenny wasn't looking at me. He stared dumbfounded at the shattered remains of his sound system. Desiring his attention, I raised my gun and fired at one of his four speakers, another direct hit. I was on a roll.

"Aw, c'mon, knock it off," Lenny said, tears welling up in his eyes. "What do you want from me?"

"If you'll pay attention, I'll tell you. I want you to tell me everything you know about George Wesley and the murders of Bill Bertram and Alison Marsh."

"Oh, George," he wailed, his eyes swelling with tears. He gestured towards the heavens, and then, as if deflating, his shoulders slumped, and his eyes turned towards the floor. He shook his head and muttered something inaudible.

"I'm waiting," I said, gesturing at another one of the mounted speakers with my gun.

Lenny looked up, exasperated. "What's there to tell? He killed them. Homicide has photos of him driving Bill's car the night of the murder, the car the bodies were found in. They found blood samples at his house. What more do you want? He killed them. Okay? Case closed."

"And you were trying to help him cover it up."

"I don't know what you're talking about. I had no idea George was mixed up in that shit."

"No?"

"No."

I raised my gun to another corner of the room, a second speaker in my sights. I was about to pull the trigger when I decided to show Lenny's sound system, or what was left of it, some mercy. I lowered the gun, and Lenny breathed a sigh of relief. I then shot his big-screen TV.

"Son of a bitch!" he screamed. "Are you fucking crazy?" He paused for a moment before crying, "Oh my God!"

"Lenny, you're just making things harder on yourself by lying. I'm going to keep shooting your stuff until I hear the truth. Now let's try this again. I was at Dantrell Miles' apartment when you and George paid a visit. I saw you there. Now, what were you two up to?"

"I don't believe you."

"No? You found some gay porn in Dantrell's bedroom and freaked George out with it. Sound familiar?"

Lenny sighed. "All right, we were there looking for some payback. George said that Miles was the one who murdered Bill."

"Because of the bar fight?"

"That and the fact that his alibi didn't hold up."

"What do you mean?"

"He told Curtis that he had been at home asleep that night, but that was a lie. A girl named Wanda was at his place looking for some money. She claims Dantrell was her baby-daddy. Wanda and her boy were outside his place all night waiting for him, and he never came home. She even started calling around to his gangbanger friends, asking where he was and when he would be back, so when Miles told Curtis that he'd been at home that night, he knew his story was bullshit. Looking back, I guess that made Miles the perfect fall guy."

I didn't know if Lenny was lying or not, but I played the heavy once more.

"And that's that?"

"I swear."

"I'd sure hate for anything else to happen to all this fine shit you got here." I raised my gun once more and aimed at his laptop computer.

"I'm telling you—"

I fired before he could finish. This time was entirely out of spite, but I soon regretted it. At first, Lenny cringed at the sound, but then his expression changed. There was a look of realization followed by an ear-to-ear grin that sent chills down my spine.

"What're you smiling about?" I said.

"I'm smiling because I can count," he said, sounding surprisingly sober.

"What do you mean?"

"Your gun holds six bullets, and you've used five. The next thing you shoot better be me because if not, I'm going to hurt you real bad for what you did to my stuff."

He was right. I was down to my last bullet. "I guess I'll have to blow your fucking head off then."

Lenny smiled. "You're no killer. I've known killers, and you don't fit the bill, not by any stretch of the imagination. Worse comes to worst, you'll shoot me in the leg or the arm and run out of here going, 'Oh my God! Oh my God! Oh my God!' And then I'll get better and show you how it's done."

He was right. I wasn't prepared to kill him. I didn't spend the last couple of years rooted to a bar stool, cultivating a gut because I was a man of action.

"That's okay," I said. "I think I've got all that I need here."

Lenny folded his arms and glared at me. I met his gaze and stared back at him, trying to look hard. He didn't seem impressed. His smile returned. It was a psychotic smile. He bared his teeth like a snarling dog, and his eyes were practically popping out of his head. I backed out of his house, watching him with a wide-eyed expression that he must've just loved.

I don't know what was worse: the fear of seeing Lenny again or knowing that I had now screwed things up beyond the point of repair. I was neither a competent investigator nor a believable heavy. I got in my car and started it, taking one last glance back at Lenny's house before pulling away.

I could see him in the window watching me, not so much looking at me but past me to a day when we'd meet again.

TWENTY-FOUR

I had an urgent appointment with a bottle of Irish whiskey back at the office. It was a little before eleven, and the fourteenth floor was quiet, aside from the ambient hum of fluorescent lights overhead. I inserted my key in the door, and as I did, someone stepped around the corner and jammed a gun into my side.

Ambushed again.

"Oh, for fuck's sake," I said under my breath.

"Don't turn around until I tell you," said a voice. A woman's voice. She spoke the words into my left ear, and I could feel her warm breath on my neck. She smelled sweet, like lilacs, and if it weren't for the gun, I might've been aroused.

"Open the door and step inside your office," the woman said.

I did as I was told. The woman followed right behind me and closed the door. I could feel her patting me down and removing my gun.

"Okay, you can turn around now," the woman said.

I turned to find Denise Bertram holding a standard-issue police revolver. It looked massive and unwieldy in her small, trembling hand.

"Hey, why don't you put that down," I said. "I'm not going to hurt you."

Denise shook her head.

"Do you mind if I sit?"

Another quick shake of the head, her expression anxious and wide-eyed.

"Go ahead," she said.

"Would you like a drink?"

"What do you have?"

"Whiskey."

"Any vodka?"

"This is an office, not a bar. Whiskey is all that's on the menu."

"No, thank you. I'm not much of a whiskey drinker."

"Do you mind if I have one? It's been a rough few days, and I could use a drink."

"No, go ahead."

"I'll have to reach inside my desk. You have nothing to worry about. You have my gun."

Denise said nothing and tensed up.

"Or how 'bout you open the desk and get me the bottle?"

"Okay, just move back and keep your hands where I can see them."

I did as she said and raised my hands above my head while scooting backward in my chair. Denise made her way to my side of the desk.

"It's in the top right-hand drawer," I said, motioning towards it with my chin.

Denise opened the drawer and retrieved the bottle, placing it on the desk. She was about to close the drawer when I stopped her. "I'm sorry, there's a cup in there as well. Would you mind grabbing that too?"

Denise placed a coffee cup next to the bottle and stepped away from the desk. She was in a bad way. I could see it on her face. She had the desperate look of someone with a million debts, and they'd all come due at once. I scooted back up to the desk, poured myself a stiff drink, and downed it. Denise took a seat in the visitor's chair. She rested the hand with the gun on her lap, the barrel still pointing at me.

"What brings you to my office, Mrs. Bertram?"

"I came here because I know you're working the case, and you're not a cop. I thought you might hear me out."

"Do I have a choice?"

"I'm sorry about the gun, but I can't take any chances."

All the color had drained from her face. Even her lips were pale. I watched them as she spoke.

"You've searched me and looked inside my desk. I'm obviously unarmed."

Denise hesitated for a moment before nodding. "Okay," she said, placing the gun inside her purse.

"That's better. Now tell me what you know and be straight with me. I can't help you unless you're entirely honest."

Denise took a deep breath and exhaled, a slight wheeze to her sigh. "I don't know what you've heard, but George didn't kill my husband, and I never asked him to. Don't get me wrong; I wanted my husband dead, but we had nothing to do with his murder."

"I take it you knew about your husband and the girl."

Denise clutched the strap of her purse, twisting it between her fingers. "Yes, I went through this with Bill before and recognized all the usual signs. I suspected something when he started coming home in the middle of the night, smelling freshly showered like he was trying to cover his tracks."

"So, you started following him."

"Yeah, and I was the one who found them in that motel room."

"So, what makes you think George had nothing to do with the murders?"

"I just know." She paused for a moment and took a deep breath. "I should backtrack a little. Have you ever heard of a man named Curtis Bledsoe?"

"I have. Why?"

"He's a drug dealer, and Bill's narcotics unit had an arrangement with him. From what I hear, the deal was Captain Morrow's idea. He agreed to ignore Bledsoe's operation for a cut of each week's profits and his guys behaving themselves, meaning no turf battles and only dealing in certain areas."

"What does this have to do with the murders?"

"I guess Bill started acting funny, and it was making Bledsoe and Morrow nervous."

"How was he acting funny?"

"I don't know. Bill was giving Bledsoe's guys a hard time, criticizing Captain Morrow and some of the other cops. That kind of stuff. I think he became disenchanted with the Bledsoe arrangement after Stephanie died. Did anyone tell you about Stephanie?"

"Yeah, Stephanie Landau, the girl who lived across the street from you."

Denise nodded. "Right, she suffered a heroin overdose, and it was one of Bledsoe's dealers who sold her the drugs. Her death devastated Bill. He had known her since she was a little girl. She used to babysit our son. Bill was constantly on edge after that, always losing his cool. From the sounds of things, he was as bad or worse on the job. I think that's why Morrow had him go on special assignment. He wanted Bill to get away and clear his head."

"But that didn't work."

"No, meeting those anti-war people just seemed to make him more disillusioned. He was worse than ever. One day, Morrow calls George into his office and says that Bill was going to get himself hurt if he didn't settle down. That night, George went home to find Bledsoe and a couple of his guys sitting in his living room. They told him much the same thing: get your partner under control, or we'll do it for you. George was sure they were going to kill him if something wasn't done fast."

"So, what did he do?"

"He tried to talk some sense into him. George tried to get him to end things with that girl. He told him she was filling his head with crazy ideas that were going to get him killed, but Bill just wouldn't listen."

"I still don't see how any of this clears George."

"I'm getting to that. The night of the murder, I followed them to the Stardust. I watched them check-in and head up to their room. They looked so happy together, just laughing and smiling as if they didn't have a care in the world."

She stopped, tears streaming down her face. I thought I should do something, perhaps give her a tissue, but I didn't have any in the office, and I didn't know what to say, so I did nothing.

Denise took a deep breath and continued. "Seeing them together, I lost it. Do you know how many nights I sat up waiting for that man to come home, worried he'd been hurt or killed on the job? I drove around for hours, just getting angrier and angrier thinking about all his lies. I stopped at home, took one of his guns, and headed back to the motel. I sat in the car for a while, just thinking about what I was going to say to him, what I was going to do. I wound up calling George, hoping he'd talk me down."

"What did he say?"

"He said I should leave him, that I deserved better. He said he wasn't worth a prison sentence and that I should think of my son."

"What did you say?"

"I asked him if he knew."

"Did he?"

"He wouldn't say, but he didn't have to. He knew, and he knew that I knew he knew, so I hung up on him. He tried calling me back, but I ignored the call. I just sat there and cried until I couldn't cry anymore. I considered going home, but then I thought about what they were doing in that motel room, and I wanted nothing more than to watch him and his little whore squirm, so I went up. I was about to knock on the door when I noticed it was ajar. It was too dark to see anything, so I flipped on the lights, and there they were in bed, the sheets soaked with blood. They had been shot several times. I'll never forget the looks on their faces like they were frozen in that moment watching it happen. It was all so horrible."

Denise broke down again. This time she reached into her purse and pulled out a tissue. She dabbed at her eyes and blew her nose.

"So then what happened?" I asked.

"I took George back to the motel room," she said without looking up. "I tried to prepare him for what he would see, but there's no way to soften the blow of seeing someone you were close to dead. Poor George turned as white as a sheet."

"What did he say?"

"He kept saying, 'I'm sorry, Bill. I tried to stop them.'"

"I take it by 'them' he meant Bledsoe and Morrow."

"It looked like a professional job. Whoever killed them had broken in and fired several shots without disturbing anyone in the adjacent rooms."

"So then what happened?"

"George calmed down and told me to go home. He said that he would take care of everything. So I went home and waited for him to call. I stayed up all night, alone."

"Where was Bill Jr.?"

"I had left him with my parents. It was just me in a big house by myself. I remember I couldn't sit still, so I just wandered about the house. I turned on all the lights. At one point, I took one of Bill's shirts out of the hamper and sat on the bed, holding it. I buried my face in it and smelled his scent. It's funny, just a few hours before, I wanted him dead, and now that he was gone, I missed him so bad it hurt. Have you ever lost someone close to you?"

"My father," I said. "We weren't close, but..."

"But he was your dad," Denise said, her voice quavering.

"Right."

We fell silent for a moment. Denise found another tissue and dabbed at her eyes.

"George came by the house a little before dawn and said everything had been taken care of. He looked exhausted. He took a seat on the sofa, and we didn't say another word to each other. I was too afraid to ask him what had happened, and he was too tired to talk. After a while, he dozed off. I still couldn't sleep, so I cleaned up around the house. I scrubbed the bathrooms, the kitchen. The next day I heard about the fire at the Stardust on the news, and I knew."

"George had destroyed the crime scene and disposed of the bodies."

Denise nodded.

"But why? I still don't get why he would cover up someone else's crime."

"At first, George was certain Bledsoe was behind Bill's murder. Just a few days before, Bill had a run-in with one of Bledsoe's men, a guy named Dantrell Miles. George figured that was the last straw and that Dan Morrow had given the hit his blessing. After I left, he called Dan and confronted him about it."

"And what did Morrow have to say?"

"He said he had nothing to do with it, and he doubted Bledsoe would act without consulting him first. But Miles, he was a different story."

"Morrow suspected Miles?"

"They both did. He's a professional killer, and it looked like a professional hit. That's why they didn't want to risk an investigation. There was no way they could just sweep the murders of a cop and a rich girl under the rug. If the investigation led back to Miles, it would only be a matter of time before their arrangement with Bledsoe was discovered."

"So it was Morrow's idea to cover up the murders."

"Yes."

"All because Dantrell got in a fight with your husband?"

"He threatened to kill him. Besides, you don't understand. These guys are animals. I don't know how many times Bill or George had to cover for them because they had beaten some poor guy half to death over a debt or for 'dissing' them. Half the time, these knuckleheads were at each other's throats. From what I've heard, Miles was crazier than most. He even stabbed his own mother."

"It was his mother's boyfriend."

"Huh?"

"It wasn't his mother. It was his mother's boyfriend."

"Right, mother's boyfriend, whatever."

Whatever? I thought about Miles and Meeks, and all the pain George inflicted on them because he played judge, jury, and executioner after only a cursory examination of the facts. Yeah, Denise, whatever.

She must've sensed what I was thinking because she lowered her eyes, her voice going quiet. "I should've said something. I should've spoken up, but George told me I would have to be quiet. He reminded me that everything I had—my house, clothes, jewelry—was bought with the money Bill had made from the Bledsoe deal and that I stood to lose everything if it was exposed. He said that he would find Bill's killer and bring him to justice himself. And you know what? I believed him because he loved Bill like a brother."

"So, now what?"

"So now I'm going to go somewhere far away. I left my son with my parents. Life on the run is no way to raise a child. I'm hoping you'll help me. Perhaps if you clear my name, I can go home and resume my life. I don't want my boy to lose both his parents, but I don't see what choice I have. I stay here, and it's prison or worse for me. Who knows what Bledsoe and Morrow will do to keep my mouth shut?"

She was right. She was as good as dead if she stayed.

"So will you help me?" she asked. "I don't have much money, but—"

"Forget about the money. I'm seeing this thing through to the end. To be honest, I'm in too deep myself to turn back."

Denise stood up. She came around to my side of the desk and kissed me on the cheek. I closed my eyes and inhaled the scent of lilacs one last time.

"Thank you, Mr. Wozniak," she said. "Hopefully, we'll meet again someday."

With that, she returned my gun and left my office. I watched her silhouette through the frosted glass of my office door. It moved to the right, out of my line of view, and then I heard the click of her heels as they faded down the hallway.

TWENTY-FIVE

I lay on the floor of a house that seemed familiar and new all at once. Somewhere in the distance, a phone rang. A door stood open before me, and a dull, natural light cast a thick V-shaped swath on the floor. A long, warped shadow formed on this small canvas, and my eyes tracked it to the dark figure of a tall, slender man. He approached, his pale white face hovering above me. Somewhere off in the distance, the phone rang again. I tried to move but couldn't, my body rooted to the floor. He reached down, long, willowy fingers stretching towards me.

For a moment, my eyes struggled to focus. The shadow of something dark and monolithic loomed above me before the scene dissolved in a hazy rush of light. Everything came into focus. I was lying on the floor of my office, staring up at my desk. My shirt was damp with sweat, my collar soaked and chilling the back of my neck. My cell phone rang, and the sound jarred me back to reality. I struggled to my feet and reached for the phone, answering it a moment too late.

I set the phone down and picked up the bottle of whiskey on my desk. Not a drop left. I tossed it into the wastebasket, and the glass struck the bottom of the metal canister with a loud thud.

I turned to look out the window. Milwaukee Avenue stretched before me, a shallow canyon of discount clothing shops, furniture emporiums, and the odd overpriced boutique catering to the moneyed young professionals flooding the area. It was late, with just a few people milling about at the bus stop across from the El and two men kitty-corner from them leaving a bar. The scene looked small and artificial, like an urban diorama.

I collapsed in my chair, exhausted, and checked the clock. It was a little after three in the morning. The phone rang again, the sound amplified tenfold by the silence preceding it. I hesitated for a moment before answering on the fourth ring. A recorded message said that I had a collect call from an inmate at Stateville Correctional Center. I accepted the charges.

"Hello?"

"Is this Glenn Wozniak?" said the voice on the other end of the line.

"Speaking."

"It's Freddy Baxter. Remember me? You visited me the other day at Stateville prison."

"Of course. What's going on, Freddy?"

"It's Dantrell. He's in trouble."

He didn't know the half of it. "You don't say. How so?"

"A cop came to visit me. A guy by the name of George Wesley. He was asking about Dantrell. He told me some of Curtis Bledsoe's boys had a beef with me, but he'd see to my safety if I told him what he wanted to know."

"So, what did you say?"

"I asked him why they had a problem with me, and he said, 'It's because you're friends with the wrong people.' I didn't want to help him, but Curtis got some scary motherfuckers up in here. Anyway, I was hoping you could give him a heads up."

Part of me felt disappointed and angry that Freddy caved and gave up his friend, but then I wasn't a young kid in prison. I didn't have the heart to tell him he was too late. "I'll see what I can do," I said.

"And could you let him know I'm sorry?"

"Yeah," I said, hanging up. I laid the phone on my desk, and an unsettling feeling came over me. I half-expected to see the silhouette of a dark figure standing in the frosted glass window of my office door. I retrieved my gun from the top drawer of my desk, loaded it, and hunkered down for a long evening. After 9/11, the government urged everyone to remain vigilant. I wondered if this was what they meant. I was ready to kill the next motherfucker who walked through that door. Shoot first and ask questions later.

God knows how long I sat like that, but my fatigue must've overwhelmed my fear because the next thing I knew, it was morning. I awoke to a bright sun warming the back of my neck and pain that felt like a jackbooted foot pressing down hard on my forehead. My face lay flat against the desk, my chin damp with drool, and when I raised my head, a piece of paper clung to my cheek for a second before releasing.

I got up and used the washroom, still paranoid enough to arm myself for the trip. When I returned, I resumed staring at the frosted window of my door, unsure what to do next.

I couldn't help thinking about George Wesley. Man, he must've been desperate. He should've laid low and stayed away, but he couldn't. He had to know if the police were getting close. He had to know if they had linked Alison to Bill and Bill to his captain's web of corruption. I must not have been a welcome sight. The last thing he needed was a private investigator poking into the case. But as it turned out, he was little more than a detour, one that almost got me killed.

I believed Denise. Someone else murdered Bill and Alison. George hunted and killed Dantrell Miles, like a man avenging the death of a friend. That was genuine.

I pulled out what few case files I had and pored over them. There wasn't a lot to go on, just some notes on the interviews I conducted, a few half-formed impressions I had scribbled down that no longer made any sense to me, and some photos of Alison's possessions and artwork. I thumbed through the pictures, stopping on one that had caught my eye the first time I saw it. A man stood in the center of the canvas, menacing a doe-eyed little girl in a frilly, baby-blue dress. He was tall with dark, spiky hair that receded into a sharp widow's peak in the front. His skin was bone-white, and his hands large with long, slender fingers like the dark stranger I kept encountering on the case, the man now haunting my dreams. Alison knew him, but from where?

I pictured him outside the Meeks' home, dragging George Wesley's body, his face streaked with blood, looking primal and sinister. I couldn't believe this was the same meek, kind-hearted man I'd encountered at the anti-war meeting, the same civic-minded square that chastised him for drunk driving. What had he said? "The next time, it might not be a tree. It might be a person. You might plow into a mother of two and orphan her kids."

Then it hit me. Erica had mentioned Edgar's first wife dying in a drunk driving accident, one in which she struck and killed a mother of two. I turned on my computer and searched the Web for information on the Marsh family. I found articles about Edgar's philanthropic work, the sale of his business, and the sad fate of the areas surrounding the company's industrial campus after Federated Components moved operations to Mexico. I kept searching until I found what I was looking for: the obituary for Edgar's first wife,

Leslie. One sentence caught my eye: Leslie is survived by her husband, Edgar, and her son, Jeremy.

I picked up the photo of Alison's painting and studied the pale, dark-haired figure at its center, remembering that I had mistaken him for a young Edgar Marsh the first time I had seen it. I thought back to Alison's memorial service. Not one person in that room full of family and friends ever so much as mentioned Jeremy. It was as if he had never existed, but then I remembered a photo I saw that evening of Alison as a young girl, sledding down a snowy hill in the arms of a boy with dark hair and a fair complexion. The boy was maybe five or six years her senior, the approximate age difference between her and her half-brother.

I put in a call to Erica Whitcombe. She sounded surprised to hear from me.

"What are you doing this evening?"

"Nothing. Why?"

"You want to meet for a drink?"

"Okay, or if you'd like a quiet night in, you could come over here, and we could rent some movies."

That was no good. I wanted to make a quick escape. "Let's start with drinks and take it from there."

"You want to meet at McGinty's? That was the bar we went to after Alison's memorial."

"Oh, right, sure."

"How does eight o'clock sound?"

"It's a date."

We hung up, and I resumed searching the Internet. A few minutes passed when I heard voices in the hallway. I grabbed my gun and went to the door. I opened it a crack and could make out the voice of the dentist from down the hall.

"Glenn Wozniak's office?" he said. "It's right around the corner, number 1414."

"Thanks," said a voice I didn't recognize, a man's voice.

I ducked into the washroom across the hall. Heavy staccato footsteps sounded in the corridor. I peered out through a crack in the door to see a man in a beige trench coat stop outside my office. He was a young guy with a crew cut and a build made for busting heads. I pegged him as a cop. The only mystery was who had sent him and why. Was it one of Morrow's boys, sent to tie up another loose end? Or perhaps Captain Montanez had decided to run me in for telling Gerry Lombardo about Bill Bertram.

Crewcut leaned against the door frame and rapped on the frosted window with his knuckles. A few seconds passed before he tried again and, hearing no answer, went inside. That was my cue to leave. I zipped past my office to the stairwell at the end of the hall and clambered down the stairs, taking them two at a time. I didn't look back for fear of seeing Crewcut, or worse, following behind me. When I reached the bottom, I burst through the door into the vestibule. A few old ladies waiting to enter the bank on the first floor eyed me with suspicion. I must've been quite a sight in dirty, rumpled clothing—my face covered in cuts and bruises, my hand clutching a revolver. I stuffed the gun down the front of my pants.

"Ladies," I said with a bow.

They looked at each other and scurried into the bank. Seconds later, a barrel-chested man in a security guard outfit stepped into the vestibule and gave me the evil eye. I headed for the door, breaking into a jog the moment I got outside. It was a brisk, windy day, and my coat was back in the office.

I headed to my apartment, parking a couple of blocks from my building. Something told me I wouldn't be going home, that I'd need to make a quick getaway. Sure enough, as I approached my place, I noticed a blue sedan—a late nineties Ford that had seen better days—idling across from my building. Two men sat in the front seat. I recognized one of them as Doug Greshing. Part of me wanted to get his attention, because as old and out of shape as I was, Doug was older and in worse shape, and making him run would give me one last satisfaction before the fucker could bring me in. I saw my future, and it involved hours of answering questions in a small, uncomfortable room, Doug playing all the same mind games I had played once upon a career.

I cut through a neighbor's backyard and peeked into the alley. Just as I expected, a second sedan sat idling behind my building. I waited a few minutes until I could no longer stand the cold and returned to my car.

Where next? I wondered. My date with Erica was not for another few hours. I started the car and drove east until I came across the Cabrini Green housing project, or at least what was left of it. Developers had moved in and seized the prime real estate linking Wicker Park to the Gold Coast. They moved in with talk of the housing project's failure and promises of mixed-income alternatives, accepting a few of the less objectionable poor into their condos and town-houses while displacing everyone else. Only a few buildings remained occupied, the place a virtual ghost town. I'd be safe there.

I turned onto a side street bordering a stretch of row houses. An old black woman, hunched and twisted, passed by pushing a shopping cart in front of her. A young boy, no more than eight years old, trailed behind her. One of his small dark hands gripped the bottom of the woman's dress. He swung the fabric from one side to the other. The old woman looked back at the child and smiled.

I watched them as they headed down the block out of sight, feeling nostalgic for the days when I was a boy spend-ing the day with my grandma. It wouldn't be too long be-fore that child's life became more difficult. Dantrell Miles was once a boy, as were Julius Meeks and George Wesley; everyone was once somebody's baby. I thought about the child I had encountered at Wanda Briggs' apartment. Young Malcolm already lived in a world of pain, raised amongst the violence of a drug trade that had already claimed his father's life. Bill Jr. had lost one parent and would soon lose another.

An overwhelming sadness settled in the pit of my stomach. It felt like acid gnawing away at my gut. I slapped an open palm against the steering wheel in frustration.

This was rock bottom—the nadir of a sad, unremarkable life. I had so little, and now it was all gone: my business, my home, my meager possessions. I had an eight o'clock date with Erica Whitcombe, but then what? Where would I go? What would I do?

I switched on the radio, turning to the news. The president stumped for war. "In Iraq, a dictator is building and hiding weapons that could enable him to dominate the Middle East and intimidate the civilized world, and we will not allow it," he warned before I switched him off.

I peered up at the sky. It was another gray day, dark clouds casting a pall over everything. Somewhere in the distance, a siren blared, and I wondered if it was meant for me.

TWENTY-SIX

I arrived at McGinty's about an hour early and desperate for a drink. Part of me was thrilled to be in a bar, any bar. Another part of me wished I had accepted Erica's offer of a quiet night at her place because I kept checking the front door for cops. Two beers and two shots later, I settled down and watched a Blackhawks game on the big-screen TVs, my forearms resting on the bar. Erica arrived just as I was finishing my third beer. She looked the same as she did at the funeral, dressed in a black blouse and skirt, her dark hair mussed in a way that could only be intentional.

"Hey," she said, giving me a playful shove. "Been waiting long?"

"I'm still somewhat sober, so no, not too long."

Erica's eyes widened at my swollen nose and the raccoon mask surrounding my eyes. "Oh my God, what happened to you?"

"It's a long story, and I'd rather not get into it right now."

She leaned down, studying my collection of cuts and abrasions. "Are you okay?"

"I've been better, but I'll be all right. I don't think I've suffered any permanent damage."

Erica straightened and flashed a smile. "That's good."

I bought us a couple of drinks, and we moved over to a table. Small talk killed a couple of minutes before awkwardness and silence settled in.

"It's good to see you," I said, breaking a particularly long pause.

"Thanks, it's good to see you too."

"I was hoping we'd have a chance to talk."

Erica nodded, with a tight smile on her face.

"I wanted to ask you a few questions about your cousin."

Her expression changed. She frowned, and her face drooped as though that tightly wound smile were the only thing keeping her features from crashing to the floor. "Is that why you called me?"

"No, I wanted to see you."

I could almost see icicles growing from her eyes. "You have about three days' worth of stubble; your clothes look like you slept in them, and, frankly, you smell a little ripe. If this is how you act when you're interested in a girl, I'd hate to catch you on one of your more casual days."

"I can explain," I said, my mind going blank.

"Well?"

"Look, I like you. I do. I think you're an attractive girl."

Erica sighed. "Just tell me what's going on."

"What's going on is I need some help with your cousin's case."

"What do you mean? I thought they had found the killer. It's that Wesley guy. They have photos of him driving the car the bodies were found in, and they discovered the victims' blood in his house."

"They did, but that doesn't necessarily make him the murderer. I believe someone else killed your cousin, and I was hoping you might be able to help me find him."

"I doubt that, but I'll try. What do you want to know?"

"What can you tell me about Alison's brother?"

Erica stiffened in her seat.

"What's wrong?"

"Nothing," she said, avoiding eye contact. "Alison doesn't have a brother?"

"Yes, she does."

"He's her half-brother."

"Okay, half-brother. What can you tell me about Jeremy Marsh?"

"What's to tell? What does he have to do with anything?"

I told her about the painting and my various encounters with him. "It's my only remaining lead."

Erica bit her bottom lip, the flesh turning pale between her teeth. She shook her head. "Would you excuse me for a moment?" she said, standing up. "I need to use the washroom."

"Sure, go ahead."

I watched her walk away. She stopped outside the corridor leading to the women's room and glanced in my direction before disappearing inside. I got up from the table and followed her. I placed an ear to the washroom door but couldn't hear anything over the jukebox and the noise of the crowd. I opened the door a crack and listened.

"Do you know when Uncle Edgar will be back?" Erica said, adding after a pause, "Okay, will you tell him I called?"

I returned to my seat. The place was hopping, lines of people gathering three deep around the bar to order drinks. The Pixies' "Velouria" came on the jukebox, and a couple of women in their early thirties let out a shriek of appreciation.

Erica returned. "Sorry, I just needed to freshen up," she said, sitting down.

I smiled. "Not a problem. So, where were we?"

"I think we were about to order a couple more drinks. Irish whiskey, right? I remember you carried a flask with you at the funeral."

"The drinks can wait. I'd rather talk about Jeremy."

Erica shifted in her seat, looking like she'd rather be any place in the world than sitting across from me at that moment. "I don't know what to tell you. He's her half-brother. We weren't close. I haven't seen him in years."

"What's wrong?"

"What do you mean?"

"You look uncomfortable."

"No, I'm fine. It's just been a long day." Erica stood up. "I'm going to go get us some drinks, okay?"

I didn't answer. I just looked at her and watched the tension build in her features, watched it collect and intensify in her eyes.

"What?"

"Is it because of your uncle?"

Erica sat down. "What do you mean?" she asked, her voice getting quiet.

"Are you afraid to say anything because of your uncle?"

"Say anything about what?"

"About Jeremy." Erica was about to speak, but I cut her off. "The mere mention of his name sets you on edge."

She shook her head, her eyes downcast. "I don't know what you're talking about."

"Listen, Erica, Alison's killer is still out there, and he'll get away with murder, perhaps hurt someone else, if you don't help me. Jeremy's the key."

Erica paused for a moment, her dark eyes welling with tears. "Okay, I'll talk, but you have to promise me you won't tell Uncle Edgar I told you any of this."

"I promise."

"What do you want to know?"

"Did Alison and Jeremy grow up together?"

"Yes, they were close at one time. I think Alison was his only friend. To be honest, he was kind of a loser. He had a lot of interests but no real dreams or ambitions. I remember him always collecting stuff—action figures, model cars, comic books—like he was a little kid. He dropped out of college and moved back home after one semester. Uncle Edgar gave him a job at Marsh Enterprises. He worked in the warehouse. I think he said he was a foreman. I'm not sure. It was a while ago. Jeremy and Ally were pretty much inseparable, which wasn't exactly the best for her social life. After all, what teenager wants to hang around with a weird, nerdy guy in his twenties? I know I found him creepy, and we were related."

"So what became of him? He wasn't at the funeral."

"I don't know. As I said, no one's seen Jeremy in years. From what I hear, he had a falling out with my uncle and disappeared."

"Did your uncle ever say what happened?"

Erica ran an index finger through the condensation her glass had left on the table. "No, he didn't want to talk about it, though I have my suspicions. Alison went into the hospital, the psych ward, shortly before Jeremy disappeared, and her hospitalization coincided with my uncle throwing Jeremy out of the house. But here's the interesting part: a couple of weeks later, she snuck out of the hospital and ran away. Guess where they found her?"

"I don't know."

Erica leaned across the table. "In a motel room with Jeremy," she whispered. She leaned back in her seat and looked at me, eyebrows raised.

"You think Jeremy was sleeping with his sister?"

"Half-sister, not that that's any better. I told you my family was fucked up. That was the last anyone heard of him. Uncle Edgar sent Alison away to a boarding school in Vermont, which is where she stayed until she graduated. She then came home and enrolled at the Art Institute. You know the rest."

I rose from my seat.

"Wait, where are you going?"

"I've got to go. I've got to talk to Mr. Marsh."

Erica stood up, a panicked expression on her face. "You promised you wouldn't tell him I told you."

"I won't. I'm a private investigator, remember? I find things out for a living."

"But I thought we were going to have some drinks, maybe go back to my place." She trailed off before perking up. "You know what? I just called him, and he's not home."

"Then I'll do something I've meant to do for the last couple of weeks and talk to his wife."

Erica sighed.

"Look, I'll call you," I said. It was the worst possible line, a boilerplate brush-off, but I was in a hurry.

Erica slumped back into her seat and folded her arms in front of her. "Fine."

"I'm sorry, Erica."

She looked up at me. "Where's your coat?"

"I don't have one. I left it in the office, and I can't go back there right now."

Erica's expression changed from disappointment to pity. She reached into her purse and withdrew a few dollars. "Here, take it."

"That's not necessary."

"I insist."

I didn't have time to argue. "Thanks. I'll call you. I promise."

Erica nodded and flashed an expression that said, 'Sure you will, pal.'

I returned to my car and sat in the dark for a moment, letting all I had learned sink in. I couldn't help but feel cheated. The old man hadn't played straight with me. Jeremy's existence didn't just slip his mind. Marsh had only told me what he wanted me to know and hoped I'd only tell him those things he wanted to be true. Those days were over. One way or another, I was going to get some answers.

TWENTY-SEVEN

I headed northwest towards my employer's home in the suburb of Inverness. Traffic was heavy within the city. I crawled along, catching red light after red light, creeping towards the expressway and the hope of an open road.

I thought back to the day I met Edgar Marsh. "I'm a private man," he had said, "and I don't wish to have my affairs discussed with anyone other than myself."

Yet he hired me, a total stranger. Why? Marsh must have had a stable of guys he could turn to in a pinch. After all, he hired someone to tail Erica when she had a drug problem as a teenager. The thought gnawed at me as I sat in stop-and-go traffic, this inescapable suspicion that all was not as it seemed. I couldn't help feeling cheated and used. It was a queasy sensation, a corrosive emptiness in my gut.

When I finally made it out of the city, it was a relief, a chance to clear my head and focus on the road before me. My car plunged ahead, the traffic thinning enough for me to maintain a steady rate of seventy miles per hour. I accelerated, racing through the shallow canyon of the Edens Expressway. Billboards loomed overhead on either side of me, hawking chain restaurants, cell phone carriers, and hard liquor.

Before long, I was in Inverness. The Marshes moved there after selling the family business. They used to live near their factories on the southernmost edge of the city. After the deal, it appeared they wanted to put some distance between themselves and their former business. So, off they went to the northern suburbs, and a four-story mansion built new for a family dwindling in numbers. It was a sizeable colonial-style structure nestled among a field of recently planted trees. These were young saplings with trunks too thin to obscure the house as much as intended and spaced so uniformly, the estate couldn't help but look artificial.

I pulled up at a gated archway outside the building. The mansion sat atop a small hill, and a long driveway wound its way from the gate to the house. It was an intimidating structure. I peered up at it. The house loomed above me, its sheer size telling me I didn't belong. There was an intercom system at the gate. I rolled down my window and pressed the buzzer. A few seconds later, a man answered.

"Yes?" he said.

"Hi, this is Glenn Wozniak here to see Mr. Marsh."

"Who?"

"Glenn Wozniak. Mr. Marsh hired me to investigate his daughter's disappearance."

There was a pause before the man answered. "Oh, yes, I remember. Mr. Marsh is not in right now. I will let him know you stopped by."

"May I speak to Mrs. Marsh then? It's urgent."

"Do you have an appointment?"

"Tell Mrs. Marsh I'm here to speak with her about Jeremy."

The line went silent. A few minutes later, the gates parted. I headed up the hill, parking behind a burgundy town car. Two rows of well-manicured hedges lined the walk from the driveway to the front entrance. I rang the bell, and the housekeeper answered. She was a heavyset woman with a short, graying natural.

"You here to see Mrs. Marsh?" she said.

"Yes, ma'am," I said, hoping my politeness might win me some brownie points.

The housekeeper told me to follow her. I entered the house and crossed a large hall with a marble floor and high ceilings. There was a staircase to the right and a sitting room to the left. Straight ahead was an archway leading to a long corridor. That's where the housekeeper headed, with me trailing behind her. We stopped at a heavy wooden door with an S-shaped brass handle. The housekeeper opened it, revealing a dark room lined with floor-to-ceiling bookshelves. A bay window overlooked a backyard filled with more of the young saplings I had seen in front. A burgundy sofa sat across the room next to a fireplace and opposite a black leather easy chair with a matching ottoman. A woman reclined in the chair, drinking brandy from a snifter, with her feet up. She wore a silky robe and pajamas. The fire's dancing flames reflected on her glass as warped bursts of orange and white.

Though Margaret Marsh seemed to have aged several years since our last meeting at Alison's funeral, I could now better see a resemblance to her daughter. Perhaps it was because she had lost weight, giving her features the gaunt, haunting appearance I had seen in so many of the girl's photos.

"Let me know if you need anything, Mrs. Marsh," the housekeeper said. "Eugene and I will be right in the kitchen."

"Thank you, Felicia," Margaret said, her voice just above a whisper.

The housekeeper backed out of the room, eyeing me with a distrustful look on her face. Mrs. Marsh sipped her brandy and watched as I took a seat on the sofa. Judging by her expression, she would've been happier to have discovered a cockroach in her drink.

"Thank you for seeing me, Mrs. Marsh."

Margaret didn't respond, her expression a mixture of fear and resentment.

"I wanted to talk to you about your stepson, Jeremy."

"That's what I heard. Look, Mr. Wozniak, I believe you settled on a fair rate with my husband at the beginning of the case, so if you think you're going to come in here and pressure us for more money, you are sadly mistaken."

"Is that what you think this is about?"

"Isn't it?"

"No, this isn't about money. It's about the case."

She stood up. "The case is closed, Mr. Wozniak."

"If only it were that simple."

"Isn't it?"

I straightened in my seat. "No. Why wasn't Jeremy at his sister's funeral?"

Margaret sat back down. She closed her eyes for a moment as though meditating on the subject. "She was his half-sister, and I have no idea. We haven't seen him in a long time. He probably doesn't even know what happened."

"Is that so?"

"Yes."

"What if I told you I had seen him?"

"I wouldn't believe you."

I described him, and Margaret slumped in her chair. "I still don't see what he has to do with anything," she said, her eyes downcast, staring at the remnants of her drink.

"You don't? From what I hear, they didn't have a conventional brother-sister relationship."

Margaret looked up, still not quite making eye contact, one hand clenched tightly into a fist. "I have no idea what you mean."

"No, you know exactly what I mean. Jeremy was sleeping with your little girl."

Margaret looked as though I had slapped her. Tears welled up in her eyes. "Sleeping with her? Is that what you call it? He raped her. He raped her over and over and over again from the time she was a little girl until she turned seventeen. This wasn't something she did willingly. That monster molested her."

"I'm sorry, Mrs. Marsh. I—"

"Mr. Wozniak, this conversation is over."

"Mrs. Marsh, I apologize. I should have chosen my words better."

"Yes, you should have. Now please leave."

"I'm afraid I can't do that. I'm in too deep to just drop things and walk away. Now you have a choice: You can talk to me, or you can talk to Inspector Greshing with the Chicago P.D. It's up to you."

Margaret's eyes narrowed. She regarded me in a way that made me squirm. Her expression, her stance, and the sound of her breathing all told me she wanted me dead. But then she softened, all the fight draining from her face.

"Okay," she said.

"Okay?"

"I'll talk."

"Okay then; why don't you start by telling me more about Alison and Jeremy's relationship. You said Jeremy molested her for years. How did you find out?"

Margaret shifted in her seat and cleared her throat before answering. "Alison began seeing a boy shortly after her seventeenth birthday. Jeremy became jealous and ambushed him one day after school. He beat him with a baseball bat until he was unconscious. The poor kid lost vision in his right eye because of the attack. Edgar, of course, paid a great deal of money to keep things quiet and Jeremy out of jail. When we confronted him about the incident, he said that the boy just wanted to get in Alison's pants, and he wasn't going to let him hurt his little sister. A couple of weeks later, we received a call from one of Alison's teachers. Alison was so shaken by what happened that she confided in her about the abuse. The teacher told Edgar and me."

"What did you do when you found out?"

"We threw him out of the house, and Edgar fired him from his job at Marsh Enterprises. Jeremy pleaded with us to forgive him. He said he was sick and needed help, but Edgar held firm. I mean, how could he ever forgive something like that? How could we ever trust him around our little girl again?"

Margaret stopped. She grabbed a tissue and blew her nose. "I'm sorry, but whenever I think of that monster with my little girl, it just sickens me."

"I understand."

Margaret downed the rest of her brandy. She shuddered, closing her eyes for a moment before continuing, "A few weeks later, Alison tried to commit suicide. One of our servants found her in the tub with her wrists slashed open. There was a letter from Jeremy in her bedroom. I don't know how she got it. We never let her out of our sight. Judging from the letter, Jeremy had no intention of changing. He pledged his undying love to her and said that he'd never let her go.

"We put Alison in the hospital, and things seemed to settle down. Her doctors said she was making progress in her therapy, and as far as we knew, Jeremy had stopped trying to contact her. Then one day, we got a call from the hospital. Alison had gone missing. So, Edgar called someone to find her."

"A private investigator?"

"I guess so. I mean, my husband had a man he'd call for these kinds of situations. Don't ask me his name or what he looks like. I never met him. Edgar said it was best I didn't associate with people like him."

I wondered if she directed that remark at me, if I was 'a person like him.'

"So then what happened?"

"This man found Alison and Jeremy in a motel on the south side of the city, just a couple blocks from Marsh Enterprises. He called Edgar, and the two of them collected Alison and brought her back home. Edgar wrote Jeremy a check. He gave him enough money to start over someplace else. He told Jeremy to leave town and stay as far away as possible from Alison, or else. Later that night, the private investigator, or whatever, came back around with a couple of big guys from the plant. They let Jeremy know in no uncertain terms that there would be consequences for sticking around. That was the last we ever heard from him."

"Why didn't your husband tell me any of this?"

"I guess he didn't see what bearing it had on the case."

"His son molested his daughter for several years and had shown a history of violent behavior. If I were him, Jeremy would have been the first person I thought of when Alison disappeared."

"We didn't think it possible."

"Please be serious."

"I am serious."

"How could you not think it was possible?"

Margaret didn't answer.

"Mrs. Marsh, you can tell me, or you can tell the police. It's your choice."

"Jeremy called Alison a few weeks before her disappearance, so..."

I leaned forward in my seat. "Yes?"

"I told you my husband had a man he called for these kinds of things. We thought..." She paused for a moment, unsure of how to continue. "We thought it had been taken care of."

We both fell silent for a moment. There was a clock on the mantel. It read 10:30 PM.

"Where's your husband, Mrs. Marsh?"

Margaret turned to me with a dull, faraway look in her eyes. "I don't know. He told me he had some urgent business to attend to."

"He's gone looking for him, hasn't he?"

Margaret didn't answer, turning once again to the fire. I'd had enough. Enough lies, enough dodges. I jumped out of my seat and grabbed her by the shoulders. "Listen, this isn't a game, Mrs. Marsh. Your husband could be in danger. Now, where'd he go?"

Margaret peered up at me with that same faraway expression. She was in her happy place, my words just white noise, wind and crashing waves.

"Mrs. Marsh," I said, tightening my grip on her shoulders.

She snapped out of her stupor, her expression changing from placid to irate.

"How dare you touch me," she said, her voice loud and guttural.

I let go of her just as Eugene entered the room. He had graying hair and a beard, well built, the fabric of his plain white button-down shirt straining to contain some formidable biceps. He burst through the door, his eyes locking on me. His face took on a stone-cold-serious expression, the kind that promised a beating.

"Look, I don't want any trouble," I said, putting my hands up.

Eugene stood at the ready, like some old-time pugilist. He balled his hands into a pair of massive, club-like fists.

"Eugene, it's all right," Margaret said. "Please escort Mr. Wozniak to the front door. We're finished speaking."

Eugene slapped a thick, meaty palm on my shoulder and began dragging me towards the hallway. I pulled out of his grip. "Please, Mrs. Marsh, reconsider. This is your husband we're talking about."

Margaret gazed into the fireplace. "Good night, Mr. Wozniak," she said in a singsong voice.

Eugene was about to grab me again, but I raised a hand to let him know I was ready to leave of my own accord. We headed outside into the cold and stopped in front of my car.

"I always knew that boy would turn up again," Eugene said.

"Any idea where I might find him?"

Eugene peered back at the house. "Did Mrs. Marsh tell you about when they found Alison and him in that motel room?"

I nodded.

"Mr. Marsh paid Jeremy a lot of money to go away, and he sent some big, strong guys from the plant over there to give him the beating of a lifetime. Between the money and the beating, I would've thought that boy would have every reason to go as far away from Chicago as possible and never return. But you know what? Every so often, I'd see him in the neighborhood. At first, I figured he was crazy, but then I realized that boy's world was never much bigger than the home he grew up in and his father's business. It's like all those people back in the day who thought the world was flat. Jeremy would no sooner leave the world he knew than those folks would venture beyond what they believed to be the end of the world."

Eugene looked back at the house. "I better head inside before Mrs. Marsh gets suspicious."

He didn't have to say anymore.

"Thanks," I said.

Eugene smiled and nodded. "Good luck," he said before heading back into the house.

I got in my car and drove back to Chicago, to an industrial site on the south side where a man and his son once worked together during more innocent times.

TWENTY-EIGHT

Marsh Enterprises used to occupy a vast industrial campus, covering several city blocks on Chicago's far south side. It was an impressive operation, employing over 1000 people and comprising multiple production facilities, a warehouse, and a four-story office building.

In late 2000, with profits on the decline, Edgar got out while the getting was still good and sold the business to a large multinational. By the summer of 2001, the buildings of the former Marsh Enterprise industrial campus sat empty. Gangbangers and vagrants took advantage of the abandoned facilities. They became places where people dealt and used drugs, where the homeless squatted, and where a sixteen-year-old girl was taken and raped one November morning on her way to school. The city condemned the buildings. One by one, they were leveled until all that stood was a single structure: the warehouse where Jeremy spent part of his young adulthood as an employee. That too was slated for demolition, its continued survival a mere oversight.

Unemployment devastated the community, and small businesses dependent on Marsh employees' dollars soon went under or moved away. The surrounding area was a ghost town or as close to a ghost town as you'd find in Chicago. It reminded me of an article I had read in the eighties about the neutron bomb. The story was in some weird, fringe magazine, anti-authoritarian in a vaguely right-wing kind of way. An old friend from high school left it at my house after a night of drinking, awkward pauses, and melancholy reflections on adulthood, his idea of catching up on old times. Frank, my friend, was a sucker for conspiracy theories and a general bore, yet the magazine was interesting. Or at least I found this particular article morbidly fascinating. It described a weapon designed to destroy the Soviet army, a bomb that killed humans with radiation while leaving buildings and machinery relatively unscathed.

If I didn't know better, I would've thought a neutron bomb had been dropped here. The area was almost entirely devoid of humanity, making the bus stops that appeared every couple of blocks seem anachronistic. The neighborhood was no longer a destination but a place to pass through on the way to other parts of the city.

The streets grew more desolate the closer I got to the old Marsh Enterprises campus, as though I were approaching the blast's epicenter. I drove down deserted throughways, my headlights illuminating the remnants of better times. Darkened storefronts bore weatherworn signs with the names of now-defunct businesses. I passed vacant apartment buildings, their windows either broken or boarded up, and couldn't help but feel uneasy when I arrived at my destination and saw the last remaining relic of a business that destroyed so many lives, a dark monolith casting a long shadow across a field of prairie vegetation.

The warehouse resembled an airplane hangar or a military installation. It was a long, two-story structure made of cinder block with a curved metal roof and few windows. The building stood behind a tall fence topped with razor wire. Someone had taken a bolt cutter and opened a flap in the enclosure. I pulled up to the opening, collected my gun and flashlight from the glove compartment, and shut off the engine. The vehicle's headlights went dim, and darkness enveloped me, a smattering of functioning street lamps providing meager illumination. I exited the car, switched on the flashlight, and ducked sideways through the flap in the gate. A chill wind whistled across the dried milkweed, thistles, and goldenrods of the prairie. I crept towards the warehouse, crouch-walking like a soldier sneaking up on the enemy, the building little more than a hazy, dark mass in the distance.

The frozen prairie turned to blacktop as I reached what was once a parking lot. I imagined trucks and forklifts heading to and from the loading docks, big guys dressed in denim driving them, and Jeremy—thin, pale Jeremy, the boss' son—among them.

That's why I was there. It was like Eugene said: Jeremy's world never extended too far beyond the family and their business. When told to go away, he hung about on the periphery like a mosquito around a porch light, waiting patiently for a door left open just a little too long or a small tear in the window screen. It was inevitable that Jeremy would end up here. He wasn't allowed back home, and even if he were, it wasn't the house he grew up in. Alison was no more. The only remaining shred of his past life was this empty monument to Marsh Enterprises.

I gazed up at the building again. The pale face of a man materialized in one of the second-floor windows before dissolving into the shadows, darkness engulfing his features as though he were sinking into a turbid pool of water. I shuddered at the sight, and for a moment, contemplated turning back. But it was too late now. There was only one way to go: forward. My path was as inevitable as Jeremy's. Enough people had died, and if I was right, Edgar Marsh was in mortal danger inside that warehouse.

I resumed my walk, my fingers tightening about the grip of my gun. The warehouse loomed above me. I stopped and studied the windows, searching for the face I had just glimpsed, the darkened hollows betraying no evidence that anyone had ever stood there.

On the right side of the building, I found an entrance just a few yards from the dock doors. I tried the door, but it wouldn't budge. A gentle breeze again rustled the dried prairie vegetation. I looked back at my car, unable to shake the feeling that someone was watching me. The pale face I saw while approaching the building kept appearing in my periphery.

I crept around to the back of the building in an agitated state, startled by the sigh of the wind, the rustle of the weeds, and the sound of my own footsteps. I found another door. Locked. There was a broken window about eight feet off the ground. A large blue dumpster sat underneath it. I climbed on top, and from there, I could reach the opening. I gripped the windowsill and hoisted myself up. My back ached, and a sharp pain emanated from somewhere in the pit of my stomach out to each of my extremities. I swung a leg up through the opening so that I was straddling the window, half of me inside and the other half out. My body protested the maneuver with every nerve ending. I peered through the window, finding nothing but darkness. I swung the other leg over and turned around so that I could grip the windowsill and begin my descent. A cold breeze blew through the window, chilling my fingers. They stiffened, and

I feared I might lose my grip. I hung for a moment with my face pressed against the cold wall before dropping the last few feet.

The thud of my landing reverberated throughout the cavernous space. Once again, feeling eyes on me, I spun around, finding only darkness. My flashlight searched for signs of life—for Jeremy, Edgar, or George Wesley—but found nothing but broken glass and some graffiti scrawled on the walls. A concrete staircase with red steel railings sat in each corner of the building. They led to a series of offices that once housed middle-management types, mostly number crunchers and shipping clerks.

I headed upstairs. The second-floor opened in the center to overlook the activity at ground level. I peered across the walkway to the other side and found a broken window. A chill wind blew through the opening, the warehouse cold enough that I could see my breath. I listened, and somewhere underneath the wind, I heard a sound like someone gasping for air, soft but audible. At first, it seemed to come from behind me, and then from down the hall.

To my right, there was a door leading to one of the old offices. I raised my gun and entered the room, finding only a file cabinet and a wooden chair. An old girly calendar from 2001, all muscle cars and cheesecake, adorned one of the walls. Miss July stared back at me from atop the hood of a black El-Camino. She was on all fours with her back arched, wearing hot pants and a low-cut T-shirt tied to reveal a bare midriff. It had been a couple of years since she had regularly greeted anyone in this room, her page brittle and covered in a layer of dust. I backed out, closing the door, and checked the next room. It was emptier than the last, with just a wastepaper basket in the corner. I imagined if I kept going, I'd find enough furniture to fill a single office: a desk here, a chair there, a lamp from one office, a phone from another.

I backed into the hallway, and again I heard gasping, this time a little louder. I tried to determine the direction of the sound's origin, craning my neck in one direction and then the other in anticipation of hearing it again, but all was silent. Another door. Taking a deep breath, I readied my gun and entered to find an empty office. I backed out of the room and ran my flashlight along the opposite side of the walkway, hoping to spot something. No luck. Another gasp, this one distinctly audible, the sound of someone in pain. I tried the next room, and then another, each one empty. By this time, I had traversed almost the entire floor.

I tried another door and was met with the pungent smell of decaying flesh. The room was pitch black. I ran my flashlight along the floor, finding what was left of George Wesley. He had been shot repeatedly, and his body dismembered. His killer had arranged his head and severed limbs around his torso—the head just above the neck, his arms at the sides, and his legs below. His skin was stark white and looked almost plastic. The whole grisly tableau looked artificial, as though I'd come across a life-size doll disassembled by some sadistic child.

I backed out of the room, my stomach pitching at the fetid smell of George's remains. Somewhere in the distance came the sound of another gasp, this one louder than the others. I stood still and listened. I heard it again to the right of me and turned, finding an air vent. I placed my ear against it, and the gasp grew louder as if it were broadcast over a PA system.

Only one room left: a utility closet. I turned the doorknob and burst inside. A thick, musky scent with a tart undertone permeated the air. My hands trembled as I searched the room with my flashlight. Some of Alison's artwork hung on the walls, paintings of urban environments with the people represented in silhouette. The rest sat stacked neatly against the wall, including the collage depicting Jeremy towering over a doe-eyed little girl. Just to the left, I found the figure of a man sprawled out on the floor, the sight making me start. He lay facing an open vent, half on his side, half on his stomach with his legs spread apart. His right hand raked at the concrete floor, his fingers scraped raw, leaving a trail of blood in their wake. He gasped for air, the sound a sickly wheeze.

"Mr. Marsh?" I whispered. My voice was raspy, tremulous, and only a little more audible than the groans I had heard since my arrival on the second floor.

The man stirred, turning over onto his back. It was Edgar Marsh, though he was almost unrecognizable under a death mask of purple welts, streaks of blood, and flaky clumps of dried gore as dark and thick as tar. His legs lay broken and askew. The bone of his left forearm was visible below the elbow, a white protuberance in stark contrast to the exposed tissue. His hair was slick with blood, much of it in thick, dark clumps. His shirt was damp, and a sucking sound issued from his chest—a knife wound. Perhaps several.

I stepped into the room and knelt beside him. Edgar peered up at me through a pair of swollen eyelids, his pupils vast dark pools. He tried to speak, wincing every time his lips moved.

"Take it easy," I said. My voice cracked as I spoke, the scent of blood choking me. "Everything's going to be okay. I'm going to get you some help."

Edgar opened his eyes as wide as they would go. His face wore the panicked look of a dying man. I offered my hand. He took it and squeezed hard. His lips strained to form words, a hissing sound emanating from his mouth. He looked desperate to speak, to tell me something. I leaned in, my ear just above his lips. He gurgled and sputtered, his words drowning in the blood, flooding his throat. I pulled away, but he drew me closer. He spoke, the words hissed yet audible, “Behind you.”

TWENTY-NINE

I felt a sharp pain in my right shoulder. A knife wound. The shock left me gasping for air. My arm went limp, and I dropped my gun.

I turned to face my attacker, dropping into a sitting position. My eyes filled with tears, and everything appeared hazy and distorted. I raised my flashlight, illuminating the tall, slender figure of a man. The light reflected off his knife, my blood glistening on the end of the blade. He raised the weapon to strike again, and I scooted back a couple of feet, directing the flashlight at his face. My assailant stumbled backward, momentarily blinded, and I reached for my gun. My fingers felt the cold metal of the barrel. I dragged the weapon to me, raised it, and fired.

My attacker howled like a wounded animal and fled from the room. I remained quiet and listened. Silence, just the beating of my heart and the faint, labored breathing of Edgar at my feet. He was fading fast, the rise and fall of his chest slowing until it was almost imperceptible. If he was going to survive, I needed to get him help, and soon. I tried my cellphone. No signal.

I got up and headed for the door. Outside, I dropped into a half-crouch, my weapon extended. I pivoted, first left and then right, finding no one. The wind whistled through the busted window at the opposite end of the walkway, and a chill ran down the back of my neck. Two offices down, I noticed an open door. I approached, crouch-walking, my gun extended before me, and stepped inside. I ran my flashlight about the room, finding Jeremy Marsh sitting hunched in a corner, hugging his long legs to his chest.

I was immediately struck by how accurately Alison had depicted him. His ivory skin gave him an almost spectral appearance, and his moist, cat-like eyes glimmered in the light. He peered up at me, a look of beseeching on his face, almost childlike in its innocence, as if to say: *How could you do this to me?* I noticed a delicate hand pressed against his right ear. Blood, as dark as tar in the dim light, seeped between his long, slender fingers.

"Are you a ghost?" he asked, a wide-eyed expression of wonderment on his face.

"No, I'm very much alive," I said, trying to sound calm.

"I saw you at that house on the west side, and I was sure you were dead. I touched you. You were ice cold."

"I can assure you I'm not a ghost."

Jeremy stood up. He was a tall, long-limbed man, and I took a step back, momentarily overcome by an irrational fear that he could reach me from clear across the room.

"Why are you here?" he asked.

I noticed the knife in his hand. He held it with the blade pointing downward. Seeing it reminded me of my latest injury, the pain now a dull, steady throbbing in my shoulder. I raised my gun, my hand trembling. Jeremy took one look at me and smiled.

There was no malice in his expression. It was a placid smile, which made it all the more unsettling. For a moment, I envisioned him torturing Mr. Marsh while humming something saccharine like Lesley Gore's "Sunshine, Lollipops, and Rainbows."

"I just came here for your father," I said. "You let me take him with me, and I promise I won't bother you again."

Jeremy shook his head. "No, that's not going to happen."

He looked me up and down, and the childlike quality I first noticed faded, replaced by an adult bitterness and anger. A second later, that was gone as well, his face becoming a blank slate.

"Did you see Joe downstairs?" he asked, concern in his voice.

I shook my head. "Joe? Who's Joe?"

"Joe Wilcher," Jeremy said. "He worked for my dad."

I knew a Joe Wilcher. He was a contemporary of Doug Greshing, an old red-nosed drunk with a gut and white thinning hair as light and wispy as down. He left the force several years before I did to start a private investigation business. Word had it, CPD had asked him to resign on charges of impropriety, kickbacks from some guy pimping Eastern European girls on the south side of the city.

"Joe Wilcher's here?" I asked, surprised.

Jeremy became agitated. "I've got to go. I've got to check on Joe. He might've been faking like you."

Jeremy took a step forward, and I raised my gun. "Joe can wait."

Jeremy stopped, with a look somewhere between a pout and a scowl on his face. "My dad sent him to hurt me," he protested, his eyes welling up with tears.

"I'm sorry to hear that, Jeremy."

"No, you're not. You work for my dad. You want to hurt me, just like all the rest."

Jeremy stared at me, his eyes dark and cold. I tried to stay calm and speak in a level voice. "Are you kidding? You saved my life, Jeremy. Another minute and Wesley would've killed me. Don't think I've forgotten that. I appreciate what you've done for me. That's why I want to help you."

He stared at me, his grip tightening around the handle of the knife.

"What I don't understand is why you were there."

"Did you see what that cop did to my Alison?" Jeremy paused, his shoulders rising and falling with each breath. "I did. I saw that fat, stupid cop hauling trash bags into the car they found. My Alison was in those bags. He cut her into little pieces and dumped her in the river. He had no right. No right!"

"But she was already dead."

Jeremy's face reddened. The beam from my flashlight reflected in the darks of his eyes like a flame. "What do you know about it?" he asked, taking another step forward.

I backed up. Jeremy then took another step, and I backed up again.

"That's enough," I said. "Stay right where you are."

He stopped. "They betrayed me. Do you know what it's like to be abandoned and betrayed by your own family? Alison said she'd always love me. She promised, and then she slept with another man. She told me she never wanted to see me again. What could I do? I had no choice."

Part of me wanted to run, but I had to know. "What happened?"

"She hurt me," Jeremy said, his voice breaking.

"What happened that night at the motel?"

"She let him touch her. I used to touch her like that."

Jeremy closed his eyes for a moment. A hint of a smile formed on his face before fading. His expression turned serious.

"He had his hands on her body," Jeremy said. "He was touching her. They were touching each other."

He stopped and winced as though in pain.

"Then what?"

Jeremy looked up at me, something in his eyes going dark. "I made them stop."

He took another step forward. I retreated, stopping when I felt a cold metal railing at my back.

"Jeremy, it doesn't have to be this way. I can help. I can get you help."

"Help me?" he asked. Then, gesturing with his head towards the utility closet, "You're here for him."

"Jeremy—"

"Do you really think I'm going to let you leave with my father? This is his fault. He did this. Were it not for him, Alison and I would be together. And now he's going to suffer, suffer like I've suffered these last few years. He's going to die, and then I'm going to join him. Him and Alison."

Jeremy moved closer. We both stood outside the room, the younger Marsh illuminated by my flashlight and everything else in darkness.

"That's enough," I said, raising my gun. My hand trembled, the barrel quivering before me.

Jeremy eyed the gun. "What are you going to do? Shoot me?"

"I don't want to."

"My father is not leaving here alive."

Jeremy took another step forward, that same placid expression on his face. Neither of us spoke. For a moment, all was silent, and then Jeremy's eyes widened and his lips parted. He howled and lunged at me. I raised my weapon and fired, but I was too slow.

Jeremy's shoulder slammed into my chest, knocking the air out of me. My whole body went slack as I toppled over the railing. The gun and the flashlight dropped, lost in the abyss. For a moment, I felt like I was floating in space, and then I crashed hard. There was a flash of light followed by nothing at all. I knew I was still alive because, unfortunately, I could feel my body, feel the pain coursing from my head to my toes.

Footfalls somewhere off in the distance. The sound rushed in and out as if in a dream. I opened my eyes, seeing only black. I looked to the left and then to the right. Off in the distance, I could see my flashlight. Damaged, it flickered on and off, illuminating a small triangle of concrete a few yards away.

I struggled onto my side and rested for a moment. The concrete felt cool against my cheek. Footsteps sounded somewhere not too far away. I slithered on my belly like a worm toward the light. Footsteps from the left, no, the right. I wasn't sure, too scared. My palms slapped against the cold concrete floor as I dragged myself forward. I heard a heartbeat and wasn't sure if it was mine or Jeremy's. All the while, the footsteps grew louder, and I knew I would have to move if I was going to live.

Somehow, I struggled to my knees and then my feet. I hobbled towards the flickering triangle of light, got close enough that I could see the flashlight itself. Another step in its direction and I caught on something in my path and fell forward, skinning my hands on the rough cement floor. Panicked, I writhed about, my hands scrambling for the flashlight. It illuminated a man's face, pale green and gnarled. My predecessor, Joe Wilcher, lay before me, his head caved in, dead eyes staring out into the darkness.

I grabbed the flashlight and searched for my weapon. I spotted it a few yards away, a pair of long, slender legs moving in my direction not too far beyond that. The flashlight cut out. I lunged forward in the darkness, my hands outstretched, my fingers finding cold metal. Footfalls close by. I rose to one knee and fired a few rounds, each squeeze of the trigger followed by a burst of bright light, creating a strobe effect. One flash revealed a jet of blood issuing from Jeremy's chest. The one after that, my assailant slumping to the floor.

I stopped firing, knowing that the next time I pulled the trigger, there'd be no blast, just a loud click that would reverberate throughout the cavernous room. I didn't want to let on that I was out of ammo, so I remained still and listened. Just a few feet in front of me, I heard the muffled sounds of Jeremy sobbing. I tried my flashlight. It flickered before once again cutting out. I tapped it, and it clicked on. I trained the light on Jeremy. He lay face down on the floor, crying into the crook of his arm.

"Mom," he said. "I'm scared."

THIRTY

The cavalry arrived in time to find me pointing an empty gun at Jeremy. Eugene had suffered a crisis of conscience and risked angering his employer by notifying the authorities. Good thing too, because Jeremy had that horror-movie vibe of a guy you just can't keep down, and I'd had more than my fill of suspense for one night.

Two ambulances transported us to the hospital, with Jeremy in one, Edgar and I in the other. My employer died en route, going into cardiac arrest on the gurney beside me. I glimpsed his dead eyes staring back at me before, overcome by exhaustion, I drifted off into a deep but troubled sleep.

I spent the next few days convalescing at Northwestern Memorial Hospital, two floors below a heavily guarded room holding Jeremy Marsh. He suffered a single wound to the chest, all but one of my shots missing their target. One was enough. Just inches to the left, and I would've struck his heart, sending him to join his father in the morgue.

The doctors pumped me full of drugs, and I spent a day slipping in and out of consciousness. The following morning, I awoke to find Dan Morrow sitting across from my bed. To my left, I saw an oversized yellow helium balloon covered in smiley faces on my nightstand—the words "Get well soon" written across it in plump rounded letters, a peace offering of sorts, though I doubted Morrow's sincerity. I guess I should've just been happy I didn't wake up to find him or some other cop smothering me with a pillow.

I sat up in my bed. "How long have you been here?"

"Just a few minutes. I thought I would stop by and pay you a visit. I wanted to let you know how sorry I am for everything that's happened."

"I don't see what you have to be sorry about, other than your guys trashing my place and George attempting to murder me."

"I never told anyone to harm you or your property."

"Thanks, but that's not exactly comforting news. It seems you have little control over your people."

"Emotions have been running high since Bill's disappearance. You kind of poked a hornet's nest when you started investigating this case, but you won't see any more trouble out of me or anyone in my narcotics unit. We're just looking to put all of this behind us."

"Meaning?"

"Meaning enough blood has been shed."

"Okay."

We both fell silent for a moment. Morrow shifted in his seat. "All right, let me lay my cards on the table. You know things, and you could make a lot of trouble for me and my guys. I know that. I don't want to see anyone else get hurt, so I'm asking you to let this go."

"Or?"

"That's it. There is no or. I didn't come here to threaten you, Glenn. I came here to appeal to your sense of decency."

"Decency? Are you fucking kidding me? What's decent about letting you get away with this shit? George Wesley killed two men to keep your little arrangement with Bledsoe a secret. He covered up a murder and destroyed a man's business. He trashed my apartment, *and* he almost killed me."

Morrow put up his hands as if in surrender. "Okay, you're right. Things got out of hand, and I can't claim any moral high ground here. By and large, we did what we did for the money, but it wasn't *just* about the money. I know it might sound crazy to you right now, but a lot of good came from my arrangement with Bledsoe. It ended the pointless turf wars in my district. It turned an entire gang into an army of street informers. It was impossible for anyone not affiliated with Bledsoe to deal in my precincts without my guys hearing about it. We made a lot of arrests, good arrests, and, more importantly, we kept the peace."

"C'mon, man, it's not like you were working in some kind of urban war zone. This isn't Lawndale or Englewood we're talking about. This is the North Side."

"Why does that matter? How much violence are you willing to tolerate? How many unnecessary deaths do you find acceptable? Let me tell you a story. There was a 67-year-old woman named Deidre Carter who used to live in my precinct. Lovely old black woman. She ran a daycare center out of her home. Kind, generous, sweet as can be. She'd sometimes bring lemonade out to the kids slinging drugs outside her building on hot summer days. And not because she was some clueless old lady who didn't know what was going on, but because she thought showing these lost kids, Bledsoe's kids, some kindness was the Christian thing to do. Anyway, one day a turf battle blew up in front of her building, and she caught a stray bullet while standing in her kitchen. It killed her instantly. No one ever found the perpetrator or the gun that killed her. For all anyone knows, one of those kids she used to bring lemonade to in the summer had shot her."

"That's fucked up."

"That's the drug war. It's senseless and unwinnable, and people like Deidre Carter keep getting caught in the middle."

"So, is this how you sold the arrangement to Bill?"

"There was a time when I didn't need to sell it to him. We were all burned out. We were tired of the hamster wheel, tired of running kids in and out of jail without it making one iota of difference."

"Why Bledsoe?"

"Good question. There was a time when I wanted nothing more than to nail that guy. He was going to be the arrest that defined my career. But that was before I saw the man in person. Before that, he was just some abstraction, a name representing some kind of drug-dealing bogeyman."

Morrow leaned forward in his seat. "You see, Bledsoe doesn't make all his money from drugs. He owns a bunch of dry cleaners he uses for money laundering. Bledsoe once told me he wanted to grow up to be George Jefferson when he was a kid. I guess, in a way, he did. Anyway, one day I was out with Bill and George doing some surveillance of one of his cleaners, and I caught my first glimpse of the man. And you know what I saw?"

I shook my head.

"I saw a man with the same tired expression I greeted every morning when I looked in the mirror. I saw someone looking for a way out, just like me. So, I paid one of his dry cleaners a visit and left a message asking him for a sit-down. He agreed, and when we met. I offered him a way out. *Us* a way out."

"You should've just quit. That's what I did, but then you've done a lot better for yourself than I ever have."

"Glenn, I guess you're just going to have to ask yourself what good will come from turning me in. Whatever you decide, you can rest assured that my narcotics unit means you no harm. You have my word on that."

"Thanks. For what it's worth, I've never believed in the war on drugs. Then again, at this point, I don't know if I believe in much of anything."

"Thank you. I'm going to get out of your hair now. I'm sure you could use some rest."

Dan stood up and extended his hand. I shook it, and we said our goodbyes.

I drifted off, waking up an hour later to find another visitor in my room. This time it was Doug Greshing.

"How you feelin'?" he asked.

"Like it's time for a career change," I said.

"Look on the bright side; now you know how much punishment you can take."

I sat up, pain coursing from my shoulder all the way down to my toes, making me wince. "I'm truly blessed. It's like I always say, the good Lord doesn't close a door without opening a window—and pushing you out of it."

Doug smiled and pulled up a seat. "I spoke to our friend Jeremy. He issued a full confession, including a full account of what transpired on the night of the 29th."

He paused, waiting for some kind of reaction.

I peered at him from under swollen eyelids. "Aren't you going to tell me what he said?"

"I didn't think we had that kind of relationship, Glenn. Sharing's a two-way street, and you weren't exactly forthcoming on this case. In fact, I get the sinking suspicion you've been ducking me."

I turned on my side, facing away from him. "Make sure to close the door behind you on your way out."

Doug cleared his throat and shifted in his seat. "I guess it would be cruel of me to bring it up and not fill you in on all the details, especially after what you've been through. I imagine you've learned your lesson. I mean, you know as well as I do that you wouldn't be in this hospital bed looking like you muff dived a circus fat lady if you'd just worked with us and—"

"Client confidentiality," I said.

"Pardon me?"

I sat up and faced him. "I said, client confidentiality. It was nothing personal, Doug."

He smiled and opened a notepad filled with some illegible scribbles. "All right, to start, Joe Wilcher was his first victim. You remember Joe?"

I nodded. "He used to be in vice."

"That's right. Joe took a job working for Edgar Marsh after he retired, and according to Jeremy, he was his father's muscle. He did a number on the kid a few years ago, beat him up pretty bad. You know why?"

I did, but I shook my head.

"Jeremy was sleeping with his sister," Doug said. "Edgar found out and had Joe and some big guys, union stiffs, beat the shit out of him. They were supposed to put a scare into the kid, so he'd go away. Unfortunately, it didn't work. A few weeks ago, he reemerged and started calling Alison, which then progressed to him following her around. Edgar found out and sicced Joe on him. He was supposed to get rid of Jeremy, and almost did too. Joe got the drop on the kid, not more than a couple of blocks from Alison's apartment. He knocked Jeremy unconscious and drove him out to the middle of nowhere. That should've been the end, but Joe got greedy. Jeremy told him he had close to a hundred grand stashed at the warehouse and it was all his if he'd just let him live. Joe, seeing an opportunity to make some easy money, agreed or at least pretended to. I'm thinking he intended to put the kid in a shallow grave the second he collected, but whatever. As a show of good faith, he put in a call to Edgar Marsh and told him he'd finished the job. So, as far as the old man knew, Jeremy was worm food. Joe and the kid then headed over to the warehouse. It was late, and it was dark. Jeremy had been living there, so he knew the place like the back of his hand. He disappeared into the shadows. Joe tried to follow, but this time the kid got the upper hand, and well, you found the body—not a pretty sight."

I flashed on Joe's face for a moment, his dead eyes staring back at me, and nodded. "I've got a question. Why didn't Edgar get suspicious when Joe didn't come to collect his money?"

"I wondered about that myself, so I paid Joe's house a visit and found something interesting in his mailbox."

"What?"

"A locker key: Number 387. You see, it occurred to me that these two would want to complete this transaction as discreetly as possible, with no big deposits or in-person exchanges of cash. I figured the key fit a locker somewhere with a big bag of cash in it. I checked a few of the obvious places: Union Station, the Greyhound bus terminal. No luck, but then I remembered that they have lockers over at a lot of the major museums, including the Art Institute, where the Marsh girl was going to school. On a hunch, I visited the place. Sure enough, there was a locker 387 and the key fit. Inside, I found a duffel bag full of money."

"So Edgar would never have known if Joe hadn't collected."

"Right, and I don't think Marsh ever expected to see him again. Joe had bought a one-way ticket to Puerto Vallarta. I imagine the plan was for him to do this one last job and retire. As far as Edgar knew, Joe had done just that."

"Leaving Jeremy free to continue stalking his sister."

"Exactly, only Jeremy was past the stalking stage at this point. His run-in with Joe pushed him over the edge. He'd been following Alison for the past few weeks and knew her routine. Once or twice a week, she and Bill would get together at the Stardust Motel. Jeremy followed them there after his run-in with Joe. He even had a key to their room. All the rooms, to be exact. The motel owner had this old drunk doing odd jobs for him, and one day, the guy left the housekeeping cart unattended outside while sleeping one off. Jeremy came by and lifted a ring of keys off it. The night of the murder, he let himself in the front door and emptied Joe's gun into Bill and Alison. The gun had a silencer, so he was in and out without anyone hearing a thing. Afterward, he went and hid in a park nearby before deciding to return to the crime scene. You want to know why he went back?"

"Why?"

"The sicko wanted to collect his sister's body. He planned to keep it and play house with her corpse. The kid arrived just in time to see Wesley remove the bodies and torch the crime scene. That put George at the top of the kid's shit list. Jeremy started tailing him, waiting for an opportunity to make him pay for taking his little keepsake. A couple of days ago, he followed George to the home of an ex-con named Julius Meeks, ambushed him, and knocked him out cold. He then brought him back to the warehouse to finish him off. Meanwhile, Edgar figured out the kid was alive. He probably should have left the rough stuff to the pros, but I suppose he didn't have any pros left at his disposal with Joe out of the picture. So he went to the warehouse and confronted Jeremy on his own. The old man was packing an antique pistol. I suspect it was all he could lay his hands on. It was probably a hand-me-down from his father or grandfather. God knows where he got the ammo. Anyway, the gun jammed, and Jeremy overpowered him. He cut him, beat him, and left him to die in that storage closet upstairs, which was when you showed up."

"Yeah," I said, my mind still processing all that he told me.

Doug stood up. "That's pretty much that, but one thing's still bothering me. If Jeremy killed Bertram and the Marsh girl, why did George set fire to the crime scene and dispose of the bodies? Why would he cover up another man's crime?"

For a moment, I considered telling him all about Dan Morrow's little arrangement with Curtis Bledsoe, but I was tired and had lost interest in playing the hero. Morrow was right. No good would come from turning him in.

"I don't have the slightest idea," I said.

"No?" Doug crossed the room and peered out the window. The hospital was located in the Streeterville area. From the higher floors, you could view a never-ending parade of shoppers on Michigan Avenue. Giant signs bearing expensive brand names hung above their heads like thought bubbles containing pricey, often unrealistic, dreams.

"I've got to tell you, there are a lot of loose ends. A *lot* of loose ends. Meeks and another ex-con by the name of Dantrell Miles were found dead in the house where Wesley was ambushed. How do they fit into all of this? Any ideas?"

I shook my head.

Doug took a seat across from me. He leaned forward in his chair. "You know what's sad about those two?"

"No, what?"

"George killed them, and he must've committed the murders while we were searching his apartment. We just missed taking the guy into custody. We get there a couple of hours earlier, and those two are still alive. Crazy, right?"

"Yeah."

"The kid says he followed George to the Meeks residence. He saw him go inside and head back to his car about an hour later. Wesley grabbed a couple of gas cans from inside the trunk and returned to the crime scene. Apparently, George was going to torch the place, just like the Stardust. The kid followed a few minutes later and caught him off guard in the bathroom. George was a little preoccupied with stuffing some poor slob's head down the toilet, so he didn't hear the kid sneak up on him." Doug paused to catch my reaction. "Any of this ring a bell?"

I didn't see any point in telling him what he already knew, so I just shrugged and kept my mouth shut.

"No? Anyway, Jeremy took the opportunity to bean George with a ceramic figurine he found in the living room. He smashed it over his head, knocking him out cold. Jeremy then took the gas cans, doused the place, and set it on fire before making off with George. He left the poor slob George was attempting to murder for dead. But he wasn't dead, was he?"

I didn't answer.

"There's no point in playing dumb, Glenn. I know you were there. I can *prove* you were there."

Doug stood up and placed something in my hand. "You recognize that?"

I did. It was my business card.

"The fire department found Miles and Meeks' bodies in the basement and called homicide to the scene. We had an APB out for Wesley, and one of my colleagues noticed his car parked down the block from the crime scene. He called me, and I found your card in Miles' back pocket. I tried tracking you down to talk about it, but you had mysteriously disappeared. I couldn't find you at home, your office, anywhere."

I stared at the card in my hand while Doug tried to make eye contact with me.

"Glenn, look at me."

I looked up in his general direction, focusing on a spot just above his head.

"I think you know more than you're letting on."

"Look, I'm tired. Why don't you get back to me when I have a lawyer present?"

Doug scratched his head. "Hey, Glenn, don't be that way. It's not you I'm after."

"What are you after?"

"The truth."

I turned over on my side, facing away from him. "Thanks for the visit," I said, waving him off. "I think it's about time for my afternoon nap."

Doug left his card on the nightstand. "Okay, I guess that's enough for now. Call me if you think of anything."

Within minutes I was asleep again. An hour later, I awoke, and this time I was alone.

THIRTY-ONE

Maya visited me a couple of days before my release from the hospital. We exchanged an awkward good-bye, and she kissed me on the cheek before walking out of my life for good. Upon leaving the hospital, I returned to my trashed apartment and a massive stack of unopened mail. It included my final check from the Marshes. Between what George and Lenny destroyed and my hospital stay, I had just broken even.

I went back to drinking myself stupid and sleeping late. Somehow, it didn't feel right. I couldn't stop thinking about the Marshes and the case. I found myself asking questions impossible to answer. Who was Alison Marsh? How did a girl like her, an artist and activist, fall for a married, corrupt, middle-aged cop like Bill Bertram? I would never know for sure, but a part of me hoped Bill became the kind of man a woman like Alison could love, a man of ideals, and not the cynical, compromised, government bureaucrat that had become all too familiar to me over the years. Perhaps in her, he had found his redemption. After all, he had stopped reporting on her anti-war group's activities.

Two weeks later, I ran into some of Alison's old friends while drinking alone at Cleo's. It was March 20th, the last day of winter, the air cold and damp, gray skies threatening rain. Tim and Phillip of the ILS sat a few stools down. The activists talked in hushed tones, their shoulders slumped. Tim recognized me and nodded. I nodded back. A few minutes later, I had to make the short trek past them to the men's room. I stopped and said hi on the way back.

"What brings you two out to my neck of the woods?" I said.

"We're meeting a friend here, and then we're headed downtown for a protest," Tim said.

"Oh yeah? How's the anti-war business going?"

"You're kidding, right?" Phillip said.

"I guess business isn't the right word. Movement?"

"That's not what I meant." Phillip motioned with his head to one of the TVs above the bar. A graphic on the screen read: "America at War." Beneath that, a ticker reported battles and quotes from military officials. The U.S. was at war with Iraq.

"When did this happen?"

"It started last night," Phillip said. "Where've you been?"

"I'm a late sleeper."

"Must be."

"Hey, I had a little too much to drink last night." I paused and scratched my head. "Now that you mention it, I thought I heard someone say something about Iraq yesterday."

The two nodded and returned their attention to the news.

"I'm sorry," I said. "You guys fought the good fight. I guess they just didn't want to listen."

No response. The ticker ran off reports from cities I had never heard of before. I had expected this for months, and yet now that it was happening, it all seemed so unreal.

"We tried, Alison," Phillip said, his eyes still on the TV. "I wish we could've done more."

"You did your best," I said. "That's all you can do. Stopping a war is a pretty tall order."

Phillip nodded.

"Hey, let me buy you guys a drink," I said.

I ordered a round of Jäger shots, and the bartender lined them up before us.

"To peace," I said, raising my glass.

"To peace," the activists repeated.

We downed our shots. A couple of minutes later, their friend arrived. He was a tall, skinny guy in his early twenties with shaggy hair and thick, black-rimmed glasses.

"Hey, you guys ready to go?" he said.

The activists nodded. "Thanks for the drink," Tim said, shaking my hand.

"No problem."

I don't know what came over me, but they were halfway to the door when I slapped some money on the counter for my tab and shouted, "Hey, wait up!"

They stopped and watched me approach, looking perplexed. "What's going on?" Phillip said.

I wanted to be a part of this. Perhaps I wanted to feel something for a change, to be a part of something bigger than myself. Perhaps, like Bill, I sought some kind of redemption. A man can only sit idly by and watch the world go to shit for so long before he's had enough.

"I want to come with you," I said. "Is that okay?"

They all paused for a moment before nodding.

"Yeah, sure, of course," Tim said.

He introduced me to their friend. "Glenn, this is Paul. Paul, this is Glenn Wozniak. He was the guy who investigated Alison's murder."

Paul's eyes widened. "A cop?"

"Private investigator," I said.

Paul did not look reassured.

"Don't worry," Phillip said. "He's cool."

We rode the El downtown together, our car packed with protesters carrying signs. A petite blonde stood across from me, her hair in a ponytail. She had a large puppet of the president. The effigy's simian-looking face wore a sly grin like some asshole kid who had just left a burning bag of dog crap on his neighbor's door. A sign hung from its neck reading: Warmonger. The blonde looked at me and smiled. I smiled back and thought about Alison. She was about this girl's age. She should've been there. The thought saddened me.

We all gathered at Daley Plaza. It was six in the evening. The air was chill and damp. Hundreds of people stood pressed together, side by side. They were young and old and of various races and ethnicities. Their collective outrage was palpable. When the protest moved from Daley Plaza onto the street, I knew it would come to an ugly end, and yet I couldn't pull myself away. Adrenaline filled the emptiness left by the case. I felt alive and a part of the world. At that moment, I couldn't help but care about the bombs raining on Baghdad and those unlucky enough to have been born inside a bullseye thousands of miles away.

A sea of humanity stretched before me. Picket signs and banners, like the sails of boats, dotted the horizon. We walked in a dense cluster, shoulder to shoulder, never more than a couple of feet separating one person from another. A few people fell off as we headed east through the canyon-like streets of the Loop while others joined—many, judging by their dress, coming straight from work. Our voices reverberated off the buildings on either side.

Somewhere along the way, I got separated from my friends. Tim had moved towards the front. I could hear him leading the crowd in a chant: "One, two, three, four, we don't need your fucking war!"

We reached Michigan Avenue and kept heading east, the procession choking off traffic. In the distance, I could see cops in full riot gear moving with the crowd, backtracking, retreating. The protesters had shut down the city, or at least part of it. We kept on moving east, the line of police resisting for a moment before giving way.

The next thing I knew, we were on Lake Shore Drive. At first, we shut down the northbound lanes, but before long, the procession had bled into the southbound lanes, stopping traffic in either direction. Some protesters climbed atop cars and waved banners. Police on horseback appeared, looking like futuristic knights in their black riot gear, their faces hidden behind dark Plexiglas visors. I caught a warped reflection of my face in one before retreating into the crowd.

Drivers sounded their horns all around me, some out of frustration and others to support the protest. A young black man rolled down his window as I passed and gave me a high five. Helicopters swirled overhead, the evening news catching aerial shots of the crowd. The protesters looked up and greeted them with a cheer. The entire world would see what we thought of the war. "No blood for oil!" someone shouted from behind me.

The entire scene took on an almost festive quality. A young, shaggy-looking man danced with a white-haired old woman to some jazz music blaring out of a nearby car, the driver looking on, amused. A thirty-something woman dressed as if she had just come from a workout walked by with a young boy perched on her shoulders. The child surveyed the scene with a look of awe on his face. It was the kind of look I wore as a child on those rare occasions my parents allowed me to stay up late with the grownups.

The cops moved in and began shepherding protesters off the outer drive. It was now close to eight o'clock. I caught sight of Tim talking with one of the police officers. The conversation seemed somewhat amicable from where I was standing. Perhaps the cops didn't like the war either, I thought.

Little by little, the crowd began evacuating Lake Shore Drive. We headed west, stopping when we hit a police barricade at Michigan Avenue. A line of officers in riot gear blocked our path. Behind them were several police vans and some cops on horseback. We backtracked on Lake Shore Drive, hitting Chicago Avenue. From there, we headed west to what another protester told me was a rendezvous point. Once again, the police stopped us at Michigan Avenue. This time they surrounded us. A line of cops in riot gear choked off traffic west on Chicago Avenue. Still, more officers guarded the way to the east. Lines of buses blocked the north and south intersections. The cops had herded us into a pen.

Protesters attempted to leave, and each time they were either rebuffed or arrested. A few yards from me, the police led a skinny, colorfully dressed woman with short brown hair away in handcuffs. She made herself go limp, and two large officers, their faces obscured by their helmets, dragged her like a rag doll, her feet scraping the ground.

"We've been peaceful. Let us go!" the crowd chanted.

The police watched us with indifference. They advanced, pushing us closer and closer together. Before long, the entire crowd huddled together within a one-block radius. Everyone tried to stay as far away from the cops as possible for fear of being arrested. One after another, the police began grabbing people and herding them onto the buses.

I noticed a familiar face on the opposite side of the street. I didn't know her name. She was a regular at the Foot, a petite, pretty redhead. She usually sat at the far end of the bar nearest the exit with a guy I imagined was her husband or boyfriend. She was talking on her cell phone, perhaps to him, a concerned look on her face. A bewildered-looking couple stood next to her. They were holding shopping bags, obvious tourists inadvertently caught in the police snare like dolphins in a tuna net.

I turned around to see Paul walking towards me. "Have you seen Tim?" he asked.

I shook my head, and he kept going, plunging into the crowd, making his way towards the line of cops on the western border of the pen. I looked back toward my fellow Club Foot patron only to find she had disappeared.

I no longer felt the exhilaration I had experienced earlier in the evening. We were all tired and scared and wanted to leave. I worked my way through the crowd, searching in vain for some way out. The going was rough. I pushed forward, lost my footing, and regained it. I stood on tiptoe and scanned the crowd, spotting Paul in the distance. The police had him. They forced him to his knees and cuffed his hands behind his back.

I don't know what came over me, but I broke into a sprint and threw my body, still tender from all the abuse it had taken during the case, into one of the arresting officers. Before I knew it, I was under a pile of cops, batons raining on me from every direction. Blood streamed down my head into my eyes, coloring everything scarlet.

"You think you're a big man?" an officer said.

"I'm going to fuck your stupid ass up," said another.

I tried to look for Paul, but all I could see were my assailants' black-padded uniforms. Another blow to the head and the world slipped away. I was drifting through space, rushing towards oblivion. I didn't quite go under. I could hear voices, see fuzzy shapes. I could still feel the batons striking my body. I rolled over onto my side into a fetal position.

"He's got a weapon," said a voice. "He's going for a weapon!"

"No! No! No!" responded another voice. "He's unarmed! He's unarmed! Back off!"

I felt a pair of firm hands gripping my shirt and a familiar voice calling my name, "Glenn! Glenn! Pull yourself together, man."

The lights and commotion came rushing back in a flood. I was standing, Todd holding me up, his face inches from mine, looking at me concerned. "You all right?" he said.

"Wait," I murmured, "What just happened?"

"You almost got yourself killed. That's what happened."

I looked behind me. The police continued hauling protesters onto buses and police vans. Somewhere in the distance, I heard Tim screaming at the top of his lungs, "We're not going away. You can't silence us with batons! We'll never go away, never give you a moment's peace until we've ended your fucking war!"

Todd dragged me to the western edge of the pen. A pair of cops stood in our way. "Move aside, guys," he said.

They stood their ground.

"You can't just let this guy go," said one of them. "You saw what he did."

"This man used to be a cop," Todd said. "He was my partner for several years. You want to take him in, you're going to have to go through me."

The cops thought for a moment before clearing a path. We walked through.

"You owe me one," Todd said.

"What just happened?"

"You know Lenny Friedhof?"

"Does he work for Dan Morrow?"

"Yes."

"I'm familiar with him."

"He thought he saw you going for a weapon. You were almost shot to death back there."

"Is that right?"

"Yes, and now it's time for you to get the fuck out of here." Todd spun me around and pushed me in the direction of home.

I looked back for a moment, unsure of what to do.

"Go!" Todd shouted before heading back into the chaos.

I turned, took a couple of steps, stopped, looked back, and took a couple more steps. Cops herded people by the hundreds onto buses bound for jails all over the city. I stood and watched for a moment before turning to leave, breaking into a run as soon as I was safely out of the police's view. I ran until my side hurt. Helicopters rumbled overhead, and sirens blared in the distance, but otherwise, everything appeared normal. Traffic crept by as it normally would in downtown Chicago. Pedestrians headed out to bars and restaurants, few paying me any mind, even as I doubled over in pain, out of breath, my face covered in blood.

My head swam, the street lamps above hazy and haloed, everything dreamlike. I took a seat on the curb and tried to collect my thoughts. So much for Morrow's men leaving me alone. Lenny wasn't about to let bygones be bygones. I got out my cellphone and made a call.

"Doug Greshing speaking," said the voice on the other end of the line.

"Hi, Doug, it's Glenn."

"What can I do for you, Glenn?"

"I was thinking about our conversation the other day."

"Yeah?"

"Yeah." I paused for a moment to spit blood into the street. "George worked with an officer named Lenny Friedhof. You might want to keep an eye on him."

The line went silent for a moment. "Is that it?" Doug asked. "That's what you called to tell me?"

"That's enough," I said, hanging up.

Another helicopter buzzed overhead. I peered up at it, blood dripping into my eyes, and all I could see was red.

Thank you so much for reading *Forgotten Boy*. Reviews mean everything to authors. If you've enjoyed this book, please consider rating it and reviewing it on the platform where you purchased your copy.

Glenn Wozniak will return. For exclusive content and updates about new releases, visit the author's website and sign up for his VIP mailing list at toddluchik.com.

About the Author

Todd Luchik is the author of *Forgotten Boy*. He has worke as a writer, editor, and digital marketer. This is his firs novel.

Todd lives in Chicago with his partners in crime writing: his wife, Rachel, and his dog, Nicky. When not writing about private eyes and murderers, he enjoys chatting with other crime fiction fans and writers. You can follow him and find out about upcoming projects at toddluchik.com.

http://toddluchik.com

https://twitter.com/ToddLuchik

https://www.facebook.com/todd.luchik.author

www.ingramcontent.com/pod-product-compliance
Lightning Source LLC
LaVergne TN
LVHW041102080826
845145LV00007B/1665

* 9 7 8 0 9 9 6 8 5 0 9 2 6 *